continued . . .

"A fantastic duo of stories from Katie MacAlister. . . . If you are a fan of MaryJanice Davidson's Betsy series, then I think you will definitely enjoy *Zen and the Art of Vampires* and *Crouching Vampire, Hidden Fang*."
—Joyfully Reviewed

"The story line is fast-paced, filled with humor and action as Katie MacAlister balances the two nicely."
—*Midwest Book Review*

Zen and the Art of Vampires

"A jocular action-packed tale . . . [a] wonderful zany series."
—*Midwest Book Review*

"A fast-moving read with sizzling chemistry and a touch of suspense."
—Darque Reviews

"Pia Thomason just might be my favorite heroine ever. . . . An entrancing story and a very good escape."
—*The Romance Reader*

The Last of the Red-Hot Vampires

"MacAlister's fast-paced romp is a delight with all its quirky twists and turns, which even include a murder mystery."
—*Booklist*

"A wild, zany romantic fantasy. . . . Readers will enjoy this madcap tale of the logical physicist who finds love."
—The Best Reviews

"A fascinating paranormal read that will captivate you."
—Romance Reviews Today

THE SILVER DRAGONS NOVEL

Me and My Shadow

"MacAlister delivers the fun, even in the drama. The characters are engaging, quick, and inhabit a universe that only a genius can imagine."
—Romance Reader at Heart

"Laugh-out-loud funny . . . a whimsical, upbeat, humor-filled paranormal romance . . . delightful."

—Romance Junkies

THE AISLING GREY, GUARDIAN, NOVELS

Holy Smokes

"[A] comedic, hot paranormal caper."   —*Booklist*

"A wonderfully amusing relationship drama . . . a laugh-out-loud tale."   —*Midwest Book Review*

Light My Fire

"Crazy paranormal high jinks, delightful characters, and simmering romance."   —*Booklist*

"A nonstop thrill ride full of sarcastic wit, verve, and action right to the end."   —A Romance Review

Fire Me Up

"[A] wickedly witty, wildly inventive, and fiendishly fun adventure in the paranormal world."   —*Booklist*

"Who knows where she will take us next? . . . [A] fascinating and fun writer."   —The Best Reviews

You Slay Me

"Smart, sexy, and laugh-out-loud funny!"

—Christine Feehan

"Amusing romantic fantasy. . . . Fans will appreciate this warm, humorous tale that slays readers with laughter."

—The Best Reviews

IT'S ALL GREEK TO ME

Katie MacAlister

A SIGNET BOOK

SIGNET
Published by New American Library, a division of
Penguin Group (USA) Inc., 375 Hudson Street,
New York, New York 10014, USA
Penguin Group (Canada), 90 Eglinton Avenue East, Suite 700, Toronto,
Ontario M4P 2Y3, Canada (a division of Pearson Penguin Canada Inc.)
Penguin Books Ltd., 80 Strand, London WC2R 0RL, England
Penguin Ireland, 25 St. Stephen's Green, Dublin 2,
Ireland (a division of Penguin Books Ltd.)
Penguin Group (Australia), 250 Camberwell Road, Camberwell, Victoria 3124,
Australia (a division of Pearson Australia Group Pty. Ltd.)
Penguin Books India Pvt. Ltd., 11 Community Centre, Panchsheel Park,
New Delhi - 110 017, India
Penguin Group (NZ), 67 Apollo Drive, Rosedale, Auckland 0632,
New Zealand (a division of Pearson New Zealand Ltd.)
Penguin Books (South Africa) (Pty.) Ltd., 24 Sturdee Avenue,
Rosebank, Johannesburg 2196, South Africa

Penguin Books Ltd., Registered Offices:
80 Strand, London WC2R 0RL, England

First published by Signet, an imprint of New American Library,
a division of Penguin Group (USA) Inc.

First Printing, December 2011
10 9 8 7 6 5 4 3 2 1

This book is an oddity (in many ways, but we'll move past most of them), particularly because while writing it over a period of six days, I regularly popped onto the Shoutbox on my message forum and cackled maniacally to all the ladies who were hanging out there.

Luckily, they are familiar with how deranged I am when the muse has me in her grip, and they not only tolerated my giddiness, they encouraged me to continue on. It is to the ladies of the Shoutbox that this book is dedicated, with special recognition to Janet Avants, Vinette Perez, Shawna Szabo, and Sara Thome for their heroism in the face of a semihysterical author.

Chapter 1

The man in front of her was crazy. That, or he was having some sort of an attack, one that involved dancing up and down and gesturing wildly, all the while talking a mile a minute, his words tumbling out with such speed, they all ran together into one dense, unintelligible stream.

Not that Harry could have understood the words even if the man had been speaking slower. She stood up from where she'd been seated on a wooden lounge, enjoying the peace of the balmy Mediterranean night. "The temptation to say, 'I'm sorry, but it's all Greek to me,' is almost overwhelming—you do realize that, right?" she asked the man.

He continued his dancing-gesturing-babbling routine, this time adding a peculiar plucking motion with the hem of her linen tunic.

She glanced around, wondering if she'd misunderstood. "Am I not supposed to be here? Is this garden off-limits to us? Derek said it was the garden area on the other side of the house that was for guests only. Did I get that wrong?"

The little man—and he was little, at least a good ten inches shorter than her solid six feet—evidently grew distressed at her inability to understand, for he grabbed her wrist and hauled her toward the massive bulk of the house.

"Is Timmy in the well?" she asked, a little smile curling her lips before her gaze moved from what she thought must surely be one of the servants to the house itself. "Only 'house' doesn't quite cut it as a description, does it? It's more like a palace. Houses don't have wings—palaces do. And I defy you to find a house sitting by its lonesome on its very own Greek island. No sir, this is a palace, pure and simple, and although I'm sure you have a good reason for dragging me to it, I should point out that the only people who are staying in its palatial confines are guests, and I'm with the band. We have the little bungalow on the servant end of the island. Hello? You really don't speak a word of English, do you?" Harry sighed.

The man continued to drag her through a very pleasant garden filled with sweet-scented flowering Mediterranean shrubs that were unfamiliar to her, attractive hedges, and pretty, neoclassical statues. The night air was balmy; the heavy scent from some flower mingled with the sharper, and to her mind more pleasing, tang of the sea. It was everything she imagined a rich man's private island paradise should be. Well, with the exception of the wizened little man who gripped her wrist.

"I couldn't just sit quietly somewhere?" she asked the man. "I promise I won't bother anyone. I don't think

I could—I'm so jet-lagged I can't even think straight. Look, that's a nice little bench right over there in the corner next to the statue of the guy with a really big winky. I won't be in anyone's way. I'll just go sit and contemplate his gigantic genitals, and all will be well."

"Harry!" A man appeared suddenly at a window, hanging out of it and waving frantically. "There you are! Hurry!"

"Derek, *what* are you doing in the house?" Harry thinned her lips at the sight of the young man. "You said we weren't supposed to go near it while the guests were here."

"That doesn't matter now! Hurry up!"

"If you think I don't have anything better to do than to fly halfway around the world to bail your butt out of trouble because you can't follow a few simple rules—"

"No, it's not me." He pulled back inside the window. "It's Cyn! She's been attacked!"

"What?" Her bellow took the little man still attached to her wrist by surprise, causing him to drop her hand as if it were suddenly made of fire. Adrenaline shot through her with a painful spike, adrenaline and a fury that almost consumed her. She leaped forward, easily hurdling the low stone balustrade of a patio area as she bolted for the nearest entrance to the house, wrenching open a pair of French doors. She didn't stop to apologize to the small group of people standing around a pool table as she raced past the men and women in elegant evening clothes and made a beeline for a door that was bound to lead to a central area of the house.

The little servant trailed her as far as a marble-tiled corridor, where he veered off to who-knew-where.

Harry didn't care—her mind was blank except for the horror of the words that kept repeating in her head. *It's Cyn! She's been attacked!*

"Harry, thank god—" Terry emerged from a side hall, gesturing toward a curving staircase, his face tight with worry. "We didn't know where you were. She's up here."

Harry ground off a good layer or two of enamel as the pair of them pelted up the seemingly endless stairs, one distracted part of her mind finding it ironic that now, of all times, she should be thankful for both her height and long legs. "What happened?" she managed to get out as they crested the stairs and Terry pointed to the left.

He cast her a worried look, but said nothing. Derek almost collided with her as he burst out of a room. "In here! Harry, you have to do something! The bastard ... he ... he ...!"

"I'll kill whoever it is," she said, her blood running icy at the thought of whatever atrocity had occurred. She shoved Derek aside and entered the room, her breath ragged, her heart about ready to leap out of her chest. She'd heard the phrase "seeing red" before, but had never thought it could be taken literally. For a few seconds, though, she would have sworn that everything in the room had an ugly red tint to it. It was obviously a bedroom; a quick glance took in the usual occasional chairs, a large bureau with matching wardrobe, and a big bed swathed in some sort of filmy draperies that fluttered in the breeze drifting in through open French doors. Her attention narrowed to the bed as she dashed to it, immediately taking into her arms one of the two huddled, sobbing figures there.

Dimly, she was aware there was another person in the room, but his identity faded to insignificance. "It's all right, Cyndi. I'm here now," she said, her fury rising as the younger woman sobbed onto her shoulder. "You'll be OK. We'll make whoever did this pay."

"He's evil! He's horrible!" Cyndi pulled back, tears spilling over from already red, bloodshot eyes. She was naked, a sheet clutched to her bare breasts, her face unmarked but blotchy from the tears. There were some nasty-looking raw marks on her neck and chest, but it was the petulant purse of her lips that suddenly chimed a warning bell in Harry's brain.

"What happened? Did someone attack you?"

Cyndi drew in a long, trembling breath and glanced over Harry's shoulder. "Yes! Well . . . more or less. He dumped me, Harry. *Dumped* me!"

Harry blinked for a few seconds. "He what?"

"Dumped me, cruelly and . . . and . . . viciously. I came up to his room, and I thought we were going to hook up, and everything was going along very nicely, and before we could get down to, you know, really doing it, he told me to leave. Just like that!"

Harry passed a shaking hand over her eyes. Slowly, her heart rate dropped back to a reasonable level. "So you weren't attacked?"

"Verbally I was. He told me that he didn't want to have sex with me, and that I should leave because he wanted to sleep." Cyndi gestured at the bed. "If it's not verbal abuse to entice someone to your bed, and get them naked, and then kiss them all over before telling them to leave, I don't know what is!"

"He enticed you?"

"Yes! Not so much in words, but he looked at me several times tonight, and a woman knows what that look means," Cyndi said with a peculiar lofty coyness. "He *wanted* me. So I came up here, and then everything was really nice until he went totally crazy and told me to leave. That's just not right, Harry. It's traumatizing! You have no idea how traumatizing it is to come up to someone's room intending to have fabulous sex and then be told to leave because that someone wants to sleep. I'm not a slut! I should sleep here, too!"

Harry took a deep, deep breath to keep from strangling the young, self-centered girl in front of her, reminding herself that her whole purpose in being here was to watch over the kids and see that they came to no harm. Her eyes lit on the red marks on Cyndi's chest, and a little spurt of anger burned in her stomach.

She turned, moving aside the hovering forms of Terry and Derek. Amy clung to the latter, her eyes huge and wary. Across the room, a man leaned drunkenly against the wall, dressed in a pair of obviously hastily donned pants, the waistband undone, his face slack and devoid of emotion as he watched Harry walk toward him. He was a little taller than she was, obviously of Greek ethnicity, with dark eyes and hair, and what in any other circumstance would be a classical sort of beauty that she would have had to be dead not to appreciate.

"I don't know what the hell you did to her to leave those marks, but I feel it's important to point out that she's only eighteen years old. Couldn't you have gotten her out of the room without touching her?" she asked, fighting with the need to yell at both Cyndi and the randy stallion before her. He had to be a guest at the party—for which the band had been brought out at great expense to entertain—but at that moment, Harry couldn't have cared less if he was the owner of this vast palace of sin; she just wanted to get Cyndi out of there without any further drama.

"I—" The man blinked at her, swallowed visibly, and shoved himself away from the wall to take a step forward. "The little bint threw herself at me. She was in my bed, waiting for me. I didn't screw her, if that's what you're all hot and bothered about."

"Bint!" Cyndi roared, and would have lunged at the man but for the sheet in which she was still tangled. "You bastard! I'm not a bint! Terry, what's a bint?"

"I don't care who tried to seduce whom, you should have known she's too young. You're just lucky she's legal. And obviously, you were playing a bit too rough if you left marks like those."

"I'm wounded!" Cyndi cried, grasping at that thought. "He hurt me! He's a beastly, horrible man who hurt me and abused me! I think I may faint."

"You're not hurt, you little—" The man wisely bit off the word as Harry frowned. "I didn't hurt her."

"Oh my god, I'm bleeding!" Cyndi cried in a dramatic voice, and clutched at Terry. "I need to go to the hospital!"

"Look, this has gone far enough. I just want you to promise to stay away from Cyndi for the rest of the weekend, OK?" Harry said with an attempt to take control of the situation.

The man scowled at her. "Who the hell are you to tell me what to do? I bet you planned all of this with that little bint, didn't you? What a setup you had, getting your friend there to try to screw me and then pretend she's been attacked. What's next? Blackmail? You can just drop that idea, because there's no way I'm going to fall for your little scheme."

With every word, anger built in Harry. Oh, she knew full well that Cyndi was milking the situation for all it was worth, just as she knew that Cyndi had pursued him and not vice versa, but his slander left her itching to punch him in the nose. Behind her she heard the whispered hush of the door opening, but she ignored it, saying simply, "Who am I? I'll tell you who I am. I'm your worst nightmare."

"I don't know." He leered in that sloppy way drunks had. "I'm willing to give you a try. Bet you know a few things that your little friend doesn't."

The man reached out and grabbed her breast. Harry saw red again before she knocked his hand away, stomped as hard as she could on his bare foot, and swiftly brought up her knee into his groin. When he doubled over with a scream, she punched him as hard as she could in the eye. His head snapped back, his face frozen in shock and pain for a moment before he fell over backward.

"What the hell is going on here?" a voice roared from behind her.

She spun around to behold an absolutely furious man coming toward her. She blinked at the sight of him, amazed for a moment that such a glorious specimen of male beauty existed outside the pages of glossy fashion magazines. He was taller even than the man she'd just knocked out, a good six inches taller than she was, with a broad expanse of chest that wasn't at all disguised by a black silk shirt open at the neck, revealing a bronzed stretch of skin that she suddenly wanted to lick. The little indentation where his neck met his collarbone beckoned to her with an unholy fascination, and she stared, bemused for a moment, wondering what on earth her mind was doing demanding that she taste this strange—if terribly beautiful—man.

"Who are you?" he demanded, his black eyes blazing with a fury that looked familiar somehow. "What the hell did you do to my brother?"

"Your brother?" Suddenly all the rage, and anger, and fury filled her again with righteousness. "I was seriously considering beating him to a bloody pulp. You're a big guy—I'll let you help if you like."

His ebony gaze raked over her in a manner that left her both hot and cold at the same time, instantly dismissing her as not being worth his consideration. He shoved her aside and marched over to where the other man moved groggily against the wall. "I believe the phrase is 'over my dead body.' Get up, Theo."

"You want on my list, too? Fine," Harry snarled, and would have rolled up her sleeves except the fawn-colored linen tunic she wore was sleeveless. "You can be second. Go ahead, Theo, get up so I can knock your block off."

The big, incredibly handsome man hoisted his brother to his feet, one of his lips curling. "You're drunk."

"Not drunk," Theo protested, his eyes glazed. "Barely had anything. That little bitch—"

Harry moved faster than she had ever moved, intent on slapping the word right off his lips, but the other man caught her as she lunged toward his brother.

"Who the hell are you?" he snarled, his arm like steel around her waist.

"I already used the 'your worst nightmare' line," she yelled at him, her fingers curling into a fist. "But you'd better believe I am!"

He stopped her fist just as she was about to punch him in the nose, shoving her backward into the small clutch of people standing next to the bed. His black-eyed gaze crawled over all of them. "You're not on the guest list. What are you doing here?"

"They're the band," Harry said, jerking her thumb toward where the four of them, Cyndi now standing wrapped in the sheet, pressed together in silent amazement. "The one your sister hired for her eighteenth birthday, assuming you are the owner of this house of debauchery."

The man's eyes returned to her, scorn just about dripping from his voice as he said, "You look a little old to be in a teenage band."

"I'm not old," she said, straightening up. Behind the man, Theo collapsed into a chair, slumping over to rest his head in his hands with a pathetic groan. She narrowed her eyes on him, wondering if she could distract his brother long enough to get a really good punch in. "I'm only thirty-three, and I'm their manager. Kind of. By proxy. I'm a writer, really, but I'm acting as their manager because Timothy's appendix burst, and Jill had to stay with him because she's about due to pop any minute with their first child, and there was no one else to watch over the kids, so she asked if I would do it for just this one gig. And, idiot that I was, I thought, how hard could it be to watch over things while they played for some obscenely rich oil billionaire's party? No one told

IT'S ALL GREEK TO ME

me your brother was a drunkard who doesn't have the common sense God gave a potato bug!"

Harry glared at the man as he glanced from his brother to the huddled girl, now thankfully silent. He took in her disheveled appearance before his eyes narrowed on Harry. "I made my money in real estate development, not oil."

She stared at him for a second. "Does that matter?"

"It does if you're going to consider the source of my wealth as material for an insult. As for this situation"—he gestured with distaste at Cyndi—"Theo has never had to force a woman into his bed. Usually it's the other way around."

"Are you saying I came up here on my own, without him asking me first?" Cyndi gasped with a sniff and a jerk of her chin. "He *asked* me to come up here. Not in so many words, but he asked me by his actions."

Harry frowned. "What actions?"

"He smiled at me twice, and winked once, and then he brushed my arm when I walked by him. I'm not dense, you know! I can tell when a man wants me! So I came up here to wait for him, because it's clear he thinks I'm steaming hot."

Harry closed her eyes for a moment, then took Cyndi by the arms, fighting to keep from shaking her. "I don't even know where to start, Cyndi."

"Start with what? I'm not the one who's wrong here. Theo is!" Cyndi answered with yet another righteous sniff.

"I thought so. This wouldn't be the first time some enterprising young lady has tried to, shall we say, benefit financially from Theo's lack of common sense," the irritating man said.

"Bullshit!" Harry snapped, releasing Cyndi in order to march over to the man. His eyebrows rose at the obscenity. She couldn't remember what his name was—it was one of those long names with a seeming overabundance of vowels—but she vaguely remembered hearing Jill mention something about his being on some world's most eligible bachelor list. If his appearance was anything to go by, she could certainly believe that. "I'm willing to admit that Cyndi has shown a huge lack of intelligence this evening—"

Cyndi gasped again, outraged.

"But neither she nor I are trying to blackmail your precious brother. It was just a case of a young girl—a very young girl, who is just barely legal, I might point out—obviously being dazzled by the situation, and making some bad judgment calls."

"I'm not dazzled," Cyndi protested. "I'm hurt! I'm bleeding all over!"

The man made a disgusted noise and looked like he wanted to roll his eyes.

"There's no actual blood, Cyndi," Harry pointed out. "Although I will admit that your playmate was far too rough with you. And though rough play is not a crime, it's certainly not a pleasant little roll in the sack, either."

"No *crime* has been committed, other than that of poor judgment," the man snapped at her implication, his scowl shifting for a moment to an expression of surprise as Harry poked him in the chest when she spoke.

"She's got marks all over her upper chest! Just look at her! What sort of a man does that?"

Iakovos Papaioannou couldn't believe that the Amazon in front of him had the nerve to poke him in the chest, just as if she had the right to chastise him. For a moment he was speechless at her utter and complete disregard for his consequence as she continued to lambaste him, throwing the most absurd accusations at his head.

He allowed her to continue just for the pleasure of watching her, admitting to himself that although his preference in women seldom extended to anything but slim, elegant, cool blondes, this woman, this earth goddess with her abundant curves and wild brown hair spilling down her back, stirred something deep inside him. Something primal, some urge, woke and demanded that he claim her in the most fundamental way a man could claim a woman.

His gaze dropped to her mouth, and he watched with fascination as her lips moved while she continued to lecture him. A faint scent caught his attention, and he breathed deeper, hoping to catch it again; when he did, the analytical side of his mind noted that it was just the scent of a sun-warmed woman, as if she had been out lying on the beach. It was nothing extraordinary, nothing unusual, and yet it seemed to go straight to his groin, firing his desire as the most costly perfume had never done.

"—and you're not even listening to me!" the goddess yelled, drawing his attention from his contemplation of laying her down on his bed and burying himself in her glorious body. She gave him a particularly hard jab in the chest, and he captured her hand without thinking, idly rubbing his thumb over her fingers.

"Of course I'm not," he said dismissively. "There's nothing further to discuss. The woman pursued Theo, not the other way around. She is not injured, despite her claims to the contrary."

She stared at him with stunned surprise for a moment or two, thick black lashes blinking over eyes he had first thought were gray, but now he could see were more hazel, the irises seeming to darken slightly as she looked at his hand. "What are you doing?"

"Trying to point out the obvious," he responded, his eyes on her lips, wondering if she tasted of the sea. She certainly looked like some goddess who had risen from the sea in vengeance, a tempest in human form.

"No, your hand. Your thumb. It's . . ."

Her gaze lifted to his, and he watched with primal satisfaction as her pupils dilated in sudden awareness of him as a man. How easy it would be to arouse her, this tempest. "What is your name?"

"Harry," she said, suddenly giving a little shiver as she pulled her fingers from his.

He frowned. That was not at all fitting for a goddess from the sea. "You have a man's name?"

"It's a nickname, actually," she said with a rueful smile. His gaze moved instantly to her lips, a drawing in his groin warning that if he continued contemplation of her mouth, what he'd like to do to it, and what he'd like it to do to him, he would end up carrying her off to his bed. While that idea seemed just fine to him, there were other things to attend to . . . at least while Elena's party was under way.

"My name is actually Eglantine, but no one but my mother calls me that. It's just such a mouthful that everyone calls me Harry. What's your name?"

"Iakovos Panagiotis Okeanos Papaioannou," he said with a slight frown, as if he was surprised she didn't know it.

That floored her. She grabbed onto the first part. "Yackydos?"

"Iakovos. It's Greek for Jacob." When she gawked at him, he continued, "My name is quite a bit more than a mouthful, yes. I would suggest that since you are this young woman's manager, you escort her back to her proper lodgings. I will attend to my brother."

"I'm hurt! I want to go to the hospital!" Cyndi cried.

"Don't be ridiculous. You don't need a doctor's care," Iakovos told her.

"I'm their *acting* manager, and if she wants to go to the hospital, then I'll take her to the hospital." Harry poked him in the chest again, not, she told herself, because she wanted to feel his fingers on hers again. Oh, sure, he was the walking epitome of sex on two legs, your standard gorgeous hunk, but he was also an extremely obtuse hunk, one who had a very large surprise coming if he thought he could just brush Cyndi's (albeit minor) injuries away.

"May I remind you that you are in *my* house," Iakovos said, his voice low and incredibly arousing. "On *my* private island."

Harry had never really thought of voices as being sinfully sexy before, but the way this man's rumbled around in his chest made the hairs on the back of her neck stand on end. It was like he was a god, a Greek god come to life, standing right there in front of her, doing all sorts of things to personal, intimate parts of her that she didn't want to think about. He was a drunkard's brother, for heaven's sake! How could she find his voice arousing? "Look, Yacky—"

"Iakovos!"

"We may be in your house on your precious island, but we're also in a country that I'm willing to bet you doesn't tolerate abuse of women, especially American citizens, and double especially when the American citizen in question is just barely eighteen." Harry took a deep breath and leveled the Greek god a look that should have felled him. "I'm assuming that since we had to take a boat to get out to Smut Island, we're going to need one to get Cyndi to the hospital on the mainland. And since I also assume you own all the boats here, I'd appreciate if you could have one of your lackeys fire one up for us."

"And if I don't?" Iakovos asked, his black eyes damn near spitting fire at her.

"You're going to be one sad little panda," she snarled.

"Are you *threatening* me?" He looked completely outraged at such a thing.

"You bet your incredibly attractive and probably hard enough to bounce a quarter off ass I am!" she snapped back.

An indescribable look flitted across his face. "You are the most irreverent woman I've ever met."

"And you're the handsomest man I've ever seen in my life, but that doesn't mean I'm going to lick you!" she yelled.

He stared at her in outright surprise.

"Sorry. That came out wrong." Color warmed her face as she mentally damned that odd twist in her mind that led her to speak without thinking. "Sometimes the dialogue I write in my head comes out of my mouth instead of staying where it belongs."

"You wish to . . . *lick*?" he asked, the same odd expression on his face.

"Not *all* of you!" she said with dignity, straightening her shoulders. "Just that spot there, where your neck meets your collarbone. Where that little indentation is . . ." Her voice trailed off as he continued to look at her as if dancing boobs had just appeared on the top of her head. "Never mind. It's not important."

He opened his mouth to say something, shook his head, and with a dismissive glance at Cyndi and the others still clustered together in silent shock, pulled out a cell phone and spoke rapidly in Greek. "A boat will be waiting for you at the east dock." His lips tightened as he looked at his brother before jerking him upright. "I trust that a visit to the hospital will reassure you that your charge has no injury beyond that of her pride."

"Pride?" Harry grabbed his arm as he was about to leave. He spun around and pinned her back with an outraged glare that she more than met with one of her own. "She's battered to hell and back again."

His black gaze flickered over Cyndi, who thrust out her chest and gave him an antagonistic look. "I see no signs of battery."

"She has red marks all over her chest and neck!" Harry said, pointing at Cyndi.

He looked at her steadily for a moment, and she could have sworn one side of his mouth twitched. "Have you never had a lover who had heavy whisker growth?"

"Huh?"

"It is common among Greek men to have to shave

more than once a day, and my brother and I are no exception to that fact."

She eyed his jaw, squinting slightly. He did have a slight darkness on his lower face, as if he was about to sport some manly stubble. He also had extremely attractive lips, the lower one in particular, with its sweet, oh, so very sweet curve, and the upper with a deep indentation up to a long, straight nose. Like the spot on his neck, she had the worst urge to taste that upper lip dip. She actually licked her own lips thinking about it before she remembered that ogling a drunk's brother, especially one who should be on the cover of *GQ*, really wasn't the thing to do. "Er . . . what was the question?"

He sighed. "Whisker burn. That is all the red marks are."

"They are?" She turned to Cyndi. "Cyn?"

"He hurt me," she said, her eyes filling with tears. "Even if it was just his rough cheeks, I need to see a doctor."

Amy, Derek's girlfriend and the other singer of the group, immediately hugged her, her blue eyes worried. Even Terry, bright, cheerful Terry who always had a joke on his lips, looked somber as he moved closer to the two women. All four sets of eyes watched Harry with an obvious plea in them.

"Whisker burn." She turned back to face the annoying god with the sexy lips. He raised an eyebrow, and she was thankful that he was clearly beyond such mortal things as saying I told you so.

"I told you she wasn't hurt," he said with a slight smirk.

She pointed a finger at him. "You just knocked yourself off your pedestal, buster. All right, I'm willing to accept that your brother didn't intentionally hurt her. But she's very upset, and she does have some nasty rashes, so I think it probably would be better for everyone's peace of mind if she saw a doctor. If you and Mr. Grabby Hands over there would just get out of here, I'll get Cyn dressed and we'll take her to the mainland."

His lickable lips tightened as if he wasn't used to receiving orders, a thought that gave her immense pleasure. Oh, how fun it would be to take him down a peg or two, to remind him that he might think himself a god amongst lesser folk, but in reality he was nothing more than a man. An extremely rich, urbane, sexy, and probably quite fascinating man, but still a man.

She looked at the dip of his collarbone. Her tongue cleaved to the roof of her mouth. "Temptation is a bitch."

"You can say that again," he muttered, giving her a dark look before turning on his heel and leaving the room, dragging his brother with him.

Chapter 2

There was no reason for him to be there. There was absolutely nothing wrong with the woman with whom Theo had gotten a little overly amorous, and yet there he was, standing in a hospital hallway, waiting to hear exactly what he knew—that she hadn't been attacked.

So why was he there, when he should have been at home keeping an eye on Elena and the guests who filled his house? The party celebrating his sister's birthday aside, he had a million other things he'd much rather be doing than standing in the antiseptic surroundings of the small hospital his father had endowed eight years ago, after the death of his beloved second wife.

Nurses hurried past him, most giving him nothing but the deferential acknowledgment due the local benefactor, a few casting warmer gazes that lingered with pleasure. He thought little of the attention they paid him—women had fawned over him since the time he grew hair between his legs.

"I think I'm going to die," Theo murmured, his head

hanging low between his knees as he hunched over in the chair. "That woman broke my nuts."

"Next time you can't keep them in your trousers, pick someone a little more experienced," Iakovos told him, his voice rich with the grim sense of injustice he was cherishing. That woman had poked him in the chest! She had *yelled* at him!

Theo looked up with a lopsided grin. Even half-drunk and suffering a black eye, he possessed the famed Papaioannou charm that had a passing female nurse gasping. "Couldn't help myself, Jake. She was so hot. Pretended to be shy, but she was rubbing herself all over me, and she had tits that drove me wild. Everything would have been fine, but then she got demanding, and next thing I knew, that skinny little bit was there screaming that she'd been attacked, and then the two others came in. Even then I could've explained that the shy bird was going off about nothing, but then they had to get that . . . that . . . ." One hand cupped his testicles.

"Amazon?" Iakovos asked.

"She-devil. Did you see how she looked at me? I thought she was going to skin me alive until you stopped her."

"It would have served you right if I'd let her." His jaw tightened as he looked down at his scapegrace brother. An only child until his father's second marriage fifteen years after his birth, Iakovos was almost twenty years older than Elena, while thirteen years stood between Theo and him. Sometimes, he felt old enough to be their father. "I told you to lay off the alcohol."

"I wasn't drunk," Theo protested. "I just had a little buzz going."

"Your little buzzes are going to land you in the hospital with liver failure if you don't cut back. Or jail if you ever again try a stunt like the one you pulled tonight—don't bother protesting that you didn't attack that girl. I know you didn't. You still shouldn't have had her in your room."

Theo gave him another smile that oozed with charm. "Come on, Jake," he said, using the Anglicized nickname that made Iakovos' lips thin. "All Papaioannou men have to do is smile, and women fall all over themselves to crawl into our beds. It's not like you haven't ever succumbed to a sweet little thing."

"There's such a thing as fouling your own nest, and I most certainly haven't succumbed to the temptation of any woman in Elena's set. I'd rather not be known as a cradle robber."

Theo made a rude face. "You're thirty-nine, Iakovos, not eighty-nine. There's nothing wrong with Elena's friends. Some of them are—" He stopped speaking, the smug look on his face swiftly changing to one of horror. "It's the she-devil! I'm getting out of here before she attacks me again."

Iakovos turned to watch the woman who was marching down the narrow hallway of the hospital toward him, her long legs eating up the distance, her hair rippling behind her like a banner. She looked exactly like the personification of a summer storm at sea, one that was about to descend upon him. For a moment he wondered if he'd be the same once the storm hit, but dismissed it as a fanciful thought, one not worthy of consideration. Especially, he noted to himself as he allowed his gaze to roam over the approaching woman, as there was such a better use for his attention. The woman—he couldn't bring himself to think of her by that appalling nickname—what did she say her name was? Rose? No, the French version of that word, Eglantine . . . an unusual name, an old-fashioned name, one that suited her.

She was tall, almost as tall as he was, and plentifully formed, not at all his usual type. She was dressed simply in neutral linen pants and a sleeveless tunic that might have hid her form from other men, but his sharp eyes picked up the alluring curve of her hip when the bottom of the tunic fluttered back momentarily. Her breasts were decently covered, but nothing could disguise their abundance, or the soft sweep of her upper arms, covered lightly in freckles. Her face wouldn't be considered beautiful by the standards held by the women he usually dated, but he found it pleasing nonetheless. She had a round little stubborn chin, that glorious wide mouth that his gaze returned to again and again, a short nose with freckles, and two eyes that were at this moment looking as if nothing would make her happier than to see him drop dead on the spot.

"Eglantine," he said, acknowledging her when she stopped in front of him, her hands on her hips.

Her nostrils flared. "Yacky."

He closed his eyes for a moment. "My name is Iako-vos. If you are unable to remember that, you may address me as Mr. Papaioannou."

She looked incredulous. "You're not serious."

"I am. It is my name. It is not that difficult to say. I'm sure that you could master it with little effort should you put your mind to it."

"Yeah, and monkeys might fly out of your butt, but since neither is likely to happen, we'll just move on, shall we?"

"*What* did you say?" he asked, outraged to the tips of his toes. Delightfully irreverent as she was, he had the desperate sense that if he did not take control of the conversation, he would be lost in the storm that seemed to accompany her.

"I said we should move on, and I—"

"You said—" He breathed heavily through his nose for a moment. "You said something about monkeys flying out of my ass. That is the second time you have mentioned that in conversation."

"Your ass? So?" Her eyebrows rose. "Do you have a problem with your butt?"

"No, I do not have a problem with it!" The sense of control slipping away from him grew stronger. He took a deep breath, and was aware of her unique scent even over the antiseptic odors of the hospital. "But you seem to have one."

She looked surprised, and before he could ask her how the young woman was, she walked around behind him, startling him by pulling up the back of the coat he'd slipped on for the ride over to the mainland. "What are you doing?" he demanded, feeling more and more as if he were a bit of flotsam caught in a whirlpool.

"Seeing if I have a problem with your ass. I don't seem to. Do you mind if I touch?"

Iakovos looked over his shoulder at her, speechless for the first time in his life. Before he could demand that she treat him with the respect due a man in his position, she put out a hand and cupped one cheek. Instantly, his groin was flooded with blood, leaving his sex heavy with need.

He was absolutely, utterly, and completely out of his depth with her.

"Well, it's kind of hard to see because you're not wearing skintight pants, but from what I can feel, no, I don't have a problem with your ass." Harry dropped his jacket as he spun around to face her, her fingers tingling from the contact with his warm behind.

She badly wanted to use both hands on him, but suspected that would be pushing things too far. As it was, he had another one of those indescribable looks on his face, as if he couldn't decide whether he wanted to throttle her or kiss her silly.

"I really hope it's the latter," she told him.

"What ladder?" he asked, his eyes taking on a bit of a wild look.

"Sorry, inner monologue again. It's not important. Is the situation with your ass settled? Good. Now, if we could address the issue of Cyndi, the doctor says she's suffering from the abrasions on her chest and neck, her blood pressure is sky-high, and she's had to be sedated because she was close to completely losing it. I don't think she's in any real danger, but she had worked herself up to such a state, it's probably better if she spends the night here," she said, lifting her chin. She dared him— she just *dared* him—to tell her she was being foolish.

A muscle in Iakovos' jaw flexed a few times, but all he said was, "I don't care if she spends a month here so long as she stops throwing herself at Theo."

"He didn't have to accept what she offered. Not to mention he was stinking drunk, and way too rough with her, as petite as she is," Harry told him, dragging her mind away from thoughts of what his butt must look like to more important things. "Amy said she'd stay with Cyndi. The doctor wants Cyndi to remain overnight, but evidently it's going to take some time to get her into a room. He said they're run off their feet because half the hospital staff went to another town where there was a train accident, so it could be a few hours. I'm sure you want to get back to your party."

His brows, straight slashes of ebony against his warm bronzed skin, lowered. "Are you giving me orders, Eglantine?"

"No, Yacky, I'm not. I'm simply suggesting that since it's going to take some time to get Cyndi settled, you probably want to go home. There's no sense for you to stay here, too. I assume you came over in another boat?"

He nodded, his eyes searching her face as if he sought some answer there. "You are tired."

"Oh, I'm well beyond tired," she agreed, giving him what she hoped was a bright smile as she rubbed her arms against the chill in the air. The hospital was very modern, if small, with an obviously quite efficient air-conditioning system. "I've been awake for over twenty-four hours." His frown asked a question. She answered it with a shrug. "The kids flew out a day before me. I wasn't called in to pinch-hit until this morning. Er . . . yesterday morning. Sometime. I've lost track of what time it is since I left Seattle."

He stared at her for a moment, not saying anything, just looking at her. She couldn't help but stare at his lips, and wondered what sort of miracle she'd have to pull off to taste them.

Without a word, he took off his suit jacket and draped it around her shoulders before turning and striding off down the corridor. The jacket was warm from his body heat, and smelled like him. The scent of his cologne—lemony and woodsy at the same time—teased her nose as she watched him walk away. "Oh, I have *no* problem at all with your butt," she said softly before melting into a chair, suddenly so exhausted she didn't have the strength to do more than huddle into the jacket and wish she was back home, in her little apartment that was completely devoid of sexy, arrogant, rich playboys with incredibly fabulous butts.

She woke up to find she was slumped sideways in the chair, drooling on the lapel of Iakovos' nice jacket.

"Come," the man himself said, holding out a hand to her.

"Where?" she asked, averting her face so he wouldn't see her wipe off a tendril of slobber on the wet patch on his coat.

"There's a handkerchief in the inside pocket," he said with martyred resignation.

"Sorry," she said, dabbing at her lips before offering him the jacket.

He looked at it as if she'd just wiped out a cesspool with it. "Keep it. I have others."

"I didn't mean to fall asleep and slobber all over it. I'll have it cleaned and sent back to you." She stood slowly, feeling as if she were a hundred years old.

"You'll need it in a few minutes. The wind is cold on the water at night."

"I told you I wasn't going to leave until Cyndi got settled in a room." He tried to herd her toward the elevator. She dug in her heels.

He made an annoyed click of his tongue. "You are exhausted and you need to rest."

"Yeah, well, you may be Mr. Fabulous, but you're so not the boss of me."

"Mr. Papaioannou, not Fabulous," he corrected her.

"I am never going to be able to pronounce that!"

"You will. It's not that difficult. Say it slowly. Papai-oan—"

"Argh!" she yelled, as her emotions of the past two hours—combined with a pretty severe case of sleep deprivation—more or less robbed her of what few inhibitions she had. She knew that, and yet there was nothing, absolutely nothing, on this good earth that was going to stop her from doing what she had wanted to do the second she saw the annoying, aggravating, incredibly sexy man in front of her.

She grabbed his head with both hands, pulled his face down to hers, and sucked his lower lip into her mouth.

He stood frozen for a second, then pulled back, his eyes glittering like polished onyx. "I do *not* like aggressive women!"

She stared at him, stunned by her own brashness but absolutely flabbergasted by the brief taste of his mouth. Before she could even begin to stammer some sort of an apology, he was on her, the cool, hard planes of the wall behind her holding her up while hot, hard man covered her front. His mouth was like fire, a sweet, sensual fire that threatened to burn her up, leaving nothing but a Harry-shaped smear of ash on the wall. He didn't ask permission for his tongue to visit hers—it was just suddenly there, sweeping around as if it owned the place while he groaned into her mouth.

She put both hands on his chest, gathered every ounce of strength, and shoved him backward.

His expression was as black as his eyes, but that didn't stop her. "And *I* don't like men who don't bother to ask permission before they stick their tongues down my throat!"

Those beautiful, glittering eyes narrowed. "How many men have stuck their tongues down your throat?"

"None! But that's beside the point!"

She panted, literally *panted*, from the fire of his kiss, and the heat of his body, which seemed to sink into her very pores, leaving her burning with the desire for more. More of his mouth, more of his body, just *more*.

He gritted his teeth. "I have never been forced to ask permission to kiss a woman. It does not happen! And I will not—"

Harry threw herself on him. She just leaped on him, wrapping both arms around his head and her legs around his waist. He caught her, pulling her higher so that her mouth was directly in front of his, his fingers digging into her behind. "Shut up and kiss me."

His eyes opened wide with indignation. "Did you just tell me to shut up?"

"Yes. Yes, I did. Do you want to make something of it?"

The promise of retribution shone brightly in his eyes, but before he could answer, Cyndi's doctor emerged from the elevator. He stopped, looking at them, blinking a couple of times as if he couldn't believe what he was seeing.

"Hi, Dr. Panagakos," Harry said, trying to think of a viable excuse for her clinging to one of the world's most eligible bachelors, her legs wrapped around his waist, his hands on her butt.

Iakovos shot her a glare. "Oh, you have no difficulty pronouncing 'Panagakos'?"

"*He* put consonants in his name," she said with a pointed look.

He growled deep in his chest, his eyes almost scorching her flesh.

The doctor edged around them, murmuring something about seeing to a patient.

"Well?" she asked Iakovos.

The muscle in his jaw twitched. "Well, what?"

"Are you going to kiss me or not? I mean, we are in this really compromising position, and despite the fact that you don't appear to have back problems, I imagine holding me up like this for any length of time is bound to wear you out."

"Do you always talk this much?" he asked, his gaze now on her lips.

"Always."

"Good." He kissed her, pushing her against the wall once more, his tongue moving with slow, sensual strokes over hers.

He felt as if he was caught in the middle of her storm, life turned upside down, everything that he knew and felt and believed completely overturned by this irritating, unreasonable, desirable woman. She tasted of the sea, of lost hopes and dreams, of woman. She was sweet and salty and so hot that he felt the prickle of sweat as it formed on his brow. He wanted her with a need that he hadn't felt since . . . well, since ever. No woman had ever threatened to overset his mind the way she had. There was no rhyme or reason to his immediate and consuming passion for her—it was like the tempest she represented, sweeping over him with a madness that he never wanted to end.

"Jake, I'm going home. I'll send Spyros back with the launch—"

Reluctantly, Iakovos released Harry's tongue, pulling back from her, allowing her legs to slide to the floor, but keeping a hold on her hips as she staggered into him. Her eyes were glazed, her expression one of stupefaction, her lips as red as ripe cherries, and he felt immense male pride in the fact that a kiss could so affect her. At least he wasn't alone in his sense of being overwhelmed.

He turned his head to look at his brother. Theo's expression of shock melted to a slow grin. "Or maybe you'll be wanting to come back sooner rather than later?"

"We'll be returning to the island now, yes," he said, eyeing Harry with some concern. She blinked several times, still clutching his arms as if she was stunned. "I'm good, but not that good, sweetheart," he told her softly.

She blinked those impossibly thick black lashes at him a few more times, then suddenly straightened up, releasing the death hold she had on his arms. "I don't know—that was pretty spectacular. But I can't go with you."

Her gaze skittered over to Theo. She straightened even more, squaring her shoulders. "What are you smirking at? Haven't you ever seen someone kiss your brother?"

"Lots of women," he answered, his grin widening.

"I've changed my mind," he told Iakovos in Greek. "She's not a she-devil. She's a witch."

He rolled his eyes and put his hand on Harry's back, gently shoving her toward the elevator. "It is late. We will return now."

"Look, Yacky, I just told you—"

"Yacky?"

Iakovos gritted his teeth at the snicker that followed the word.

"I just told you that I wasn't going to leave until Cyndi is settled in a room."

"She's in a room. Her female companion is with her. I sent the other two over on the first launch."

Harry stopped arguing and looked at him with those big eyes that were now a dark, mysterious gray-brown. "She is? But the dude in Admitting said it would be a few hours."

"Wealth and fame have their use sometimes," he told her, pushing her onto the elevator.

"Wealth, yeah, but fame? Eh. Not really. Let me just check and make sure she's OK."

Iakovos waited until she had satisfied herself that her charge was being well taken care of before asking, "What do you know of fame?" He was very much aware of her standing next to him in the confined space of the elevator as they left the hospital. "You said you were not the band's regular manager."

"I'm not." She slid him an odd glance, a little smile curling the edges of her lips. He wanted to strip her right there and take her on the floor of the elevator. "Do you guys get new U.S. movies out here?"

"Yes."

"Did you see the one that came out a couple of months ago?" She named the title of a popular movie that he had particularly enjoyed.

"I took Elena to it, as a matter of fact."

"Ah. Well, that was based on one of my books."

Both Theo and he stared at her in surprise. She smiled. "I told you I was a writer. I write thrillers under the name of M. J. Reynolds. That was the first one made into a movie, although they totally changed the story from the book. Still, it was fun to see it."

Iakovos made a mental note to remove the latest M. J. Reynolds book that sat on his nightstand before he got Harry into his bed. That she would find herself there was not a point open to debate—he wanted her with a need that rocked him, and she obviously was in a similar state. Before the night was over, he would tame the tempest, or die trying.

Chapter 3

Harry made no objection when, upon reaching Iakovos' island, he guided her into the house rather than escorting her to the staff quarters. Theo said nothing, as well, just disappeared into the back of the house, where strains of music could be heard. Elena's friends, Iakovos knew from experience, would be happy dancing until the sun rose. Without a word, he took Harry's hand, leading her up a flight of stairs and turning to the north, to the family wing. He was painfully aware of her scent, her nearness, the heat of her, and was far too busy planning all of the things he was going to do to her when he finally got her naked and into his bed to expend any energy on actual speech.

Luckily, she didn't seem to need conversation. She just gave him a long look when he opened the door to his personal rooms and gestured for her to go in. She studied the room, then him, her attention seeming to be divided between his lower neck and his mouth. After a moment's consideration, she gave a little nod as if she'd come to a decision, and entered his sitting room. He led her through it, through the dressing room, past his lavish bathroom, to his bedroom. The doors were cast open, so he could watch the waves crash onto the rocks below, on the north side of the island, the wildness of the water always stirring an answer from something deep inside him.

"Are you using some form of birth control?" he asked politely, fighting with the need to simply shred the clothes off her and pounce.

"Pills, yes."

He reached for her, then paused, a horrible thought occurring to him. "There is a man in your life?"

She shook her head, staring at his upper lip. With one finger she touched the indentation between the lip and his nose. "So sexy," she murmured.

"Then why are you taking birth control pills?" he demanded, his skin prickling at the thought of any other man attempting to capture his tempest.

"Convenience, mostly. I only get a couple of periods a year that way."

"There is no man you are seeing? No man who you desire?"

"Oh, yes, there's a man I desire," she said. "Can we get on with it? Because I feel like I'm going to explode or something if you don't touch me soon."

"Who is this man?" The words came out in a snarl. "What is his name?"

A little smile turned her mouth up. "Yannykos Papamomo . . . er . . . nope. Sorry. Still not able to say it."

Him. She wanted him. She desired him. Of course she did; she'd literally thrown herself on him at the hospital. "Remove your clothing," was all he said.

Her eyebrows lifted before she smiled a long, slow smile that he seemed to feel in his gut. "You like a strip-tease, do you? OK. I don't know how good I am at it, but I can try."

He removed his shirt and shoes, but left his trousers on as she slowly unbuttoned the line of buttons down her tunic. He was aroused, his erection heavy and hot, taking on a level of hardness he didn't recall ever achieving before. Even though she had flung herself on him, he didn't want to startle her with the sight of just how much she had affected him.

She paused, her attention fixed on his groin. "Holy Mary, mother of god. You, sir, are packing wood. That looks like it hurts. You'd better let that loose before you do some sort of permanent damage to yourself."

So much for not startling her. He debated demanding that she unzip his trousers, but decided there was no way he'd be able to survive her hands anywhere near his groin, so he shucked his pants and underwear with quick efficiency.

Her eyebrows rose at the sight of him, but she said nothing, her gaze moving from his genitals to his neck to his mouth.

"Do you need help with those buttons?" he asked after another few minutes had passed and she was still working down the long line of them.

"Yeah, why don't you start at the bottom and work up, and we'll meet in the middle."

He smiled a smile filled with manly intentions, and reached for her. "As you like."

"You know, ripping the buttons off wasn't quite what I had in mind when—oh, hello!"

He tore off the tunic, his hands instantly on her breasts. Unable to keep from diving into the plump little offerings presented just for him, he buried his face in them, breathing deeply of her scent, his fingers stroking the sensitive peaks until she clutched his bare shoulders, her eyes wide.

He lifted his head, his hands busy on her linen trousers. "This is going to be close, sweetheart."

"You're telling me," she said, shivering as she stroked a hand down his chest. "I'm sorry, can you stop what you're doing?"

He pushed her pants to her feet, frowning as he looked down at her. "What?"

"Thanks."

She leaned forward and licked at the base of his throat, moaning as she rubbed herself against him. His eyes crossed as his erection pressed into the soft silk of her belly.

"Finished?" he asked in a strangled voice when she gave his collarbone a little kiss.

"For now. There's still that spot above your lip, but I'll save that for dessert. You can have a turn if you like."

"Thank you," he said gravely, and without further ado, he yanked off her underwear, releasing her breasts from the warm satin confines of her bra.

"I like a man who gets right down to business," she said, squirming as he pulled her against his body, dipping his head to claim that delectable mouth once again.

The way she moved against him set off all sorts of warning bells in his mind. If she wiggled just once more to the left, it would all be over for him.

"You taste of the sea, my little tempest," he murmured into her neck as he lifted her, carrying her to his bed and then following her down onto it.

"Salty, you mean? It's the heat, probably. I'm not used to it."

"Wild," he corrected. "You taste untamed. Endlessly changing."

"Oooh, pretty," she said on a long breath, her body lying with languid grace.

He nibbled on her breasts, drinking in her soft little sounds of pleasure as he licked first one nipple, then the other before moving lower.

He kissed her belly, the scent of her driving that strange, primitive need within him to possess her. He had to have her now, or burst. He moved her thighs open for him, settling himself at the entrance to her paradise, his arms braced next to her, dipping his head to take her mouth as he prepared to slide into her warmth.

She gave a long, slow sigh, her eyes drifting shut with pleasure as he kissed a path to her breasts, gritting his teeth against the need to bury himself within her. He would do this slowly, giving her the time needed to rouse her passion. He kissed his way around to her ear, nibbling on the line of her neck, his penis so hot and heavy that he honestly thought it might kill him. "It is good, is it not, sweetheart?"

She made no answer. He bit her earlobe gently, then realized something was wrong. He rose up enough to look down at her. She was flushed with passion, her eyes closed, her mouth rosy and well kissed ... and slightly open. The tiniest of snores emerged from between those delicious lips.

She'd fallen asleep? While they were making love? It

was true they weren't actually engaged in intercourse, but this certainly counted as foreplay. Iakovos stared down at her in complete disbelief. He'd never, *ever* had a woman fall asleep while he was foreplaying. Perhaps not all of them were as wild with arousal as they said they were, but he had always done his best to be a thoughtful lover, taking pleasure in making sure his companion received her full share of attention before he succumbed to his own climax.

And now this tempest, this storm of a woman who consumed his mind and body so effortlessly, had the audacity to fall asleep while he was attempting to bring her pleasure.

He gently nipped her shoulder to see if she had just drifted off. Perhaps he had been too considerate by taking it slow? Perhaps there was too much foreplay? Her nose wrinkled. He nipped again.

She snored.

What was the etiquette of a lover who fell asleep in such a situation, he wondered, loath to leave her lying there so warm and enticing, but not wishing to continue if she wasn't going to participate.

"Eglantine," he said in a tone of voice that was perhaps tinged with just a shade of desperation.

She scowled in her sleep.

"Harry."

"Mrrf?" Her eyes opened. "Hmm?"

"You fell asleep."

"I did?" She blinked a few times, then glanced down to where his chest was resting on her belly. "Oh! I'm sorry! It's no reflection on you, Iakovos, honest. I guess the jet lag caught up to me. Do you want to proceed?"

"Only if you can spare me the time," he said, wasp-ishly, he knew, but he felt that he was due a little wasp-ishness given the situation.

"I'm all yours," she said, stroking her hands down his back to his ass cheeks as he moved up to possess himself of her mouth again.

He groaned into her mouth at her heat, watching the passion make her eyes go soft. Her lips were sweet, like fresh berries tipped in seawater, and her neck and shoul-ders beckoned to his mouth. He bit gently on her ear, licking the path to her jaw, murmuring words of plea-sure as he did so.

She was asleep again.

Iakovos looked down at her face, the storm serene now as she lay sleeping, a little smile curling her mouth, the thick lashes resting against the honey-sweet skin of her cheeks.

He rolled onto his back with a sigh, and cast a regret-ful look at his erection. "We're on our own tonight, it would appear."

Harry murmured something unintelligible, rolling over to drape herself halfway across his chest, her leg wrapping itself around one of his. She gave a contented sigh, pressed a kiss to his cheek, and snuggled into him, snoring gently into his neck.

Oh, he'd tamed his tempest all right. He'd tamed her right into insensibility.

The sunlight woke Harry, simply because she wasn't used to seeing it in her western-facing bedroom. She opened her eyes, looking with sleepy confusion at the sight that greeted her. Wide doors were opened to catch the breeze off the sea, through which she could see the blue-jade water of the Aegean as it surged against the rocks. A long, low bureau sat next to the doors. Muted pictures hung in tasteful clusters on the wall. She was in a room, a masculine room, a room that could probably hold her entire apartment and still have extra space. . . . Suddenly she remembered where she was.

She rolled over to find Iakovos lying on his side, his head propped up on one hand, watching her with un-readable black eyes. In the light of the morning sun, however, she could see that they weren't really black; they were a dark brown, streaked with black and shiny gold flecks.

"Awkward," she said after a moment of silence.

"You think so?" he asked, his voice sliding along her skin like silk.

"You don't?"

"Not particularly, no."

"Yes, well, you've probably woken up to legions of women, but I'm not a famous world's most eligible Greek playboy. I don't know what I'm supposed to do. You'll have to let me know what's normally done in this situation. Should I act all casual, like I wake up to a new lover every day? Should I blush and avert my eyes shyly from your naked form? Should I pounce on you? What's standard in this situation?"

A little frown creased the area between his brows. "You weren't a virgin. You must have woken up to a lover before."

"A lover, yes. But not tons of them like you have."

"Who says I have had tons of lovers?"

"Magazines. Newspapers. Internet celebrity sites, no doubt," she said, ticking them off on her fingers.

"They exaggerate."

"Uh-huh. Just out of idle curiosity, how many women *have* you woken up to?"

He looked like he wasn't going to answer for a few seconds, then frowned in concentration. "I haven't ever counted them."

"That many, huh?"

"No, I just don't feel the need to count them. Once a relationship is past, it's past. I do not concern myself with it anymore."

"*Not* the sort of thing someone who wakes up for the first time in your bed wants to hear," she said, pushing him over onto his back as she straddled his hips. Immediately his hands went to her breasts. "I have a horrible feeling that you had to wake me up at some point last night. Did I really fall asleep on you?"

"Twice," he said, his fingers teasing her breasts.

"Have I wounded your manly pride?" she asked, arching her back as he set her afire with just the touch of his hands.

"Extremely."

She put her hands over his, stopping him for a moment as she leaned down to kiss him. "I really am sorry, Iakovos. The jet lag must have nailed me. Did you at least . . . finish?"

"No."

She winced. "Sorry," she repeated.

"It's not something I care to experience again, but you are welcome to make amends, if you desire," he said, his eyes lighting with a darkly sensual glint that warmed her to the tips of her toenails.

She squirmed against him. "Oh, I think I owe you at least that much. Do you like to be on the top or the bottom?"

"What?" He looked like he couldn't believe what she was asking.

"Do you want me to ride you like a rented mule, or do you prefer to be Mr. Missionary Position? I'm fine with either, so it doesn't matter to me." She stroked her hands down his chest, greatly enjoying the soft hairs that tickled her fingertips. His chest hair narrowed below his belly button, leading in a glossy trail down to his penis.

His lips twisted. "Are you always so irreverent about sex?"

"Sure. It's supposed to be fun, isn't it?"

"Enjoyable, yes." He slid his hands up her thighs, rubbing his thumb against sensitive flesh. She saw stars for a moment before rocking her hips against him. "Hot and sweaty and fulfilling, absolutely."

She moaned, rising up a little as one of his fingers curled into her depths. "Oh, very, very fulfilling."

"Harry?"

She moaned again, her back arched as he slid a second finger in with the first. "Hrrn?"

He flipped her over onto her back, coming on top of her, pulling her legs around his hips. "I prefer to be on top."

"Definitely works for me," she gasped as he slid into her. Her hips rose to meet his as he pistoned forward, his mouth suddenly on hers, throwing her into sensory overload. He tasted so good, so hot, she just wanted to stay there forever, reveling in him, her body welcoming the hard thrust as he invaded her depths. "Harder," she whispered, her lips trailing along his neck, tasting the saltiness of his skin as he obliged, moving against her with more force. "Faster."

"My little tempest," he moaned into her ear. "I should have known you would like it this way, wild and uncontrolled."

"Uncontrolled is definitely better," she groaned, her legs tightening around his hips, dragging her nails gently down his spine. "Oh dear god, what you do to me!"

"If it's anything like what you're doing to me—"

The rest of his words were lost as she suddenly froze, her entire body perched for one endless moment on the edge of something momentous before she yelled his name and came apart in his arms.

He followed, his hoarse shout of completion sweet in her ears, almost as sweet as the weight of him when he collapsed on her. She stroked his back, not minding that it was slick with sweat, for he definitely had earned it. His breathing was as ragged as hers, hot little puffs of it on her neck as he regained his senses.

He rolled off her, his eyes wide and staring up at the ceiling, his breath still uneven. Harry felt like someone had replaced her limbs with ones that lacked bones. She looked over at Iakovos, about to comment that he could be on top anytime he desired, when she suddenly realized just how big the bed was. "Glorioski, Yacky. This bed is huge."

His head turned to look at her, his eyes disbelieving. "Pardon?"

"Your bed." She gestured at the space between them.

"You could house a family of five here. It's massive. What do you need such a gigantic bed for?"

He was back to looking at her as if the boobs were dancing on her head again. "I am a large man. I like to spread out."

She bit back a smile. She'd noticed that fact in the middle of the night, when she had to use the bathroom. He had been asleep, one arm thrown over her as he lay facedown, spread-eagle on the bed, taking up an enormous amount of space. "Yes. I like that about you. You make me feel feminine. Not a lot of guys can do that because I'm so big, you know. In fact, I don't think any of them have ever done so to such a high degree."

"Eglantine," he said, his lips tightening as he pulled her across the vast miles of his bed to his chest. "I thought we agreed to not discuss our previous lovers."

"No, you couldn't count yours, there were so many. I can count mine on one finger."

His lips pursed. "You've had only one lover?"

"Yes. It lasted three years, though, so I think that should count as three. 'One' sounds so pathetic, don't you think?"

"No," he said, pulling the sheets over them. "I don't think that sounds pathetic at all. Go to sleep."

"It's morning," she protested, aware of a languid sense that made it seem wrong to want to move out of the soft, warm bed. "I have things to do."

"It's early and you've only had a few hours of sleep."

"I should check on the boys. They are probably wondering what happened to me last night."

"You can speak to them later."

"I should check on Cyndi and make sure she's OK."

"I will call the hospital for you. Sleep now, little storm. You need to build your strength for later."

"Ha-ha. Very funny." She snuggled against him, her body relaxing against his warmth, wondering what it would take to stay in his arms forever.

Chapter 4

"Harry Knight, you're an idiot, falling for a guy you just met." The words hung in the air as she made a clean dive into the narrow pool she'd found tucked away in a corner of the garden, hidden by tall shrubs. The water wasn't heated, and shaded as it was, the shock of cold had her gasping for breath as she surfaced and shook the water from her eyes before she picked one of the four lanes and settled into an easy crawl stroke meant to wake her up after a morning of lovemaking so mind-bogglingly good, her body still hummed with aware- ness.

Not awareness of herself, but of him.

Iakovos. She let the name roll around her mind as she swam lazy laps, trying to pinpoint just what she thought of him.

He was sexy, definitely. Just looking at him literally had her drooling, and made her feel somewhat giddy, like she was fifteen and in love with a rock star.

He was caring. He didn't just use her body, giving nothing of himself. He made love to her with his whole being, his whispered words of what he was feeling, what he was thinking, how much he liked her response almost as wonderful as the touch of his body. She didn't have a lot of experience with men, but instinctively she knew that Iakovos' behavior in bed went above and beyond the call of duty.

She flipped over onto her back, her arms and legs moving mechanically as she swam the laps, her attention caught up with how much she liked his mind. She had thought at first that he was a typical arrogant, stick-up-his-butt hunk, half in love with himself, and more than a little smitten with his own consequence. But by the time she kissed him in the hospital, she'd realized that he wasn't anything like that. Oh, he liked to talk the talk, but the second he realized that she saw through the facade, he didn't even bother to try to maintain it.

Iakovos was, she suspected as she watched the cloudless blue morning sky while she swam, quite simply a very nice, very intriguing man, and if things didn't come to an immediate and complete halt, she was going to fall madly in love with him.

A shadow fell over her face, causing her stroke to check and leaving her sputtering in the water for a moment.

"Eglantine. We meet again," a deep, lazy voice said.

She shook the water out of her eyes and treaded water for a moment, looking up at where he stood at the side of the pool. He was dressed in a pair of navy blue swim trunks and was carrying a towel.

"Yacky. I'm sorry," she stammered, unable to take her eyes off all his exposed flesh. "I didn't realize this was your pool."

"They're *all* my pools," he said, humor lacing his voice. "It's my island."

"No, I meant . . . I guess I didn't think. This looked like it was an unused lap pool. I didn't mean to use it without permission—"

"Sweetheart, you're welcome to use whatever you want here, and that includes me, an event that is going to happen sooner rather than later if you keep looking at me like that."

She grinned, slowly swimming away. "I can't help it. Have you ever heard of a tongue cleaving to the roof of a mouth? Looking at you makes my tongue cleave, Iakovos."

"I have better things to do with your tongue." He dove over her head into the lane next to hers, emerging from the water with his black hair slicked back. He had a slight widow's peak, and wore his hair a little longer than most men she had met, long enough that it brushed the tops of his ears. It was as soft as silk when it ran through her fingers, she remembered with a little shiver.

He was looking at her with an indescribable expression, his eyes glittering like the morning sun on the cool water. "If you keep looking at me like that, Harry, I'm going to make love to you again."

"Oh, I have no problem with that," she said, giving the idea her full vote of approval.

He started to move toward her, then stopped and shook his head. "I always swim in the morning."

"Then by all means, swim. Will it bother you if I do a few more laps, too?"

"Not at all."

He moved over to an outside lane, she assumed so he

wouldn't splash her. She watched him for a moment as he swam off in a smooth Australian crawl before resuming her own laps.

She had just finished four laps of a particularly sloppy breaststroke when she became aware that he was watching her. She tossed him a curious look. "Something wrong?"

"Not at all. You swim very well."

She shrugged, and went back to the previously interrupted backstroke. "I get by. It's not often I have the chance to swim, so when I do, I try to take advantage of it."

"You should do it more," he said, mirroring her backstroke. She peeked at him from the corner of her eye. His crawl was much better than his backstroke. "You could be quite a good swimmer if you gave it a little time."

It took a few seconds before his statement sank in. When it did, she stopped and glared at him. "Are you implying that just because I'm not some gazillionaire rich most wanted bachelor that I'm not a good swimmer?"

"Most eligible bachelor, not most wanted," he corrected, not bothering to look at her, damn his arrogant hide. "And all I said was that if you practiced it more, you could be quite good at it."

"Oh, those are fighting words, buster," she said, swimming to the steps that led out of the pool.

"I didn't intend to insult you—"

"Like hell you didn't!" She pulled down the back of her suit that always rode up over her butt cheeks and strode to the opposite end of the pool. "Come on, out of the water. You're going to put your money where your extremely sexy and almost irresistible mouth is."

"What exactly do you propose? A wager?" he asked as he slowly climbed out of the pool.

"That sounds good. We'll have a little race, shall we? Winner has to . . ." She paused, trying to think of a suitable prize.

"Have sex with the other person?" he suggested, a slow, sultry smile curling his lips as he strolled toward her, the water glistening like scattered diamonds on his chest.

"Deal. How many laps are you up to?"

His gaze moved slowly over her body. "I'll let you set the course, but I should point out that I have an unfair advantage over you."

"Because you're taller than me?" she asked, doing her own visual inspection. Just looking at him made her heart rate pick up. Before he could answer, she held up her hand. "Wait a second—uncleaving tongue."

He laughed and shook his head. "No, the advantage is due to me having access to a pool on a daily basis. And as for tongues . . ." He bent down and took possession of her mouth, his tongue a brand on lips made cool by the water. "As I said, I can think of so many other things to do with them."

"Well, you're going to have an advantage if you do that again," Harry said, pushing back after a few minutes of burning under the touch of his hands and mouth. "You do something to my bones to make them go all wobbly."

He lifted his hands in a show of surrender and backed

up. "I wouldn't wish to be accused of cheating. Shall we say four laps? Any particular stroke?"

"What's your strongest?" she asked. "Crawl?"

"Crawl is fine," he agreed, and she knew without a shred of a doubt that he intended to let her win the race. She smiled to herself, sure that she could change that intention in under a minute.

"You want to count us down?" she said, taking up a position at the middle left lane. He chose the one next to her.

"You can do the honors."

"OK. Dive on five." She spread her feet and dropped her hands until her fingers dangled just above the floor of the pool decking in the classic starting pose. "Ready?"

He gave her a curious glance, then mimicked her pose. "Ready."

She counted them off, giving him a half-second start before diving into the pool, adrenaline giving her a little kick as she undulated underwater for the allowable distance before breaking the surface and immediately taking up a fast but maintainable pace. After one lap, she was a full body length ahead of him. She slowed up just a hair as she did an underwater turn, so that he could catch up to see that she was having no problem outpacing him.

She knew the moment he realized that. His smooth crawl suddenly went choppy as he tried to power through the stroke to build up speed. Mentally, she shook her head and cranked her own stroke up a notch, enjoying the rush of endorphins as she made the second turn, now two body lengths ahead of him. By the time she was on the last lap, he was breathing with every stroke, a sure sign he was running out of steam.

She finished almost half the pool length ahead of him, turning around to watch him approach. He didn't bother touching the wall, just stopped next to her, wiping the water from his eyes and nose, his breath as ragged as when he had made love to her this morning, his big chest heaving with the effort to get much-needed oxygen into his lungs.

"You . . . swim . . . professionally . . ." he panted, sweeping his hair back, his eyes accusing.

"Nope. But I was on my high school and college swim teams." She smiled, and swam over to him, sliding her hands up his chest. "You've got a lot of power, Iakovos, but no style, no finesse. Your legs were all over the place, and I'm willing to bet your pull and recovery arm positions were way off."

He grabbed her, pulling her against him, his hands hard on her behind, growling into her mouth as he said, "I'll show you who has no finesse."

They didn't, much to Iakovos' dismay, make love there in the pool, but it was a near thing. He remembered just in time that although none of his family members ever used his lap pool, some of the houseguests might choose to do so, and being caught buried up to the hilt in his wonderful sea-witch had the potential for exposing her to ridicule.

That she had beaten him when he had been so sure he would easily be able to outswim her both surprised and delighted him. That's what he got for assuming she was like any other woman—it was perfectly natural that a tempest, born of the sea as she was, should swim as fast as a dolphin. He released the breast he had been suckling, pulling up the top of her one-piece swimsuit with reluctance, once again pleased with the dazed look that came over her eyes whenever he touched her.

"I can't think of a time when I've looked forward more to paying the penalty for losing a wager," he told her, possessing her mouth one more time, just because he couldn't stop himself. "But I will gladly do so tonight."

"Sounds good to me," she said, sighing happily.

He looked down at her for a moment, at her flushed face, the long tendrils of hair streaming out behind her on the water. Although he wasn't responsible for entertaining Elena's friends, they were guests to his home, and he should put in an occasional appearance. He'd put off business concerns for the few days that he'd devoted to his sister's birthday celebration, but there was always work to be done. Just because the woman whose body pressed so enticingly against his was different from all others didn't mean he had to sate himself on her. She was just a woman.

He looked deep into her eyes made warm with passion, and knew it was stupid to lie to himself. He didn't care about playing host and he didn't care about conducting business. He wanted to spend time with Harry and see what delightful things her mind would think to say and do. "Do you have plans for today?"

He had her so flustered, it took her a moment to collect her thoughts. That, also, pleased him. "Cyndi will be released this afternoon, so I should probably be there to get her."

"The others can do so. I will put a boat at their disposal."

"I'm supposed to be their manager," she reminded him.

He didn't like the idea of her at their beck and call. "I'll have Dmitri make sure they don't run into any issues."

"Dmitri?"

"My assistant." She looked like she was going to protest, so he kissed her again to muddle her mind.

"And then they're sure to want to rehearse," she said a few minutes later, clutching his shoulders, her mouth hot on his neck. "I should probably be there in case they need something."

"My staff can attend to whatever they need," he said, his hands on her ass as he gently pushed her toward the metal ladder. Dear god, how he loved that ass. "Get dressed, and I'll take you to Krokos. You'll like it—it's not too far down the coast from here, but is off the tourist path."

"I shouldn't . . ." She climbed out of the pool.

He followed her, lifting her chin in order to bite her bottom lip.

"All right," she said after a moment's hesitation, water streaming down the slick black swimsuit. He watched a couple of drops roll down between her breasts, and felt his groin grow hot. "But I warn you, if you take me anywhere private, I'm likely to ravish you."

He grinned, unable to keep from pulling her to him for one last plundering kiss. "I'm counting on that, sweetheart. I'm counting on that."

*   *   *

Harry was in heaven, or as close as she could come to it on earth. She looked back from where she perched at the bow of Iakovos' zippy little speedboat, the spray and wind whipping her hair around as if it had a mind of its own. The speed at which they were moving made it impossible to carry on a conversation without shouting, so she contented herself with admiring the view, which mostly consisted of Iakovos. He wore a pair of black pants and a thin red cotton shirt, open just enough at the neck to let her see his sexy neck spot and a hint of the chest hair that she knew was as soft as the finest silk. She loved his chest, couldn't stop wanting to touch and taste it.

He was watching her, as well, sitting with one hand casually on the steering wheel, the other resting on his thigh.

She loved his thighs, too. He had the long muscles of a swimmer, and was unexpectedly ticklish on his inner thighs. Her toes curled in her sandals as she remembered giggling earlier that morning when she gently dragged her nails up his thighs and made him squirm.

She flashed him a smile and turned back to see where they were heading, when a shimmer off the port side made her gasp. She pointed and slid back along the bow of the boat until she stood next to him, grabbing his arm to make him look. "Dolphins!"

He flipped a switch to put the boat on autopilot and wrapped his arm around her waist as he obediently looked at the three dolphins who streaked alongside and in front of the boat.

"They're riding our bow wave," he yelled.

"I've never seen one in person!" She clung to the

metal railing and leaned out to watch them, laughing as one broke the surface and leaped just a few yards from the boat. The sight of them filled her with so much joy that tears stung her eyes.

"Do not lean out too far, or you'll fall in," he warned.

She turned back to share the joy with him, suddenly caught up in the heat of his gaze. Without thinking, she moved into his arms, wrapping her own around his waist, just standing there with her body pressed against his, his mouth gently caressing her forehead while her hair whipped around them. She was content to simply be with him while she experienced this magical world of sun and sea and a man who was fast taking her heart.

An hour later, she stood at the base of stone and earth that jutted up out of the crystal blue water, the brownish red landscape dotted with patches of green, and brilliant white stone buildings clinging with impossible ease to the cliffside.

Iakovos must have called ahead, because a jeep was waiting for him when he pulled the boat up at a small dock. A couple of larger ships were anchored offshore, including one yacht, but Harry paid them no mind as Iakovos told her about the area.

"Saffron is the most valuable asset this region has, but we are here at the wrong time to see the crocus fields. Perhaps another time you will be able to see how it is processed, but for now, you have your choice of lunch, sightseeing, or I can get us a room at the hotel so that you can seduce me."

She looked around the town that rose in steps, dense green scrub balancing out the crisp white buildings with red tile roofs. The air smelled of sea and warm earth, and warmer man. She wanted to bury her face in his neck and just breathe in his scent, but since he'd gone to all the trouble of bringing her out here, she figured she'd better enjoy the opportunity.

"How about a little sightseeing, and then lunch, and then we'll see where we are on the whole idea of me having my womanly way with you."

"I know exactly where I am on that subject, but it shall be as you desire." With his hand warm on her back through the thin gauze of her sundress, he guided her around the town to see what sights there were.

"What is that?" she asked, her hand shading her eyes as she pointed to a mass of white buildings spilling over the hillside.

He glanced at them, then steered her in another direction. "Holiday villas. Come, we will see the older part of town."

They took in a pretty little white church, strolled along the main street, viewed the peculiar but beautiful square tower that was really a dovecote, and finally settled in a taverna on the fringes of the town, sitting high on the hill so it looked down on the water below.

"You're not going to get in trouble for this, are you?" Harry asked as she sat in the shade of an old olive tree.

"For feeding you, or for the things I was thinking I'd like to be doing to you? Definitely not for the former, but quite possibly for the latter."

"Oh, now I'm definitely going to want seduction time," she laughed, highly aware of his leg casually pressed against hers as they sat along the narrow edge of the taverna's patio area. "I meant just taking off and leaving your guests. As much as I've enjoyed the day, I can't help but feel guilty about taking you away from your responsibilities."

"Perhaps," he said, giving her a slow smile that made her melt into a puddle of desire, "I've made you my responsibility for the day."

"One more like that, and you're going to be in big trouble," she warned him.

"Really?" He gave her a considering look. "How so?"

She leaned forward, her breast brushing his arm, and traced a finger down his cheek. "You'd have to explain to everyone why you came in with a woman and left with a boneless, mindless blob of goo."

Before he could answer—and she could see that he was going to answer in kind—the taverna owner trotted over to see what they wanted.

"Do you have any preference?" Iakovos asked after consulting with the man.

"Not really, although I should warn you, I'm allergic to shellfish."

He looked scandalized. "That's tantamount to heresy in Greece."

"In Seattle, too. It's the bane of my existence."

He spoke again with the owner, who gave her a wink before going off to bring their food. "He thinks you're lucky."

"Me?" She opened her eyes wide. "Because I'm with one of the top ten world's most sexy bachelors?"

"Hardly. Because the dolphins welcomed you to Krokos," he answered, pouring her a glass of beer. "You've really never seen them before?"

"No. Do you mind if I touch you?"

It was his turn to look surprised, one side of his mouth

twitching a little. "I don't mind, but you run the risk of shocking the taverna owner."

"Not that sort of touching, Mr. Smutty Mind. I just want to touch you, and I didn't know if you would consider that out of line or not."

"I can honestly say that you have my full approval to touch me however and whenever you like," he said, taking a big swig of beer. "Does that put your mind at ease?"

"Yes, thank you." She put her hand on his thigh, enjoying the sensation of the hard muscle beneath her fingers and the warmth that seeped through the material of his pants. "Why do you speak English with a British accent?"

"I was educated in England. Are we playing Twenty Questions? Why has a woman as beautiful as you had only one lover?"

"Men," she said with a sigh that turned into a little shiver when he casually draped his hand over the back of her chair, his fingers gently stroking the back of her neck, "are intimidated by me. Either I'm taller than they are, which makes them all squirrely, or I'm too ... too ..."

"Untamed?" he asked, his fingers dipping beneath her sundress to stroke the flesh of her back.

"Unconventional. The ones who aren't intimidated are ... I don't know ... just not my type. They don't have a sense of humor, or they are into stuff that doesn't interest me."

"What sort of stuff?" he asked, his fingers building up a burn in a lower, much more private place. "Sports? Politics?"

"No, nothing like that. It's more the way their minds work, I guess. They just don't have that ... spark that fascinates me and makes me want to be with them."

He was silent for a moment. "Do I have that spark?"

"You," she said, leaning close enough that her lips brushed his when she spoke, "have way too much spark for my peace of mind."

Chapter 5

They didn't make it back to the island before Iakovos gave in to the need that had burned so deep inside him ever since she poked him in his chest. He wanted to blame the light, sea green sundress she was wearing, since it not only caressed her flesh the way he wanted to caress her, but also showed off the lovely long line of her legs, of her smooth arms, of her breasts, which he knew were made just for his mouth.

As they headed back to his house, the sun starting to set, he managed to believe, for a whole three minutes, that what he felt for Harry was only a temporary infatuation, pure, honest lust and nothing more.

That lasted until he watched her being his own personal figurehead, posed at the front of the boat, the wind whipping the material of her dress around, allowing tantalizing glimpses of thigh and flashes of underwear.

It was suddenly too much for him. He had to take control of the situation, or risk being lost for good. He throttled the engine way back and put it on cruise, calling for Harry to join him for a glass of the champagne that was cooling in the cabin below.

She sat on the rear bank of seats, her face aglow with pleasure as she watched the shore sliding past them, but it was when she looked at him that her eyes came alive. He liked that; he liked the way she was so honest about her emotions, not trying to hide what she thought or felt.

"How did you become a writer?" he asked, determined to get through the next hour it would take to get back home without losing control of himself in her heat.

"I used to work for a software developer, writing parts of their manuals. One day, I thought it would be fun to add a little touch of humor to the manual. The director of the program didn't agree with me. I lost my job, and I decided right then and there that I was going to write fiction, where I could make up my own worlds, and people them with characters I liked, and ones I wanted to exact a little revenge on. I sold a couple of books, and things just kind of took off from there. Is it my turn?"

He ached to have her. Maybe talking would distract him from the overwhelming need to possess her. "Yes, it's your turn. Do you want to ask how I became a . . . what did you call me?"

"Gazillionaire? Yes, that's actually what I was going to ask you. Were you born into it, or did you make it?"

He gave her a long look. "Does it matter?"

"Absolutely," she said without a second's hesitation.

He watched her, fascinated by the play of light in her eyes. She must have thought she'd insulted him because she hurried to explain. "I'm not interested in how much you have, you know. I make a nice wad of money myself, and there's just me to take care of, so I'm not looking for a sugar daddy or anything like that."

To his surprise, he didn't question that statement at all. Normally he had a very good sense of when people wanted something from him, but she didn't trigger any of those warnings in his mind.

"But there's a big difference between having something handed to you and earning it yourself," she said, hesitating.

"Do you think I inherited my money, or made it?" he asked her, curious to see how she would analyze him.

"I think . . ." Her gaze searched his face. "You're very comfortable with yourself, which makes me think you were born to affluence, and never had to worry about where your next meal was coming from. But at the same time, you strike me as a man who's made his own way, one who isn't afraid of working for a goal. So I'm going to go with you're a self-made gazillionaire."

"'Billionaire,' I believe, is the correct term," he said, struck by how well she'd done. "As it happens, I was born into comfortable circumstances, but my father lost his fortune shortly after that. When I came of age, I decided that I would restore what was lost, and I worked for twenty years to do that."

"But you went to school in England."

"And worked evenings and weekends to pay my way. My mother died at my birth, and my father grieved for almost fifteen years, until he met Elena and Theo's mother."

She looked at him with sympathy. "That must have been difficult for both you and your father. Are you close to him?"

"I was, until he died eight years ago. How about you—you said you were alone? You have no family?"

"Only child of divorced parents. They're both still alive, but I haven't seen my father since I was about two, and my mother has her own life and her own interests. She lives in Arizona; I live in Seattle. . . . We call each other once a month."

"No friends?" he asked, unable to keep from stroking his thumb over the velvety soft smoothness of her sun-warmed cheek.

"Of course I have friends. I'm not a hermit," she said, leaning into his hand. "What about you? How does a man as successful as you weed out the people who just want something from you from the true friends?"

His eyes widened at her perspicacity.

She smiled at the look. "You forget, you're talking to someone who gets e-mails from everyone who thinks they want to be a writer. Usually most of them just want advice, but some of them want to use me. I figured if it was that way for me, it must be a hundred times worse for you."

"I have a couple of close friends," he said slowly, wondering at the level of comfort he had with this child of the sea. It was almost as if he'd known her for a very long time. "And there're Theo and Elena. Harry?"

"Hmm?"

"I'm not going to be able to last all the way back to the island."

"Oh, thank god," she said, her shoulders slumping with relief. "I didn't want to just pounce on you in case you thought all I was interested in was your body, when really it's your mind that's so incredibly sexy, not that I don't absolutely love your body, because I'd have to be dead a couple of years not to, but still, I didn't want you to think that I looked at you as nothing more than an orgasm machine."

He stared at her, and the calm that he now realized came before the storm ended with a whoosh of his breath as he stood up, swung her into his arms, and carried her down to the cabin.

He didn't waste any time, either, Harry thought to herself, as with quick efficiency he stripped her of her clothes, then removed his own, laying her down on one of the two bunks that lined either side of the cabin.

"I don't think you're going to fit," she told him, looking up at where he stood bent over so as to avoid hitting the ceiling. "Look—I fill the whole thing. My head and feet are both touching the walls."

He snarled something in Greek that she was willing to bet wasn't at all nice. His gaze darted here and there, his fingers twitching spasmodically until he suddenly snatched the mattress off the other bunk, and threw it onto the floor of the cabin, along with the blankets.

"Up," he said, gesturing to her.

She got up. He pulled her mattress off, nudged it alongside the first, then flung the blankets over the top of both.

"Down," he ordered.

She slid him a look, amused by the fact that he had found a solution to the problem. Surely such problem solving deserved reward. She knelt before him, taking his erection in her hands. "Now, I'm not a big expert on doing this, so if I do something that you don't like, or do it wrong, or even if you have suggestions on how to improve the whole experience, I'm more than willing to hear you out."

He looked down at her with dawning hope in his eyes. "I'll be sure to let you know how it goes."

"Oh, thank you," she said gratefully. "Most men never talk when it comes to this, you know. They just lie there twitching and moaning, and then they go to sleep. Or at least my boyfriend did, and really, I don't know how one is supposed to improve when one doesn't have any feedback. It's just like writing, if you think about it. My goal with each book is to become a better writer, so since I'm kind of a novice at this, if you don't mind, I'd appreciate it if you could provide constructive criticism once we're done."

He stared down at her in what appeared to be utter disbelief. "You want me to criticize the manner you use to pleasure me?"

"Well . . . I've always been a big believer in critique groups," she said, taking his testicles in one hand while the other explored the length—and there was certainly a lot of it to be explored—of his penis. "Not that I think group involvement is appropriate here, but let's think of this as you being my critique partner, OK?"

"Harry," he said, his voice taking on a gravelly tone.

"Yes?"

"We're going to be in Turkey if you don't stop talking and let me make love to you. Or, alternately, you can do what you're poised to do."

She rubbed his shaft. "Not unless you promise to tell me what I can do to improve the experience for you."

He closed his eyes and took a deep, deep breath. "I promise."

"Thank you. OK, here we go, then!" He tasted hot; that was her first thought. Hot and slightly salty, and as she found a rhythm that had him clutching the doorframe, his eyes rolled back in his head, his beautiful chest heaving as his hips moved along with her, she figured that perhaps stopping to ask for his opinion wasn't the best option. Then again, one never knew unless one asked, and she was a big believer in communication.

"So," she said, with a slight pop as she released the head of his penis. "Thoughts?"

He looked down at her with wild eyes. "'Thoughts'? Is that what you said? You said 'thoughts'?"

"Yes. I know it's probably not the thing to stop in the middle of it, but really, I'd like to take this opportunity as a learning experience, so if you have some feedback to share, I want to hear it."

"Feedback," he said, as if he couldn't understand the word.

"Yes, you know, feedback. Was I too fast? Too slow? Not enough tongue swirls under the very tip? Were you go or no go on the gropage of your balls while I did it?"

He stared down at her for another few seconds, and then his Adam's apple bobbed. "I think the best feedback I can give you is going to be tactile."

"Tactile in what way?" she asked, looking at his penis. Although she normally was not at all attracted by men who had a lot of body hair, Iakovos' was anything but off-putting. "As an aside, can we talk about your hair?"

"Why not?" he said, making a gesture for her to proceed. "Do you mind if I lie down for this?"

"No, go right ahead. It's easier on my knees anyway."

She scooted over so he could have the bulk of the mattresses.

He lay down, his hands behind his head, his penis pointing straight up. "You wish to discuss my body hair, I assume? I'm sorry if it offends you, but Greek men, as you may be aware—"

"Oh, it doesn't offend me at all," she interrupted, stroking his chest. "Just the opposite. Your chest hair, for example, is so, so soft, I just want to bury my face in it."

"By all means, help yourself," he said, gesturing toward his chest.

She leaned forward, her breasts brushing his belly as she pressed her face to the center of his chest, licking the line between his pectorals. "Very soft."

"I'm glad to hear you think so," he said politely, but she couldn't help but notice his voice was starting to get rough again. "Just so you know, once you're done cataloging my body hair, I will be taking my turn."

"I'm glad I shaved before I came to Greece, then," she said, kissing first one nipple, then the other. She trailed a line of kisses over to one shoulder, then down the smooth, silky flesh of his bicep, down lower to his wrist. "Your arm hair is very soft, too. And I absolutely love your hands, but we'll leave those for another time."

He lifted up his free hand to look at first its back, then its front. "You have the oddest likes of any woman I've ever met."

"Now, your leg hair is a smidgen sturdier than your arm hair," she said, nipping at his hip before moving on to kiss a line straight down his heavy thigh muscle. "I like that you're ticklish here, too, but I promise I won't tickle you now. I think what I like most about your legs, while we're on the subject, is that you don't have beefy upper legs and scrawny lower legs. You have really fabulous calves, you know."

"I'm glad to know that all the time I've put into maintaining them has been worthwhile."

She glanced up from where she was kissing his knee and stroking his calf. "Do you do special exercises?"

"No, sweetheart, I don't."

"Oh. You're being facetious."

"I was. I apologize. Are you through?"

"Not quite. Your feet, Iakovos."

He lifted his head to look down the length of his body at them. "I have two."

"Yes. They are nice feet. I approve of them. However, I'm not going to suck on your toes, because frankly, the thought of that just makes my skin crawl. So if you harbor any fetishy sorts of thoughts about toe sucking, I'm afraid I'm going to have to disappoint you."

"To be honest, I'm not a big fan of it, either," he said. "Now are you done?"

"Almost. I haven't discussed your pubic hair."

He laid back down and started laughing, his hands making vague gestures in the air.

She propped her chin on his hipbone and waited until he was done. "You're laughing at me," she said finally, when his laughter had died down to a burble.

He wiped his eyes and grinned. "With you, Harry, not at you."

"I'm trying to have a serious discussion—"

His penis bobbed next to her head. Her lower lip quivered for a moment before she regained control. She cleared her throat. "Trying to have a serious discussion about your pubic hair, and you . . . you . . ."

An odd little snorting noise emerged from her.

He lay still, tears of laughter leaking from the sides of his eyes, waiting.

"Oh god, I can't do this," she said, bursting into laughter, leaning over him and kissing his smiling lips. "I love your pubic hair. Make love to me, Iakovos. Right now, before I go into a lecture about bouncing coins off your butt."

"You already mentioned that," he said, chuckling as he pulled her down beneath him. "But I believe I warned you that I expected to have my turn."

"You want to talk about my body hair?" She looked down at her pubic bone. "Everything important is shaved off except for that, and I feel I should warn you that what you're seeing isn't my natural state. My girlfriend convinced me that if I was going to Greece, I needed a bikini wax, and holy Jesus, Iakovos, I'm never getting another one. You have no idea how much they hurt."

He laid a hand over her pubic mound, gently touching the nicely trimmed hair. "I can't imagine why women feel like they need to go through such torture."

"Well, guys like women trimmed, or so my friend insists."

"Trimmed is one thing. Ripped out by the roots . . ." He flinched and leaned down to press a kiss into the crease of her thigh. "Do not feel as if you need to do so on my account. Now, I believe we were having a discussion of your oral technique."

She stopped squirming as he spread her legs, pulling her knees over his shoulders. "Oh, yes, please, I'd appreciate any suggestions."

"Here is my first suggestion." His head dipped as his mouth closed over her sensitive parts, his tongue and fingers gently probing until he found the spot that made her grab great big handfuls of blankets and writhe with building pleasure.

"Tell me," he said, lifting his head, an obvious twinkle in his eye, "how do you feel about it when I put a finger into you? Would you prefer two? You're too tight for three, but I believe two would fit nicely."

She glared down at him for a few seconds. "You, sir, do not play fair."

"Not even remotely close to it," he agreed, moving up her so her legs were now around his waist. The tip of him nudged her, seeking entrance. "Slow and easy, or hard and fast?"

She shifted her hips, pulling him forward until he slid into her. "Hard and fast. Always hard and fast. Make me wild, Iakovos!"

He made her see stars, and by the time they both lay panting, exhausted by the fast and furious release, she knew that it was too late. She could live without a fabulous lover, without the sex so hot it could steam a carpet, but she couldn't live without everything else that made up the gloriously wonderful, endlessly intriguing package that was Iakovos.

The trick was to convince him that he couldn't live without her.

Chapter 6

"I should check on the kids to make sure everyone is OK," Harry told Iakovos as she started up the path from the dock to the gardens.

"They're adults. They'll be fine without you for a few hours."

The western sky was still tinged with smears of red and orange from the sunset, the colors shifting into a violet that deepened overhead to velvety black. Night was settling around Iakovos' little island, the exterior lights that illuminated the great white stone structure throwing amber pools on the walls, while discreetly placed solar ground lights dotted the garden, casting just enough light to see by.

She wanted badly for him to take her hand or put his arm around her. She knew she could initiate contact, but she wanted him to be the one to make the move, wanted him to feel, as she did, that something was missing unless they were touching.

"What utter bullshit," she snapped at herself, and boldly took his hand.

His fingers tightened around hers as he stopped to look at her. "They are adults, Harry—"

"No, sorry, that 'bullshit' was for me, not you."

One side of his mouth twitched. "You were inner-monologuing again?"

"It happens a lot, I'm afraid," she said with a sigh. "I think all those years of writing short-circuited something in my brain. I was yelling at myself because I wanted you to want to hold my hand but I didn't want to initiate it myself, because I thought it would somehow mean more that you wanted to hold my hand first, but then I realized that was hypocritical, because maybe you wanted me to hold your hand, but didn't want me thinking you're nothing but a horn-dawg, and if what I really wanted was to hold your hand, then I could just stop waiting for you to make the first move, and bloody well hold your hand and stop worrying about whether or not you wanted to hold my hand first."

"I could have made love to you in the time it took you to explain that," he said, lifting their hands to his mouth so he could kiss her fingers. "Thank you for being so considerate of my feelings. Next time, I will hold your hand without worrying that you think I'm a horn-dawg."

"Good," she said, smiling at him. "I'm going to check on the kids."

"You will be joining me later," he said as she released his hand to move toward the south end of the garden.

She paused and looked back at him. "Was that a question or a statement?"

"Both."

His face was in shadow, but she could hear the passion that she knew must be in his eyes. "Wild dolphins couldn't keep me away."

"Wild dolphins?"

"It sounded more Greek than wild horses." She blew him a kiss and headed to the south.

His voice called after her. "Harry?"

"Yes?"

"What exactly is a horn-dawg?"

She laughed. She couldn't help herself—she was just so happy. A note taped to her door reassured her that not only had Cyndi recovered from her adventures with Theo, but she was evidently well enough that she had gone off with the band for an evening of fun in the mainland town.

Her happiness lasted until she opened the door to her bungalow and discovered she'd been robbed.

"What the hell?" She spun around the room, her mouth hanging open, but her suitcase was gone, the swimsuit she'd left hanging in the tiny bathroom was gone, her purse with her passport and phone—all gone.

"God damn it!" She checked the room next to hers, flinging open the door to see Amy and Derek's things strewn all over the room in the usual disarray, but everything was present. She tried the next two doors, but those rooms hadn't been robbed, either.

"Dammit all to hell and back again," she said, running across the garden toward the massive structure. She felt a little odd just barging in to Iakovos' house when he had others there, but she knew he'd be furious to find out someone had robbed her.

To her surprise, no one was strolling around the patio when she crossed it. No one was in the room with the billiards table, either. She paused, listening intently, but there was no sound of voices or music or laughter. Where the hell was everyone?

"Iakovos?" she asked as she stepped into the hall. Her voice echoed hollowly.

"Lost?"

She spun around at the man's voice, but her heart fell when the tall, handsome Greek who leaned against the doorway wasn't the one she wanted. "No, I'm not lost. I was looking for Iakovos."

Theo pushed himself away from the door and advanced on her, a grin on his lips as he gestured toward the stairs with a glass. "He's probably upstairs. You know where his rooms are?"

"Yes." She eyed him as he strolled toward her. He didn't appear to be drunk, but something told her that he was. "I hope you're not planning on attacking any other members of the band."

"I didn't attack any of them to begin with," he said, stopping in front of her. Her nose wrinkled at the smell of whisky.

He caught the gesture, glanced at his glass, then back to her with the same grin. "You want a drink?"

"No, thanks. Where is everyone?"

"Mainland. There's a club in town that Elena loves, so they all went off to dance the night away." He moved closer to her, his body language making her uncomfortable. "You like dancing, beautiful?"

She backed up a step. "Sometimes. It depends on the company. Would you happen to know if my group went with your sister?"

"Don't doubt they did. Elena likes people around her. I, on the other hand"—he traced the length of her arm with one finger—"prefer quiet time with just one special person."

He couldn't be serious, Harry thought to herself. He couldn't honestly think that she would be at all interested in him, could he? No, he couldn't. It was the drink making him act this way. "And you think I'm that person?" she couldn't help but ask, wondering just how far he'd go before she would have to deck him again.

His eyelids dropped to give him sultry bedroom eyes. "I think you could be."

It was almost too easy. She felt a little unsporting, and decided that rather than waiting to see just how much of a fool he would make of himself, she'd stop it. "You'd be wrong, then."

"Ah." He straightened up, took a swig of his booze, and gave her another sloppy grin. "You're after Jake. If I told you I've got money, too, would you kiss me like you did him?"

She stared at him in disbelief for a second, then tossed her head back and laughed. "You're drunk, willing to take a woman who is sleeping with your brother, and you don't think anything's wrong with hurting a young girl. No, Theo, there's not enough money in the world to convince me to kiss you. I think I'll go find your brother and ask if he has any brain shampoo, because, honestly, I'd like to forget I even saw you tonight."

"Witch," he spat, slamming his glass down on a half-moon table behind him.

"I think you left the 'B' off that," she said, brushing past him toward the stairs.

He grabbed her breast roughly, shoving his face in hers, no doubt intending to force a kiss on her.

Harry knocked his hand off her breast and slammed the heel of her hand into his jaw, making his head snap back. He snarled something in Greek, but she followed up with a sharp right to his nose.

"You have got to be the stupidest man I have ever met," she told him as he collapsed on the floor. Blood flowed out of his nose onto his white polo shirt. She stepped over his prone form and added, "I hope your nose is broken."

Should she mention the episode to Iakovos? she wondered as she made her way through the house to the north wing. She was of the mind that she should, because clearly Theo was close to being out of control. If the episode with Cyndi hadn't proven that, the fact that he thought it was just fine to come on to her did. The nerve of him, hitting on her when he knew she was sleeping with Iakovos.

She paused as a thought struck her—maybe he didn't know. All he'd seen was her kissing Iakovos, nothing more. Perhaps Iakovos was being circumspect about their blossoming relationship, not wanting people to know they were lovers.

She thought for a moment about the way his hand kept slipping down from her waist to her butt when they were sightseeing, and shook her head. She didn't think he was overly concerned about keeping their status secret.

His door loomed before her, and she stood in front of it for a minute, not knowing whether she should just walk in, or if she should knock. "Do both, you idiot," she told herself, and gave a light tap on the door, opening it enough to stick her head in. "Iakovos?"

The sitting room was empty. So was the dressing

room attached to it, but the door to the bathroom was slightly ajar, wisps of steam curling around it. "Anyone home?" she called loudly before pushing it open.

Iakovos stood before the mirror, a towel wrapped around his waist, shaving. "That was fast," he said, meeting her reflection in the mirror. "Everything all right with your charges?"

"I don't know; they seem to have disappeared with your sister. Iakovos—"

He cocked an eyebrow, waiting for her to continue. When she didn't, he finished shaving and wiped his face before turning to her.

"Your brother . . ." She remembered the conversation with him earlier. He was, she knew, a man who valued his family.

"What about him?"

"He's drunk," she finally said, coming to a quick decision. Theo might be a drunkard, but he wasn't stupid. She had seen the glimmer of intelligence in his eyes the night before, at the hospital. Surely he would get the point that she wasn't interested in him.

Iakovos shrugged and ran a comb through his damp hair, brushing the silken black strands off his forehead. "He's bound to be lit up with Elena's crowd here. So long as he confines himself to being drunk in my home and not in town, I'm not too worried."

"Even if he attacks another woman?" she asked, distracted by now with the play of his muscles in his arms and chest.

"He knows better than to attack any of Elena's friends, and I've told him to mind himself where your group is concerned. You haven't changed."

She looked down at her dress and suddenly remembered what had driven her there in the first place. "No,
and I'm not likely to, either. I hate to tell you this, but
either someone snuck onto your island without you
knowing it, or one of your sister's friends is a thief, because all my stuff is gone. My clothes, my passport, my
digital camera—all gone. I can replace everything but
the passport, but it just pisses me off nonetheless."

He gave her an odd look, then took her arm and
pulled her back through to his dressing room, throwing
open one of a bank of closet doors. She peered closer
and saw familiar clothing hanging next to his pants,
shirts, and an abundance of suits. "Those are my
clothes."

"I had your things moved up here while we were in
Krokos," he said with a smile that promised so much. "It
just seemed more efficient than having you go back and
forth."

"Efficient, with just a smidgen of high-handed . . .
You get eight out of ten for style points," she said, relieved that she wasn't going to have to spend the time
trying to locate her stolen passport.

"Your bag and other things are in the sitting room,"
he said. "Are you hungry?"

"For food or for you?" she asked, sucking in her lip as
she looked at his beautiful naked chest and belly.

"I'm going to be conceited and assume you're hungry
for me. I was actually referring to food."

"We just ate a couple of hours ago," she said, trying to
quell the fire that threatened to consume her just by
standing near him. Dammit, Harry, she scolded herself,
now who's being the horn-dawg? You can have a con-

versation with the man without wanting to jump his bones.

He gave her a wry smile. "I'm a big man, sweetheart, and you're a demanding woman. If you want me to continue to be able to do all those things you're thinking right now, I need to eat regularly."

Her gaze snapped up from where she had been looking speculatively at the towel around his waist, a little heat warming her cheeks. "I'd say I'm sorry about ogling you and thinking those thoughts that you seem to know I'm thinking, although I don't know how because I have a perfect poker face, but we would both know that I'm not at all sorry. Dinner sounds fine."

"Your face is many things," he said, stepping close so he could take her chin in his fingers, his thumb stroking over her cheek, "but I suspect if you were to try to play poker with me, you'd lose very badly."

"That sounds like another wager," she said, smiling at the look in his eyes.

His head dipped down until his mouth brushed hers. "One I will happily take, but I should warn you that one of the ways I supported myself when I was in school was by gambling."

"Horses?" she asked, surprised because he didn't seem like the type of man who did that.

"Cards. Poker was my specialty. All those rich boys sent off to school with fat allowances were easy pickings for a poor Greek boy who had nothing to lose."

"You were that good?" she asked, wanting to laugh.

"Better than good." The look he gave her made her toes curl. "Damned near impossible to beat."

"Oh, I do love a man who gets cocky," she said, putting her hands behind her back so she wouldn't fling herself on him. "I would have thought you'd have learned your lesson when I beat the crap out of you swimming, but no, you just seem to be begging for punishment. You're on, Mr. Card Shark."

"After dinner, then," he said, and the promise in his eyes had nothing to do with poker. He reached beyond her and pulled out a pair of jeans. "Where would you like to eat? We could have dinner in town, or I could have my housekeeper whip up something for us and I could eat it off your naked body."

She stared at him for a moment, unable to breathe for the images that danced in her head. After five seconds of trying very, very hard not to pounce on him and lick that sweet spot on his neck, and suck on his upper lip, and run her hands through that silky black hair, she managed to swallow and, without a word, she gathered up a few articles of clothing and walked past him into the bathroom.

She found the items of a cosmetic nature she'd brought with her lined up on one of the vanities in the bathroom. She showered, washed the salt out of her hair, and hurriedly dried it, impatient as ever because it seemed to take eons to dry. She was about to twist it up and out of her way when she remembered Iakovos murmuring into her ear as he made love to her on the boat about how much he liked its wild length.

"Just when I was going to cut it, too," she said, flipping it back and doing a quick check to make sure she was presentable before going off to find him.

A note was taped to the door of his sitting room.

"Getting dinner. We'll eat here. Poker chips in drawer on the left."

She smiled, then suddenly ran for her laptop that someone had set up on a small writing desk. She was frantically trying to memorize the rules of poker when Iakovos came into the room, a bottle of champagne and two glasses in one hand and an odd expression on his face.

"Eglantine," he said, setting the glasses down.

"Yacky," she said, hurriedly closing the Web browser.

"My brother is lying in the south hall, unconscious, with what appears to be a broken nose. I don't suppose you know anything about that?"

She adopted an expression of complete innocence. "Now, why would you even think to ask me that?"

His expression grew grim as he pulled her to her feet, his thumb running over her fingers. "Did he do something to make you defend yourself?"

"I told you he was drunk," she said carefully.

"What did he do?"

There was an edge to his voice that she didn't like. Although she had no intention of putting up with any crap from Theo, she didn't want to cause dissent between the brothers. An angry Iakovos would probably be less likely to see to it that his brother got help than if he was in a more understanding mood.

"He seemed to think that I was after you for your money, for one thing."

He made a dismissive nose. "You're not."

"No, I'm not, but I suppose it's a natural assumption on his part. Is he jealous of you, by any chance? Because you're more good-looking, and older, and a world's most sexy billionaire?"

"Not that I know of, and thank you for the compliment of assuming he would be jealous of me and not vice versa. What did he do to upset you, Harry?"

"Tried to kiss me," she finally said, uncomfortable with the idea of lying to him.

"I'll kill him."

She grabbed his arm as he turned away, his jaw tight, his eyes glittering. "That's overreacting a little, don't you think? He didn't succeed, after all, and I decked him good and proper. Do you really think his nose is broken? I wasn't shooting for that, but honestly, I can't help but think it might teach him a lesson if it is."

"It's broken. I set it right after I dumped him in his room."

She gawked at him for a moment. "You know how to set a broken nose?"

"Yes. Let go of me, Eglantine."

"Like hell I will, Yacky. It doesn't matter—it really doesn't."

The eyes he turned on her burned with anger, his face beautiful in its fury. "My brother tries to kiss my lover and you don't think that matters? I don't know what sort of man you were with before, but Greek men do not take kindly to others poaching their women, and I am no exception to that rule."

"Maybe he didn't know we were . . . that we've been . . ." She gestured between them.

"He knows," Iakovos snapped.

"What exactly are we? I don't quite know what to call us. Are we dating? A couple? An item? Are you officially my boyfriend, because if you are, I'm going to call up every single one of my female friends, and not only tell them that my boyfriend is the handsomest man who ever walked the earth, I'm going to send them pictures of you in your swimsuit so they can suffer exquisitely knowing that I get to lick you and touch you and sleep with you, and they don't." She took a deep, shuddering breath. "It's going to be one of the best moments of my life!"

"Harry," he said, shoving a hand through his hair, "are you trying to distract me so I won't go throttle my brother?"

"Yes. Is it working?"

"Yes."

"Good." She paused, then added, "Although I am serious about the picture thing. Would you mind posing for me tomorrow? And maybe we could get a couple of shots of us together? Because one of my friends will accuse me of just stalking you if I don't have shots of us together. Maybe one of you kissing me. And one where I'm touching your bare chest. Or would it look better to be sitting on your lap? Hmm."

He took a deep breath. She was going to kill him. He knew this. He accepted it about her. She was going to casually drop bombs like this, that his swine of a brother had touched her—and he didn't for one moment think that Theo had just threatened to do so; for Harry to defend herself by force meant that she felt threatened by the situation—and then expect him to do nothing about it.

Well, she had something to learn about him. No one touched her. She was *his* tempest, *his* goddess, and he was aware that the emotions scorching his belly went far beyond the normal anger of a man whose woman was approached by another. He knew at that moment that he would move heaven and earth to keep her safe. She was his, pure and simple, and if Theo even so much as cast an unwise look her way, he'd send him packing so fast he wouldn't know what hit him.

"Iakovos?"

He pulled his attention away from the dark thoughts of what he would like to do to Theo, and focused them again on the woman who stood before him dressed in a flowing, gauzy flame-colored shirt edged with beading, and wide, loose matching trousers that clung to her hips. He cast his mind back to what she had been saying. "You can call me whatever you want, and stop looking guilty. I'm not going to thrash Theo, even though he deserves it. We'll have some champagne, the dinner that should be here shortly, and then I will make love to you until you stop thinking about showing pictures of me to your friends and start thinking about the ways you're going to placate my anger about not telling me the minute Theo approached you."

"Are you an easy man to placate?" she asked.

"No." He reached for her, his hands in her wild mane, feeling his testicles tighten even as his sex swelled. "Feel free to be as inventive as you like with your attempt to sweeten my temper."

She giggled as she boldly cupped him, making him groan. "You're talking to a writer, Iakovos. My imagination is my stock-in-trade, and I assure you, I plan on devoting all my attention to making you crazy with desire."

"You already do that," he murmured, about to kiss

her. He stopped when a knock sounded on the door, and his housekeeper, Rosalia, entered bearing a tray, her husband, Spyros, following with another.

Rosalia flicked a look at Harry, who blushed and moved away from Iakovos.

He knew that Rosalia, originally employed as Theo's and Elena's nurse, was interested to see the woman who claimed his attention. She hadn't liked the last woman he had been with, and had made her displeasure quite clear, but if she thought she was going to do anything that made Harry the least bit uncomfortable, he would have no compunction in reminding her who paid her wages.

"This is Rosalia," he said after receiving a pointed look from that same woman.

"It's a pleasure to meet you," Harry said, offering her hand.

Rosalia set down the tray and looked at the hand for a moment before taking it and giving it a perfunctory shake.

"Here, let me help you." Harry bundled her laptop and bag off the table. "That smells delicious, whatever it is."

"This is Spyros, Rosalia's husband. He doesn't speak English."

"We've met," Harry said, her eyes dancing with secret mirth as she offered her hand to Spyros. The old man set down his tray, wiping his hands on his trousers before shaking her hand, telling her in Greek that she was a pleasant change from the last woman Iakovos had brought to the island.

Harry smiled a little uncertainly, her eyes shifting to his for a translation.

"He's saying welcome," Iakovos said, giving his employees a gimlet eye.

Rosalia had been arranging the plates and dishes on the table, her eyes on Harry. "Is this the one responsible for the mess in the hall?" She also spoke in Greek, her dark gaze piercing him with a look that would tolerate no attempt to shield the truth.

Iakovos sighed to himself. Theo was an especial favorite of Rosalia's. She had always been willing to overlook even the most embarrassing of situations that his brother found himself in. "Yes."

To his surprise, her lips curled into a smile as she nodded at Harry. "This one is not like the others."

"No, she's not."

"You do not mess things up this time," she said with a warning glance his way as she collected the trays and started toward the door. "She does not have her nose in the air like the others. She will give you strong sons."

Rosalia sailed out of the door with a grinning Spyros trailing behind her.

"Oh dear," Harry said, looking worried. "Something tells me that didn't go well. Did I do something wrong? Or does she just not like you having women here?"

"Actually, she told me not to mess things up with you."

Harry brightened up at that. "She did? What a nice woman. Intelligent, too. I hope you take her words to heart."

He popped the cork on the champagne bottle, telling himself that he would never be able to guess what would come out of her mouth next. She was a delight, a wild, unexpected delight. "Every other woman I've brought here has been concerned with keeping me happy and pandering to my every desire. Not one has ever told me I had better not mess things up."

"Seriously?" She took the glass he handed her, her eyes wide as she examined his face. "That had to get old fast."

"It did. Harry?"

"Yes, Iakovos?"

"Eat your dinner." One side of his mouth went up as he let her see the desire in his eyes. "As I mentioned this morning, you're going to need your strength."

Chapter 7

It wasn't easy, but Harry managed to tear herself away from Iakovos' bed the next morning. She was actually rather proud of the feat, since he had made noises about staying in bed until the concert that night, but she finally convinced him that she really had to honor her duties and make sure that Cyndi had recovered from her trauma, as well as ensuring that all was going smoothly for the evening's event.

She wore the same taupe linen tunic and pants that she had worn the first day, the buttons having magically been sewn back on and the clothing laundered, a circumstance that had sent her to locate Rosalia to thank her for the attention.

"It is no problem," the older woman said, standing in the middle of a busy kitchen. Despite being somewhat nervous about approaching Rosalia, Harry liked the woman. She had thick black hair streaked with white and pulled back in a bun, a face that showed her life hadn't always been one of ease, and a no-nonsense air that made Harry relax despite the circumstances.

"I appreciate you cleaning my things. I didn't bring much with me because I figured we'd be here just for a couple of days." Harry spoke carefully, not wanting to give the impression that she was taking it for granted that Iakovos would ask her to stay on when the band went home. She was pretty sure he would, but she'd never been one to assume.

"Kyrie Papaioannou, he will buy you more. You do not worry," the woman said.

"I'm sure he would if I asked him to, but there's no need to do that. If I want something, I'm sure I can get it in town. I just wanted to say thank you for the buttons and for doing my laundry."

The woman inclined her head in acknowledgment of the thanks, saying, as Harry was leaving the kitchen, "You like it here, yes? Greece pleases you?"

There was a question in Rosalia's eyes that had nothing to do with the country, and everything to do with one man. "Yes," Harry said slowly, meeting her gaze. "I love everything about Greece."

"Good," the woman said, nodding abruptly. "You go, now. We are busy for the party."

Harry smiled and left the kitchen, feeling as if she'd just passed a test.

The smile faded when, as she strolled across the grassy lawn outside the staff bungalows, she was greeted with, "Houston, we have a problem."

"A problem?" she asked Derek, who was facing her with a grim expression. "What problem? Iakovos said you guys had gone over to the mainland with his sister and her friends last night. Did something happen there?"

"Iakovos?" Derek asked, looking at her with much

speculation. Like Terry and Amy, he was in a swimsuit, the three of them lounging on a couple of chairs, the damp towels at their feet indicating they'd had a dip in the lovely blue-green water.

"Mr. Papamono . . . oh, don't ask me to say his last name, it has way too many vowels. And stop giving me that knowing look. What I do with billionaire Greek playboys who own their own islands and have incredibly wonderful butts is no one's business but my own."

"But he's, like, old," Terry said with the naïveté of a nineteen-year-old. "That secretary dude of his said that he's a lot older than his sister."

"He's not old at all! He's in perfect shape." Heat rolled up from her chest as she remembered just exactly how perfect his shape was.

"I suppose it doesn't matter since you're—" Terry shut his mouth quickly.

"Old, as well?" she asked, giving him a glare.

"Not old. Just . . . seasoned?" he asked with what she was sure he felt was a charming smile.

"It's not like I'm ancient, for heaven's sake. I could be your sister, after all."

The three of them looked at her in silence.

"OK, a really, really older sister, but a sister nonetheless. What problem do we have? And where's Cyndi?"

"Cyndi *is* the problem," Amy said, taking Derek's hand.

"She's not all right?" Harry glanced around. "Where is she?"

"She's not here, Harry. She walked out last night."

"She *what*?"

Amy nodded. "We tried to get you on your phone, but it just went through to your voice mail."

"Oh my god." Harry put both hands to her head, rubbing, as a sudden headache had blossomed there. "I left my cell behind yesterday because Iakovos said I could use his if I needed to."

"You weren't in your room, either," Terry pointed out, his eyes twinkling.

"No, I . . . er . . . I'm staying with Iakovos. Oh my god. She left? Why?"

"She said she's not going to stay here, that she can't face that guy who didn't want her, and she's a bundle of nerves, and oh, all sorts of things about needing a break from the stress." Amy looked almost scared.

Harry stared at the girl in horror, goose bumps making her back twitch. "She can't do that, can she? Don't you guys have some sort of a contract?"

"We do, and she can. She did." Terry looked at his watch. "She's booked a flight out of Athens today."

Harry sat down suddenly on a nearby chair, her legs wobbly. "Holy moly. Well, we just have to get her back. Athens is only a couple of hours away—there's still time for her to get back here before the party. I'll call her. I'll reason with her."

"It won't do any good," Amy said. "We've all tried."

Harry thought of Iakovos' delectable lips. She didn't want to see them tight with anger, and he was sure to be angry when he found out that the lead singer of the group he'd flown out at no little expense had done a runner. He wouldn't be angry with her, personally, but he wouldn't be happy. She liked him when he was happy.

He teased her with outrageous statements, and touched her, and let her lick his upper lip. She loved his lips. She especially loved them when they were doing things to her body that just thinking about made her skin feel tight. "Yes, well, you might not be as motivated as me."

Forty minutes later, Harry conceded defeat and clicked off her cell phone. She looked at the three anxious faces watching her. "She won't listen."

"I told you she wouldn't. She's really rattled by this, Harry."

"I could call Tim . . . but he was due to be in the hospital for another couple of days, and besides, Jill's about to give birth . . . Dammit. Why did Cyndi have to be such a twit and try to sleep with Theo?" Harry stood up and began to pace. "Well, we're just going to have to cope with the three of you. Let's see . . . Amy, you know Cyndi's songs as well as your own, don't you?"

She nodded. "Yes, but—"

"OK, so you just take over her role, and we'll get someone to play the keyboard in your place."

"Who?" Derek asked, waving a hand around to indicate the surroundings. "This place is great and all, but I kind of think musicians are scarce here. At least the ones who know our music."

"Well . . . we could find someone in Athens. . . ." Harry bit her lower lip, wondering how she'd find a musician to take Amy's place on such short notice, and in a foreign country to boot.

"You could do it," Amy suggested.

"Don't be ridiculous. I'm no musician," Harry said, wondering if there was such a thing as an Athens craigslist.

"Tim said you used to be in his band."

She glanced over at the three of them. "Twenty years ago, yes. Maybe one of the guests . . . No, that wouldn't be right."

"Harry."

"No!" she told their expectant faces. "Honestly, guys, it's been forever and a day since I was in Tim's band."

"You were a singer, weren't you?"

"If you could call it that. I did some vocals, but mostly I just played—" She clamped her lips shut.

"Keyboard?" Terry asked with a grin.

"Shut up. I'm not doing this."

"Well, if you want us to get sued for breach of contract, OK," he said with a negligent shrug of his shoulders.

"Now you're exaggerating. Iakovos wouldn't sue you."

They all looked at her, making a blush rise on her cheeks. She knew what they were thinking—that she could smooth the path with Iakovos so that he wouldn't punish them for breaking their contract. She'd be damned if she would use him like that.

"If you explain what's happened, I'm sure you can work something out with him. Pay back the advance, that sort of thing."

"And the money for coming to Greece for four of us? And for staying here?" Derek shook his head. "We're broke, Harry. We all pitched in to buy the recording equipment for the studio. We can't pay him back."

"Well . . . maybe I could . . ."

"We don't mind breaking the contract for you," Terry assured her. "It'll ruin our careers, and probably scar us for life, but if that doesn't bother you, then we'll try not to hold it against you."

Harry knew the inevitable when she faced it, but it didn't make the bitter pill any easier to swallow. Her shoulders slumped with defeat. "I don't even know your music."

"You've got ten hours to learn it," Derek said cheerfully, holding out his wrist so she could see the time.

"I suppose if Amy sings the songs, I could play simplified versions of the music, but really—"

"I can't sing Cyndi's songs!" Amy wailed.

"Why not?"

"Because I don't have her range! Besides, there's the dance-with-the-moon song. I can't dance at all. You know that."

"I can't, either, but that didn't stop me from taking a belly-dancing class," Harry said with a smile at the memory of her attempt to please her then-boyfriend. "Man, was that a disaster."

"You dance?" Amy's eyes widened as she glanced at the two men.

"NO!" Harry yelled at them. "Don't even think what I know you're thinking!"

"You can sing; you just said you sang for Tim. And you can belly-dance, and that's what Cyndi does on the moon song," Amy said, her hand on Harry's arm. "If you could do that song, and maybe a couple of others, then I could do mine, and . . . and . . . it would be OK."

"If you expect me to put on a belly-dancing costume and prance around—"

"Please, Harry."

"I said I'd do keyboards for you, but as for singing and dancing, absolutely not. It's completely out of the question. There is no way on God's green earth I am going to perform again. You guys got that? Good."

An hour later she was back in the kitchen, apologizing to Rosalia.

"I do not know this dress. It is what?"

"A belly dancer's outfit. Or anything like it, really. A long, flowing skirt, and a short little top that covers just the boobs. Do you think I could buy something like that in town?"

The older woman raked her with a disbelieving look. "You need this for the party?"

"Yes. It's a long story, and frankly, one that if I think about too much, will send me screaming into the night."

"Is there a problem?"

Harry spun around at the question. A man stood in the doorway, as tall as her, but wiry, with short curly black hair.

"I'm Dmitri," the man said, holding out his hand. "I'm Iakovos' assistant, as well as his cousin. You're Eglantine, aren't you?"

"Call me Harry, please."

"Is something the matter with the setup for tonight? I checked with the builders and the sound engineers, and they assured me everything is ready and working."

"Oh god, I haven't even had time to think of the sound equipment," Harry said, running a hand through her hair.

"Can I help with something?"

She eyed the man. He appeared to be in his midthirties, with warm, friendly eyes. He didn't look anything like Iakovos or even Theo, but she had the feeling she could trust him.

"I'm pretty good at problem solving," he said when she hesitated. "Iakovos doesn't keep me around just for my fabulous personality, you know."

"I'm sure you're very efficient," she said with a smile, deciding she'd risk it. "And I'll buy you a great big bottle of Scotch for next Secretary's Day if you can find me a belly dancer's outfit in the next five hours."

He didn't even blink, just pulled out his cell phone. "What's your size?"

She told him her measurements, and gave him a description of what she needed.

"You're good," she told him when, without so much as batting an eyelash, he reassured her that he would have an outfit of some sort for her. "If you can pull this off, I'll tell Iakovos he needs to give you a raise."

"If the outfit you want me to get looks anything like what I think it will, you won't have to tell him. He'll take one look at you and give me the raise himself."

She laughed and gave his arm a squeeze before hurrying off to rehearse the songs she had a horrible feeling would never be the same once she got done with them.

Chapter 8

Iakovos was impatient, and didn't like that feeling one little bit. If there was one thing he prized above all else, it was his ability to control the situations that demanded his attention and time. He had faced and triumphed over the financial ruin of his family. He'd used his wits not only to survive school as a lonely foreigner, but to emerge from university well on his way to becoming a very rich man.

He worked hard, he did what he had to do, and in the end he got lucky, very lucky, by being in the right place at the right time, having snatched up a stretch of land that turned out to be worth its weight in gold. After that, it was all a matter of applying himself to the situation at hand, mastering it, and moving on to the next task.

"Life," he said to no one in particular as he stood next to a table laden with food, staring with unseeing eyes at the people in colorful beachwear as they mingled around the largest of the three pools his house boasted, "is being particularly annoying right now."

"What's that?"

He looked up to see his sister's laughing eyes watching him. Elena was always laughing, especially now that she was eighteen and an adult, surrounded by her friends, her life lying before her like a glittering road.

"Nothing. Are you enjoying your birthday?"

"Very much so." She held up her wrist. "A very handsome man gave me this gorgeous diamond bracelet this morning."

"I'm glad you like it," he said, wondering how Harry would look wearing diamonds, and nothing else.

"I love it, and I love you for giving me such a wonderful birthday," she answered, kissing his cheek.

He murmured something noncommittal. Diamonds were too insipid for his storm goddess. She needed a gem with some depth to it, something that would match her fiery spirit. Rubies?

"So, Iakovos, Rosalia says that you had dinner in your room last night with the American lady."

No, rubies were too harsh for Harry. Her nature demanded something that would hint at the storm that could whip around her at any moment, while also reflecting the calm that followed. Ah, he had it. Emeralds.

"Iakovos?"

He looked down at his sister when she tugged on his arm.

Her grin was beyond cheeky. "Is she nice, this American lady?"

The image danced in his mind of Harry naked, spread across his bed, emeralds glittering in her hair and draped across her belly. His lips thinned even as blood that had been happily flowing through his veins stopped short and headed straight for his penis.

"I didn't see her, but Theo says she's huge, as tall as him, and built like—" Elena held out her hands.

"She's not huge at all. She's perfectly in proportion, every last inch of her, and Theo needs to keep his damned mouth shut or I'll shut it for him."

Elena looked startled for a moment, then laughed outright, the sound a light ripple, like sunlight on a brook. Harry's laugh was much earthier, a deep, throaty chuckle that went straight to his head.

"I won't tease you anymore, but I do want to meet her."

Iakovos pulled his attention back from where it had been wandering. "You'll see her and the others tonight at the concert."

"I can't wait to see them," she said, almost dancing with excitement. "And you're the best brother ever. I hope this perfect woman of yours knows just how wonderful you are."

A smug, wholly masculine smile tugged at the corners of his mouth. He certainly had left her sated by the time they managed to drag themselves out of bed.

"Where's Theo?" he asked, one thought leading to another.

Elena, sensing she'd lost his attention, shrugged. "He was in the game room when I last saw him."

"I have a few things I want to discuss with him before the day gets any older," Iakovos said with grim satisfaction, and took himself off to give his brother a piece of his mind.

By the time he had done that, been briefed by Rosalia about the dinner that would take place before the concert, and gone for a quick swim, he knew he was fighting a losing battle. He wanted to see Harry.

What was she doing at that moment? Probably she was with the band, making sure they didn't get into any trouble. Why couldn't they watch themselves? He knew from the security checks run on the group that none of them were over the age of twenty, but surely they were old enough that they didn't need to run her ragged keeping an eye on them.

"Where are you off to?" he called to Dmitri as he caught sight of his cousin heading for the east dock.

Dmitri turned back and said with the hint of a grin, "I'm going to meet a courier who just flew in from Athens."

"What courier?" he asked, not aware of anything important being brought to the island.

"The one bringing you a present."

"I've just come from a hell of a fight with Theo," Iakovos said with a long look at Dmitri. "I'm really in no mood to play verbal games. What present?"

"I'd tell you, but I don't think Harry would appreciate me ruining the surprise."

Harry bought him a present? Why was he surprised? It was so like her to turn the tables on him when he'd just made arrangements with the most prestigious jeweler in Athens to have a variety of emeralds sent out for his perusal. "Is it something I'm going to like?" he asked.

Dmitri's grin widened. "If it's as good as I think it is, you, my friend, are going to be on your knees in gratitude that I have consented to work for you."

"If nothing else, you never fail to amuse me," Iakovos said dryly. "I just hope it's worth the cost of flying it out here."

"It's not costing you anything. Harry insisted on paying for it, so you can stop worrying that she's spending your money."

"I never thought she was, and wouldn't care if she did."

Dmitri checked himself as he was about to leave, giving Iakovos a long look. "No, I don't think you do care. She's really gotten to you, hasn't she?"

"Yes. Where is she?"

Dmitri jerked his head toward the south.

"With that group?"

"Yes."

He made a face. "They should let her have some time to herself." And, more important, time for him.

"I think I'll let her tell you what's going on," Dmitri said cryptically, then left him to take a boat to the mainland.

Iakovos watched him leave, wondering how Harry had managed to win both Rosalia and Dmitri over so quickly. He couldn't recall the last time either of them approved of one of his lovers.

The noise that greeted him when he strolled across the lawn that marked the boundary of the servants' area made him smile. Far from being exhausted by their late-night and early-morning activities, Harry sounded as if she could easily call down a hurricane.

"What is going on? Why are you yelling?" he asked as he approached them, trying to school his expression into one of stern immovability, but suspecting he failed. He waited, anticipation building as to what Harry would do upon seeing him. Of all her charms, it was the sense of the unexpected that appealed to him the most. Quite simply, he never knew what to expect from her.

"I'm yelling because this whole idea is ridiculous," Harry said with a disgusted wave at her torso. "I *crushed* Terry."

Iakovos looked at one of the two slim young men. The one with long hair held a guitar in his hands, while the pale, nervous girl next to him clutched a small bodhran. The other man was on the ground, a pained look on his face as he rubbed his lower back. "On purpose, or just for a whim?"

"I thought about doing it on a whim, but decided that was too random a reason. Turn around, you lot," she ordered the three others.

They blinked at her with identical expressions of surprise. "What?" Terry asked.

She twirled her finger in the air. "You heard me. Turn around. Count to sixty. When you're done, you can turn back."

To Iakovos' surprise and wholehearted approval, Harry flung herself on him, kissing him with a passion that instantly made him hard.

"I missed you," she whispered into his mouth.

"We've only been parted for three hours," he said, both hands on her delicious ass as he gave serious consideration to the idea of carrying her into the nearest vacant room and diving into the storm again.

"Yes, but they've been long, long hours," she said, sighing sadly before releasing him just as the three others turned back to face them. The one named Terry looked like he was going to make an untoward comment until Iakovos pinned him back with a look that let him know that to do so would be the sheerest folly. "You're not going to believe what has happened. I know you won't because I certainly don't. And before you get annoyed about it, we've worked everything out, so it's all OK, at least most of it is. Crushing Terry isn't going to work, though."

His anger, always quick to spark, rose when she told the tale of the insipid little twit's latest drama.

"It is unfortunate, but not the disaster you seem to imply it is," he told Harry. "Surely the other girl, Annie—"

"Amy," Harry corrected.

"—can do all of the singing?"

"They don't work like that. Normally Derek is on guitar, Cyndi sings, Amy is keyboards, and Terry takes either the bodhran, fiddle, or another guitar, as needed. On Amy's songs, Cyndi played the keyboard. But now with Cyndi gone, they're either limited to Amy's songs, or . . . or . . . oh god, I can't believe I agreed to do this."

"Harry's going to take Cyn's part," Derek said with a big smile.

"You're a singer?" Iakovos asked her.

"No. Not at all. Just a little. Once, a very long time ago, but I hung up my singing hat many, many years back."

"That's how she and Tim met," Derek informed him. "They were in a band together."

"Twenty years ago, yes, but I haven't sung in front of a crowd since then. But it's not the singing that worries me," she said, her shoulders slumping.

Out of the blue, Iakovos was struck with a desire to protect her from the weight of responsibility that hung so heavily over her. He wanted her saying the outrageous things she said, looking at him as if he were the most wonderful being in existence, and licking that absurd spot on his neck that she had said drove her wild. He didn't want her looking like she was about to cry. "This is of no matter. We will simply cancel your contract."

Hope flared in her eyes for a moment before she asked, "Would your sister mind? I was under the impression that Illuminati was her favorite band, and that's why you had them flown out here."

"She won't mind," he lied, looking her dead in the eye. He had no idea what he would tell Elena, but he'd come up with something to turn the situation around. He always did.

Harry smiled, her heart beating faster, as it always seemed to do when she looked at him. He was so gorgeous, so unexpectedly warm and witty and completely wonderful, and there he was, lying just to save her a little grief. It was too much, just too much for her. She was madly, completely, utterly head over heels in love with him. "If I asked you to marry me, what would you say?"

She took him by surprise—his eyebrows shooting up to the top of his forehead told her that. "I would say that it's the man's prerogative to ask that question."

"Oh." She squinted against the sun at him, reveling in the warmth in his eyes. "By any chance, are you intending on asking me that question?"

"Yes."

"Now?"

His brows lowered into a straight line. "No."

"OK." She smiled again. "Then I guess in the interests of keeping your sister from wanting to gut me, we'd better go forward with the gig. Besides, the problem isn't really the singing. We've made a few adjustments to the lineup, so I'll be singing stuff I know. It's the dancing that's the really big problem at the moment."

"If I had said no, would you still sing for my sister?" he asked, taking her by surprise for a change.

She knew exactly what he was talking about. "Of course I would."

He gave her another of his unreadable looks, then said, "If you don't wish to dance, then don't."

"It's not quite that simple. See, their big song, the one that's the huge viral hit, and the one that your sister specially requested, has this part where Cyndi does a little dance with Terry, kind of a cross between a Gypsy dance and a belly dance. And at the end of it, Cyndi launches herself into the air, and Terry catches her and spins her around. It's the signature move of the song, and although I would dearly love to just skip it, leaving it out is going to be hugely jarring."

"It's just a dance," he said, frowning at her look of distress.

"You and I may think that, but everyone else assures me it's vital to the song. Here, I can show you."

Harry pulled out her cell phone and played a video of a song. "Evidently Elena told Tim she particularly wanted them to do this because it's her favorite of all their songs, and she's seen the video about a hundred times, and is looking forward to seeing it done in person."

"You don't know the dance steps?" Iakovos asked her.

"No, I don't. But I could probably fake most of them. It's the lift that's the problem. I'm built like a tank, and

I flattened poor Terry when we tried it just a few minutes ago."

Iakovos frowned, looking from her to Terry, who was trying to stand up straight. "It's simply a matter of leverage. You're not so large he shouldn't be able to lift you. Let me see you do it."

"All right, but only if we drag out a mattress first. I don't want to completely squash Terry since he has to play tonight."

Iakovos rolled his eyes, but he actually helped the two boys haul out the mattress from Harry's room. She explained that with the layout of the stage that had been set up for the evening concert, Terry would be on ground level, and she would throw herself off the steps in order to avoid the lifting part of the move.

"Show me," he commanded, and Harry, climbing onto a bench, threw herself at the grim-faced Terry where he stood braced in front of the mattress.

"Told you that mattress was a good idea," Harry said a moment later, accepting the hand Iakovos held out for her as he pulled her to her feet. "You OK, Terry?"

"Yeah, but I've changed my mind. Let's just go home," he said, groaning as he pried himself off the mattress.

"You're not doing it right. Try again," Iakovos said, moving to stand in front of the mattress, his legs braced apart. "I'll catch you this time."

"I'll squash you, too," Harry said, feeling like an elephant.

"Don't be ridiculous. Do it again."

She looked at the set expression on his face, thought about arguing with him but decided that he must be one

of those people who had to see something to believe it.
"Incoming!" she warned as she launched herself at him.

His hands were warm and solid on her waist as he
held her over his head. She gave a little shout of triumph, grinning down at him as he slowly lowered her.
She twined her body around his in a serpentine motion
until her feet were once again on the ground.

"There, you see? It's all a matter of physics. You just
need to catch Harry at the right point," he told Terry.
"Try it again. I will guide you."

They spent an hour practicing, and to Harry's surprise, and no little relief, by the end of that time Terry
was able to catch her. He couldn't hold her overhead the
way Iakovos could, but if she started her downward spiral around his body the second he caught her, the move
worked. It wasn't graceful, and it was a far cry from Cyndi's version, but it would suffice in a pinch.

"Thanks for your help. You weren't by any chance a
ballet dancer in the past?" Harry asked Iakovos as she
strolled with him toward the stage, where the band was
going to have the sound check with the Greek techni-
cians who had arrived earlier in the morning.

"Can you honestly picture me in a pair of tights?" he
asked in return.

She stopped to give him a very thorough visual ex-
amination. He was dressed casually in a pair of faded
jeans and a navy blue striped shirt that rippled against
his skin with the breeze from the beach. "Well, I couldn't
until you let me feel your butt, but after that? I can picture you in anything."

"I didn't let you feel me. You just did," he pointed

out, a tiny little twitch at the corner of his mouth telling her a lot.

"Yeah, but you liked it."

One eyebrow rose. "How do you know that?"

"If you hadn't, you would have given me one of those 'I am the lord of this castle and you are nothing but an annoyance' looks that you gave me in Theo's room. Speaking of the Romeo of the Aegean, did you have a talk with him about last night?"

His brows pulled together. "It's been taken care of."

She put a hand on his arm. "I know it's none of my business, and I really don't want to cause problems between you and him, but I think he's got a very real drinking problem. Honestly, I don't think he would have given me a thought last night except he was . . . well, drunk."

"It's been taken care of," Iakovos repeated, not looking at her, his jaw tense as he watched the engineers and sound crew while they tested the equipment.

"Is he an alcoholic? Or is that none of my business?" she asked, wanting to hold him but suddenly feeling shy. "I know lots of recovering alcoholics. Maybe if you got him into a treatment program—"

"I had ample time watching my father go in and out of clinics after my stepmother died to know that such treatment is useless if the person doesn't wish to be cured."

"Yes, but if you talked to Theo, maybe found out why he drinks so much, perhaps you could stop him from going down this path."

He turned back to her, his dark eyes burning with

passion. "You're going to make my life hell, aren't you? You're going to stir everything up until you've got it all mixed up and turned around, and completely out of control. Isn't that right?"

"That's not my intention, no," she said, stung by the unexpected accusation.

He must have seen the hurt in her eyes, for despite the fact that they were clearly visible to any of the guests who strolled down to the far lawn where the stage was set up, he took her in his arms, his breath hot on her mouth. "Sometimes, sweetheart, a storm is just what we need."

"I really don't understand you at times," she answered, her body tight with anticipation. "But if you're not going to kiss me until I'm senseless, I'm going to have to molest you right here in front of everybody, and that would shock everyone so that they'd warn you about having anything to do with me, and then you wouldn't ask me to marry you, and I'd go home and live by myself until I was a very old lady, grabbing unsuspecting passersby to tell them about the time I slept with the number seven most eligible bachelor in the world."

"Five. I'm number five, not seven."

Harry stared at him for a moment, then turned on her heel and walked away. He wondered if she'd misunderstood what he had been trying to say about needing a storm in his life, but as he watched her walk toward the stage, she lifted her hand in a rude gesture.

He laughed out loud at it, his heart and groin warming at the sight of her. He hadn't known quite how to take her proposal of marriage, and surprised even himself when he told her he intended to marry her, but he'd be lying if he pretended he had any intention of letting her out of his life.

She was his tempest, and that was all there was to the matter.

Chapter 9

Despite the lead singer's absence, the usual issues that come when strangers set up sound equipment, and Harry's general sense of giddiness whenever she thought of Iakovos, the pinnacle of Elena's party was set to go off with (Harry fervently prayed) no hitches.

"We're having a formal dinner for Elena before the concert," Iakovos had told her a few hours before the event itself. "I'd like you to be there."

"Dear god, food? Before a concert? Are you insane?" she asked him, recoiling at the thought of anything so repugnant.

He gave her a silent appraisal. "Stage nerves?"

"Big enough to stop a herd of elephants." She put her hand on his chest, right over his heart. "Thank you for asking me, though. Any other time, and I would love to, but not tonight. Not when I have . . . oh dear god, I didn't tell you about the outfit your cousin picked up for me."

"Dmitri got you clothing for me?"

"No, not you, me."

He frowned. "I thought he said. . . . Never mind."

"I should warn you. . . . Oh god. No, it's no good." She closed her eyes and shuddered. "There's just no way to brace you for it. Just . . . just remember that this was the only thing that Dmitri could find, and he did his best, and it's all so your sister can have what she wants for her birthday."

He looked puzzled, but she didn't have the courage to tell him about the outfit. "Promise me you won't hold it against me."

"I promise," he said immediately.

Her gaze held his. "You don't have the slightest idea what I'm talking about, do you?"

"Not in the least, but I promise that I won't be angry with you if Elena isn't delighted with your performance."

"Oh god," she said, half whimpering, and gave him a quick kiss before hurrying off to the backstage area.

Two hours later she stood in front of a mirror in Amy and Derek's room, and swore. "If anything pops out—"

"Nothing's going to pop out," Amy reassured her.

"Or falls off. The skirt looks flimsy. Maybe I should wear jeans underneath it."

Amy giggled. "I think it's a very nice outfit, Harry. You look great! It's very sexy. I bet Mr. Papaioannou will like it."

Harry stared at the reflection in the mirror. She was neither a vain woman nor overly modest. Her body was the way it was. She wouldn't have minded being shorter, slighter, with hair that wasn't so impossible to do anything with, but she'd long since learned to be comfortable with herself. But this . . . She stared at the breasts that were lifted and separated within an inch of their lives. The bodice was made up of a cobalt blue bra with thankfully full-coverage cups that were intricately beaded with silver and mother-of-pearl. Between the cups, a short silver fringe fell a few inches, giving her little shivers as it slithered across her flesh. The belt of the skirt rose high on her hips, dropping to a V in the center, also beaded, from which fell a longer layer of silver fringe over a long, extremely full skirt of chiffon.

It was hideously expensive, a true work of art, and although she almost fainted when Dmitri told her how much it cost to have it flown in, it was worth every cent.

The only problem was Iakovos. She had absolutely no doubt that he would, in the privacy of his bedroom, be ecstatic with it since it highlighted her good points and hid the bad, but it did its job just a little too well. She knew enough about Iakovos now to realize that he was more than a little possessive, and she had a strong presentiment that he would not care for her being onstage in such an outfit.

"He's going to have a fit," she said aloud as she bent over, making sure her breasts were going to stay put. The maker of the outfit had known what he or she was doing—nothing popped out.

"You think so? It's not that revealing, Harry."

She smoothed her hands down the chiffon drapery that hung from her hips, and gave a twirl. The material flew out, revealing everything from her toes to her underwear.

"Oh," Amy said, her hand over her mouth. "I see what you mean."

"Uh-huh. Now toss in the fact that Iakovos is very Greek, and I think you see the problem."

"Well . . . you have the scarf," Amy said, picking up

the matching cobalt blue body-sized scarf fringed with mother-of-pearl.

"Let's just hope that it won't be as bad as I think it will be," Harry said, wrapping the oversized scarf around her torso several times.

"Are you really going to marry him?"

Harry sighed at her reflection and turned away. "I plan on it, but evidently I breached some sort of Greek man etiquette by asking him first, so we'll have to wait and see what he does."

Amy giggled. "And if he doesn't ask you?"

"Oh, I'm sure I'll think of something. Maybe tattoo my name on his butt when he's sleeping, or handcuff myself to him, or superglue myself to his bed. My main concern right now is just getting through the evening without killing Terry or embarrassing myself. Do you think I should use some of that?" She gestured toward Amy's stage makeup.

"You're welcome to use what you want, but I don't think you need it."

"False courage, my dear." She picked up a kohl stick and applied it to both eyes, then tipped her head to the side. "What do you think?"

Amy gave a little chirrup of laughter.

Harry sighed. "I look like a raccoon in a dress, don't I?"

Amy chirruped again.

She reached for a tissue and cold cream, removing the kohl. "Oh well, those Beautiful People out there are just going to have to take me as I am. Besides, it's better Iakovos sees me as I am, so he knows right from the start what he's getting."

If he was getting her, Harry mused as she followed Amy out to the stage. She tried various ways to make the scarf cover more of her flesh, but it kept slipping off her, so in the end she just let it drape over the back of her arms like a stole. Iakovos, she was pretty sure, was falling for her just as she had already fallen in love with him. She wasn't stupid, after all. She knew he wanted her physically, but even though he said nothing about his emotions, his delight was clearly evident in his eyes when he looked at her. It made her feel all warm and soft inside, and she just hoped that he wasn't the sort of man who had to be hit over the head with his own emotions before he acknowledged them.

Given that, she wondered again about his prediction that she would make his life a hell, but she decided that was something she'd have to ask about later, once the evening was over.

As she walked to the back of the stage, her hands sweaty with nerves, she was aware of the laughter and excited chatter from the other side of the temporary wooden structure that had been built for the concert. The audience was there, and obviously excited. More than anything she wanted—she looked up and all coherent thought stopped. Rounding the back of the stage, two men strode toward her, one a tall, imposing figure clad in an impossibly beautiful black tuxedo. At his side, a slighter man hurried after him, a phone in one hand, his head nodding quickly as Iakovos spoke.

She froze like a deer caught in a spotlight, her heart pounding as Iakovos approached. He was so gorgeous, so incredibly handsome, he literally stripped the breath right out of her lungs. But it was something more than just the beauty of his face, and the warm, silky strength of his body that had so captured her heart. It was Iakovos himself, the odd little way he had of quirking up one corner of his mouth when she said something outrageous. It was the way he thought of her as a storm, a tempestuous element that he had to tame. It was the fact that he was sexy, and successful, and much sought after, and yet he took the time to make sure everyone else was happy.

At that moment, he looked up and saw her, then came to a stop about twelve feet away, his expression stunned. She blinked at him. He stared at her for the count of ten, then turned his head toward Dmitri without taking his eyes off her. "You're getting a raise."

Dmitri winked at her and grinned.

Harry didn't have time to acknowledge it. She was too busy trying to breathe. "You look—" She had to swallow. She was going to drool if she didn't.

"So do you." His gaze was filled with sudden, intense heat as it locked onto her chest, then drifted down to her belly, and finally spent a long time on her hips, hidden though they were beneath the chiffon skirt.

"Although I miss seeing that little spot on your neck."

"I want to rip that dress off you and make love to you right now," he told her.

She glanced at Dmitri.

He looked off into the night, whistling a little tune to himself.

"If you did that, I couldn't go onstage."

"So?" he asked, moving toward her much like a panther stalks its prey.

"Your sister would be disappointed."

"What sister?"

"Elena."

"Oh. Her." He stopped just out of her reach, a grimace twisting his face. "I suppose you're right."

"You're not ... er ... mad about the outfit, are you? Dmitri had a hell of a time finding something that would fit me, and although this shows a whole lot more skin than I'm happy about, it's really all he could get me."

His gaze scorched her skin. "Why would I be angry? It's lovely. You're ... indescribable."

"I—I don't know why," she said, relieved that it was going to be so easy after all. "And thank you. I'm sorry I misjudged you."

"Misjudged me how?" he asked, but Terry appeared from behind the cases used to hold the amps and beckoned her forward.

"Showtime, beautiful," he said with an impudent grin.

"Oh god," she said, her stomach clenching in horror, her eyes huge as she silently pleaded with Iakovos to stop her from going onstage. "I don't suppose you'd like to go sailing or something right now, Yacky?"

Dmitri snorted. "Did you just call him Yack—"

"You say it and you're fired," Iakovos said out of the side of his mouth.

"You just gave me a raise!"

"You'll be fine, Eglantine," Iakovos told her. "Stop worrying." His gaze still crawled over her body, leaving her feeling as if her skin were suddenly two sizes too small.

"Fine way to treat your own cousin, and after all I did today for you," Dmitri said with another grin, but he, too, added, "I'm sure it'll be great, Harry."

"Ignore him. He's from the bad side of the family," Iakovos said, and made shooing gestures at Dmitri.

"Good luck, Harry. I'm leaving, I'm leaving, Jake. You can stop looking like you want to drown me."

Iakovos sighed as Dmitri hurried off to talk to one of the rented roadies.

"Why *Jake*?" Harry asked, in an attempt to keep from flinging herself on him.

"They called me Jacob in England. Theo picked it up and it spread to Dmitri. They do it just to irritate me."

"Oh." She had a hard time keeping her lips straight.

His gaze instantly shot to her mouth, the intensity visible on his face causing sweat to prickle on her palms. "Did you learn the music you needed to learn?"

"I think so. I'm just taking the big finale, and doing two ballads to give Amy a little breather."

"Ah. Good."

They stared at each other.

"I suppose I should go."

"Yes," he agreed.

"I want to kiss you."

"I want to strip you naked and bury myself in you," he told her, and she believed him.

They stared at each other again, then, in unspoken agreement, they turned and walked away in opposite directions.

It took an almost superhuman effort, but Iakovos managed to leave the woman whose very presence lightened his heart and made him feel like whistling. Not that he wanted to whistle at that moment; he was hot and hard and wanted nothing more than to do exactly what he'd said—bury himself in her heat. But as he rounded the front of the stage and stood well off to the side, watching Elena laugh and chat happily with her friends gathered to watch the concert, he knew in his heart that his self-sacrifice would be well rewarded. Tonight he would raise a storm and glory in every delectable inch of her. Just the thought of her in that scandalously sexy belly dancer's outfit sent his blood pressure up several points. The way it caressed the heavy curve of her breasts, her bare midriff, the belt emphasizing the flare of her hips, those delicious hips that swayed in a deliberate attempt to entice him—and never failed to do so—those long, long legs that even now he could feel wrapped around him as he plunged himself into her again and again . . .

"You need either a cold shower or a woman," Theo murmured as he passed by, a dainty little blonde perched on one arm, while the other held a tall champagne flute.

"I have a woman," he answered, shifting to the side to stand behind a chair, wincing as his erection rubbed painfully against his now too tight trousers. He nodded toward the glass. "How many of those have you had?"

Theo smiled, allowing the blonde to pull him into the crowd. "Not nearly as many as I'd like. And you can stop looking at me like I'm something you stepped in. I said I'd apologize to Harry, and I will."

"Tomorrow. She'll be busy tonight."

"I have no doubt she will."

Iakovos frowned as the crowd burst into applause when the band took the stage. He tried very hard not to look at Harry as she took her place, but it was a lost cause and he knew it. He stared at her as she sang a ballad, later watching her graceful arms when she stood behind the keyboard, her body swaying in time with the music. The other girl was singing now, but he had eyes only for Harry. He wondered if she would wear that outfit for him in his bedroom, and decided that if she did, he'd probably rip it off her within seconds.

The way it exposed all those delicious curves, emphasizing her breasts and hips, the way her belly undulated in time with the music . . . *exposed*. Her curves were exposed. He looked around, suddenly aware of what she had meant when she asked if he was angry.

By Christ, she was practically naked up there on the stage where every man with a pair of eyes in his head could ogle her. His storm!

He swore to himself, trying to assess whether the band could continue to play if he ran onto the stage, wrapped her in the thickest quilt he could find, and carried her off to his bedroom so he could lecture her within an inch of her life.

"Not bad, are they?" Dmitri asked him just as he had decided to do that very thing.

"They're tolerable." His teeth ground together while he alternated between watching Harry and glaring at every male he could.

"Ah, looks like Harry's going to sing again." Dmitri slid him a laughing glance. "It's killing you, isn't it?"

"Yes." His hands were fists when Harry took center stage, looking suddenly vulnerable as she stood alone with Derek, who held a violin.

"I wondered if it was going to occur to you. If it makes you feel any better, I tried to get something that wouldn't give you an aneurysm. This was as decent as I could find."

"I'll kill you later, after I kill her," he growled.

Dmitri laughed. "Look at it this way: the concert is a huge success, and just look at Elena. She's practically beaming with happiness."

Iakovos cast a glance toward his sister. Her face was shining as she danced with her friends. He knew he should keep an eye out for men who might get too pushy with her, but his gaze was drawn to the stage. He trusted his sister. He didn't trust any of the men within eyeshot of Harry.

"Harry's pretty awesome, too." Dmitri said casually.

"She has a lovely voice, yes."

"That's not really what I meant, but that slow song she sang was great. She has a lot of talent."

Iakovos' fingers spasmed. "Your death is going to be slow and painful."

"I have no doubt of it," Dmitri said, laughing again. "You're a lucky bastard, you know that? You got the looks, the business savvy, and a woman you don't deserve. You going to keep her?"

"Assuming I survive the evening, yes."

"Good. I like what she's done for you."

He frowned. "In what way?"

"Made you happy. You look like you could burst into song at any moment. It's a nice change from the man who moved through life without letting anything touch him."

Iakovos was about to answer Dmitri, but at that moment the sweet notes of a violin cut through the night, followed by a high, clear voice that seemed to soar upward, to the moon that glowed overhead. Harry's head was turned slightly to the side, her gaze locked on his as she sang, the pure, lilting notes resonating deep within him. She sang of the sea, of the lovers who were separated, of the storm that brought them together again. She sang for him alone, and he would be grateful until he drew his last breath that she had chosen his life to touch.

Iakovos had never been much of a man for romance. He made token romantic gestures to lovers, since it was expected and as a rule he liked to keep his women happy. But the gestures he had considered romantic—candlelit dinners, gifts of jewelry, afternoons spent in bed—paled by comparison to the exquisite moment when he knew that Harry was singing just for him. She gave the gift of herself, and once again he felt completely out of his depth with her.

Elena caught his eye as the song ended and the crowd applauded the performance. She grinned at him, blowing him a kiss, and he knew that she would take to Harry as everyone else had. Not that he'd been worried about that, he told himself as he moved around behind the throng of people dancing to a bouncy song. Even if Elena had a violent dislike of Harry, that wasn't going to change the fact that she belonged to him. He didn't bother analyzing the whys or hows—that never seemed to matter much. What did matter was surviving the rest of this interminable evening until he could whisk Harry away to his bed.

He knew the final song was nigh when Terry, with a grim twist to his lips, jumped off the stage with a bodhran in his hands. Harry shot the young man a worried look as two remaining musicians started playing. Her voice was restrained, pleasant, but he knew she was nervous. He continued strolling around the edge of the crowd as they danced along with the music, hands clapping in time to it. Harry had a tambourine in her hand as she sang, but he could see the tension in every line of her body.

Silly woman. Did she really think he'd let anything happen to her? As one of the refrains ended, Harry tossed the tambourine in the air as she did an improvised dance. Iakovos thanked god he'd had the foresight to have the event filmed, and decided right then and there that no one but he would have access to the video. The way she moved in that damned costume should be illegal.

She threw the tambourine onto the floor of the stage and gathered herself for the leap off the steps.

He moved forward. Terry shot him a grateful look, stepping back as Iakovos braced himself. The music swelled, and Harry leaped. He caught her by her bare waist, holding her high overhead, spinning her around, his heart singing as she laughed down at him, surprise turning to delight in her eyes.

She slid in an erotic spiral down his body until her feet touched the ground. His hands were still on her hips as she bent back, balancing herself on her hands before flipping backward onto her feet.

"Nice catch," she told him over the cheering of the crowd before running back to the stage and singing with much more animation until the song ended.

He was in love with her. Wholly, completely, inexorably in love with her. How could he not be? She was everything a woman should be—warm, smart, unflappable, and very, very flexible. He had plans to put that flexibility to good use, but first he had to get through the rest of the festivities.

Once they were over, though ... then she would be his.

Chapter 10

The noise woke Harry up the following morning. It infiltrated a pleasant dream in which Iakovos, wearing nothing but a smile, taught her how to play poker. She had just lost a big stack of chips to him, and was about to pay the forfeit of kissing him senseless when the horrible noise of some poor animal in pain interrupted her.

She woke up to realize the noise was Iakovos singing in the shower. She sat up, arms around her knees as she listened to him, smiling as she recognized the tune as being one that Amy had sung last night. It had Middle Eastern overtones, and a beat that was impossible to hear without wanting to dance, but that wasn't what had her leaping to her feet, wincing as he hit a high note that never, in her estimation, should have been heard by mortal man. The fact that he was singing the entire song off-key warmed her heart, however.

"I just wonder if the people who put together that bachelor list knew about your singing," she said softly, then unable to restrain herself, pulled on the belly dancer's outfit and ran to the bathroom.

She took up a pose outside of the huge black marble shower, and let her feet go wild as Iakovos happily sang away. She didn't remember much from the few dancing lessons she'd taken all those years ago, but she didn't think Iakovos would be too harsh a judge.

The shower door opened as she was indulging in a spin, her arms in the air, hips dancing to the beat she heard in her head. He stood frozen in the door, a towel clasped in one hand halfway to his face, water streaming down his magnificent body, his eyes huge.

"Done with the shower?" she asked with a couple of hip shakes.

He stared at her hips.

"That's a shame, because after last night, I smell like you, and I thought maybe we could get cleaned up together." She thought for a moment, then tried a belly roll. His gaze shot to her belly. "Not that you smell bad or anything. I like the way you smell. I like it a lot. I especially like that you don't go in for much cologne."

She spun around again, sweeping her hands up from her waist to her breasts. His fingers tightened on the towel as he focused on her breasts.

"So when I said that I smell like you, I simply meant that I smell like I've spent the night in bed with an extremely virile man who damn near steamed the sheets, he was so hot."

"Eglantine," he managed to say at last, his voice hoarse.

"Yes, my adorable wet Yacky?"

"Take off that outfit."

"You don't like it?" She stopped dancing and looked down at herself. "You liked it last night."

"Take it off," he repeated.

She did so, glancing at his face, which was hard and frozen as he stepped out of the shower. Had she insulted him by saying she smelled like him? She did, though. She smelled like a woman who had been pleasured to the tips of her toes and back again. Surely he understood that? Maybe he thought she was mocking him by dancing while he was singing in the shower. Perhaps he was embarrassed by the fact that he had absolutely no singing ability.

She'd just have to reassure him that she found his singing charming, which she did.

"I'm sorry if I disturbed your bathroom time," she said, peeling off the bra before unhooking the belt and letting the skirt drop. "I certainly didn't mean to rush you out of the show—Iakovos!"

He flung aside the towel and fell to his knees at her feet, wrapping his hands around her upper thighs and burying his face in her stomach. "You do smell like me," he murmured, urging her legs open. "I like that."

She stared down at his head, his hair slicked back, water from it running down his back as he spread her knees, his mouth hot on her.

"You're not going to—you don't think you're—Iakovos! I haven't taken a shower yet!- I'm all . . ."

"Hot?" he asked, sliding a finger into her.

Her knees buckled. He lowered her onto the floor, his mouth kissing a steamy path across her stomach before he headed south again.

"Not springtime fresh," she said, trying desperately to

think of a polite euphemism and failing, mostly because her mind just stopped working at the touch of his mouth.

"Sweetheart, you're going to be a whole hell of a lot less fresh by the time I get done with you."

"Yes, but I didn't think men liked to do things like that afterward. And since just a few hours ago . . ."

His tongue did a little swirl against her that had her grabbing the throw rug underneath her. "You taste of passion, of a wild storm that is made up of you and me together. It inflames me, and makes me want to take you all over again."

"Oh, yes, please," she cooed, her body writhing against his as he moved up her, the wetness of his chest making little squishy noises on her stomach as he kissed her breasts, laving them with burning swipes of his tongue.

"But if you are really bothered by your lack of springtime, then I must do what I can to make you happy."

He must have shaved in the shower, she thought as he rubbed his cheek on the underside of her breast, his fingers still working their magic in her depths. Although she had a few little whisker marks from the previous night, he seemed to be stubble-free now.

"You always make me happy," she said, trying to pull him up so she could kiss him, and stroke him, and feel the wonderful muscles of his back work as he pounded into her.

He looked up at her, his eyes filled with a seductive glint that made her melt into a puddle. "Let's see if I can't push the stakes a little, hmm?"

"Push them how? Iakovos? Where are you going?"

He moved off her, getting to his feet, dangling one of

his big hands in front of her. "You made it clear that you don't wish to make love until you've had a shower."

"No, you misunderstood," she said, taking his hand and letting him pull her to her feet. "I didn't mean—" She stopped speaking at the look of his wicked smile, one that made her feel hot all over. She glanced down at his penis, which was full of enthusiasm, then over to the shower, giving it a speculative look, before returning her gaze to him. "You're not serious, are you? I'm far too big to do that. I'll break your back."

"We'll see, shall we?" He led her into the shower. It was one of those models that had several jets that came at you from all angles, and before too long, he had her wet and soaped up, giggling as he teased her with little soapy touches that did more to fire her passion than anything else.

"I'm too big," she moaned against his neck as his fingers slipped down around her butt, pulling her tight against him. He was soapy now, as well, and his penis slid against her pubic bone, making her wild with need. "You can't hold me up that long."

"I could, but if it worries you, we'll do it the easy way," he murmured, his fingers sliding down into her intimate parts, making her see stars again. "Wrap your leg around my thigh."

She slid her leg up his in one long, sensual stroke, curling it around his thigh. He urged her hips forward, saying as his hands caressed her slick breasts, "You must guide me, my wild water spirit."

He was hot and so hard, she wondered if he hurt. She knew she did, her inner muscles quivering in desperate anticipation of the feel of him. She moved her hand on him, drawing a groan of sheer pleasure from him before she tilted her hips a little more and angled him to where she knew he would find a welcome.

The soapy water ensured that he slid in despite the unusual position, the look in his eyes burning her as he sucked on her lower lip, saying, "Fast and hard?"

"Is there anything else?" she answered, sweeping her hands up his arms, down his shoulders to his back, where she dug her fingers into the thick muscles of his butt, urging him on.

"There is, but it's not nearly so much fun," he agreed, and set to work on making her mindless with pleasure.

He had to carry her out of the shower because she didn't have a single bone left in her body by the time he was done.

"Elena would like to meet you." Iakovos appeared in the doorway from the dressing room, buckling a narrow black belt.

Momentarily distracted by the sight of him, Harry froze, her hand poised in midstroke as she tried to brush some semblance of order into her hair. How on earth had she ever managed to catch the fancy of such a gorgeous man? "Is this the equivalent to being taken home to meet your parents?"

"I suppose it is." He gave her a little smile. "Nervous?"

"Of course I am. This is your baby sister we're talking about. You adore her, don't you?"

He gave a short laugh. "When she's not driving me to distraction, yes. You have nothing to be worried about—you've already met my brother and cousin. Elena will love you."

She might, Harry allowed. Then again, she might be offended by a woman who held her brother's interest. Some girls were like that.

"Dmitri assures me that my business will collapse if I don't take a few video conferences today. Elena has offered to see your friends off to the airport, but she would like to show you around Agios Nikos, the local town. Would you prefer to rest, or spend time with her?"

"Do I have a choice?" she asked, giving up on her hair.

"Of course you do." She held his gaze until he smiled. "Elena really would like to get to know you."

"I would be delighted to spend the day with your sister," she said, putting her hands on his chest just because she couldn't stop herself.

Instantly his eyes went all slumbering sensuality on her. "I will meet you in town. The taverna is run by the mayor and has quite good food."

"Ooh, I get to see how real Greeks live?" she asked as he kissed her fingers.

"I'm a real Greek," he said, biting the tip of her finger.

"You, Mr. Sexy Pants, may be real, but you are anything but typical. Until this evening, then?"

He released her fingers to pull her up to him, his mouth plundering hers with an intensity that left her feeling boneless again. "Until this evening."

Chapter 11

Harry opted to go to the airport with Elena to see the band off, not because she felt she had to finally wave good-bye to her charges, but because she wanted to have a chance to assess Elena's reaction to her with the security of others around.

"You must be Harry," Elena said as she approached the dock where the band's instruments and luggage were being loaded on one of the boats tied up there.

"I am. Hello, Elena. Happy day after your birthday."

"Thank you."

Harry was conscious of being examined by a pair of grave brown eyes, unusually astute eyes that gave her a momentary qualm.

That faded when Elena suddenly smiled and leaned forward to give Harry a big hug. "I'm so happy to meet you at last. Iakovos said you did not wish to sing last night, but did it just so I would not be disappointed. I couldn't have had a more wonderful birthday."

"I was happy to do it," Harry lied, relieved that she

had passed the Elena Test. "I'm just glad I could help out."

Terry, Amy, and Derek all burst into laughter. She glared at them until they stopped, but was forced to endure the grossest slurs against her character as they zipped over to the mainland, then drove to the nearby airport.

"Lies, I tell you, all lies," she said, pinching Derek after he described just how thoroughly she had flattened Terry until he had figured out how to catch her. "See if I ever step up to be your fill-in manager again."

"Oh, we've already told Tim that we'll take you anytime he wants to have another appendicitis," Derek said with a grin.

"Dear god, what a horrible thought!"

She kissed Amy, hugged the boys, and told them all to behave on the way home.

"I don't see why we shouldn't have some fun, since it's obvious you are," Terry said with an exaggerated wink as the others headed toward the security gate. "You'll have us back to play at your wedding, right? We'd totally be up for that."

Horror filled Harry at his teasing words. She stammered something, watching with no little sense of relief as Terry, with one last wave, joined the queue to pass through security.

How could he say that in front of Elena? Harry was certain that Iakovos hadn't mentioned any such intention as marriage to anyone, let alone his young sister. They'd known each other only a couple of days, after all, and although it was one thing for her to fall madly in love at the drop of a hat—not that she'd ever done it before, but Iakovos was definitely dropped-hat worthy—men of his position did not. They didn't put you on a world's most eligible bachelor list if you were prone to marrying women you'd just met.

Elena would think her the worst sort of gold digger. She had to—if Harry was in her shoes, she certainly would. She took a deep breath and turned to face the younger woman, but there was nothing in Elena's expression to show she'd heard the comment. Maybe she hadn't?

"Iakovos said you had never seen dolphins before. Would you like to meet some?"

"Dolphins? You mean, like a marine show?"

Elena shook her head, slipping on a pair of sunglasses as they left the coolness of the airport. The heat of the morning hit Harry with the impact of a sledgehammer. She wondered if she'd ever get used to it.

"A friend of mine is a—what is the word . . . marine biologist? He has a company that takes tourists out to see dolphins and whales, you know. Seeing them, and sailing next to them. It is very beautiful. He uses a microphone underwater to find them, and then tourists can get into the water. If the dolphins like the people, they come and play. If not, Vasilis tells you that you must stay away from them."

"Sounds wonderful. Is he taking some tourists out today?"

"No, he only does that on certain days, because he does other work, too, serious work. The tourists are just to pay for that. But if you would like to see dolphins and sperm whales up close, I will ask him if he would take us out on his boat." Elena got behind the wheel of the sporty yellow convertible that she had casually mentioned was Iakovos' graduation gift to her. "You have your swimsuit on?"

Harry looked down at the green sundress. "No, I don't. I didn't think to put it on underneath."

"You should always have your suit on," Elena said, her dark eyes dancing. "Unless you prefer swimming without it. It is very sensual, swimming in the sea without it. The water touches you all over your legs and bottom and breasts. It is very wicked, but so much fun."

Harry's jaw went slack at the thought of frolicking in the water with Iakovos. "I bet it is," she finally said, moving that particular fantasy to the top of her Things I Want to Do with Iakovos list.

"I will call Vasilis, and then we will stop in town to buy you a suit, and you can see the dolphins up close," she said, pulling out her cell phone.

Just as Harry relaxed against the leather seat, enjoying the breathtaking views from the road they were taking along the coastline, Elena said casually, "Iakovos did not tell me you were going to marry him."

Harry's blood ran cold as she glanced at Elena, noting her expressionless face. "No, I don't imagine he did."

"Has he asked you?"

Harry sighed and wished she could put duct tape over Terry's mouth. "As a matter of fact, he hasn't. I asked him."

"Oh? And what did he say?"

Really, Harry thought to herself, this is what you get for speaking without thinking. "He said he'd have to ask me the question." She'd be damned if she would admit to this young girl that she had pressed him to know if he was going to ask her.

Elena's expression might have been neutral, but there was real shock in her voice when she said, "You asked him. I don't think—no, I'm sure no one has ever asked Iakovos if he would marry her."

Harry stared out at the passing scenery, all pleasure in it now gone. "Yes, well, trust me to do things backward."

"I don't think it's backward, I just think it's... unusual."

Harry was silent, suddenly feeling like a fool.

"I think he should marry you," Elena said about ten minutes later.

Harry looked at her in surprise.

"Yes," Elena said with a nod, her attention on the road. "I think he should. It's time he has someone. I want him to be happy, and Dmitri says he really likes you, and that you make him laugh, so I think that you were right to ask him."

"I'm glad you approve," Harry said, relaxing again. Maybe Elena was right, and Iakovos wouldn't be so put off by her proposal that he wouldn't bother to ask her. Maybe he liked it.

Maybe she should just stop worrying and let what was going to happen, happen.

Three hours later, Harry gathered her nerve and jumped into the water next to the catamaran owned by Elena's friend, a pleasant young man in his early twenties who was more than happy to run them out to see the sea life.

Vasilis and Elena were already in the water, while his

partner on board manned a hydrophone, yelling instructions. At first, Harry didn't see anything, but suddenly a dark shape flitting beneath her had her sticking her face in the water to see a small pod of dolphins circling them, obviously curious about the boat and the people.

Harry was thrilled, and although the dolphins didn't come close enough to touch, she enjoyed their playful grace as they swam around the catamaran.

"Dolphins are sacred to Greeks," Elena told her an hour later, as they sat on the deck of the boat, sunning themselves while they sailed back to shore. "To see one at the beginning of a trip is good luck."

"I've heard that," Harry said, remembering her trip to Krokos with Iakovos. She sat with her chin on her knees, arms around her legs, as the beauty of the water and coast sank into her soul. She could easily see herself staying here forever . . . but that really depended on a dark-eyed man whom she suddenly wondered about. Had she been projecting too much of her emotion onto him? Was he merely being polite when he said that yes, he was going to ask her to marry him? Was he happy with the incredibly wonderful sexual chemistry that blazed between them, but not thinking of having her around permanently?

Was she setting herself up for the biggest fall of her life?

"Did you enjoy the dolphins?" Elena asked in a quiet voice.

Harry shook her dark thoughts away. She was brooding, that's all. "I loved it. Thank you so much for arranging this treat."

"It is my pleasure," Elena said, giving her a curious look. "Something is wrong?"

"No," Harry said with a sigh. "The truth is, I have this horrible imagination. It runs amok with me sometimes. That's normally a very good thing when you're a writer, because you just unleash your muse and let her run with the wind when it comes time to actually sit down and write a book, but the rest of the time, when you're not writing, it can make your life hellish."

"What's it running amok with you about now?" Elena asked, obviously genuinely curious.

Harry hesitated, not wishing to bare either her heart or her thoughts to someone so young.

"Iakovos?" Elena asked, tipping her head to the side to consider Harry.

"I was thinking," Harry said slowly, "that he would have enjoyed seeing the dolphins as well." And that although she found the whole experience thrilling, part of her regretted the fact that he wasn't here to share her joy.

It really was too much, she told herself as Elena murmured something noncommittal, to think that she, a grown woman who was more than comfortable with being by herself, suddenly couldn't go even a few hours without missing a man.

And how she missed him. She wanted to tell him her thoughts, to share the fun of seeing the dolphins, to ask him a thousand questions about the area, the ships, the people . . . everything. She just wanted him.

"Oh, no," Elena said an hour later as they arrived back in the town of Agios Nikos. Harry had gotten out of the car while Elena took a call she had said was from her best girlfriend. "Harry, it's Christina. You remember her from last night, right?"

Harry did no such thing, but she nodded.

"She's broken up with her boyfriend, and is crying. I promised Iakovos I would show you around town—"

"Don't worry about me," Harry reassured her, closing the car door. "I'll just putter around on my own for a bit. You take care of your friend."

"She's in Athens, so I can't go to her, but she wants to talk," Elena said, her hand over the mouthpiece. "Don't worry about your things—I'll take them back to the house with me. You're sure you don't mind?"

Harry let the bag containing her newly purchased, and now wet, swimsuit drop back into the car, taking a little money from her purse in case she saw a souvenir to purchase. "I don't mind at all. Go be a shoulder to cry on."

"You're so sweet. Thank you!" Elena hugged her, then pointed to the south end of town. "The taverna is down there, on the water. Iakovos said he would meet us at six. I'm going to run home to change, but I'll be back in an hour or so. You won't forget to meet us for dinner?"

As if she could. "I won't forget."

Elena hugged her again, gathered their things, and then was off, leaving her car at the garage as she ran to the marina, her phone at her ear.

Harry surveyed the town from her position at a garage located high up on the hillside. Like most Greek towns along this section of the coast, Agios Nikos was perched on land that dropped sharply to the sea. Much of it had been terraced, but the streets were still very steep, although the buildings clung to the slope of the land with apparent ease. It was hard on the calves walking up and down the streets, regardless, but Harry enjoyed the sights and sounds of a midsized Greek town. After a few hours of people watching and visiting what sights she could find, the heat started to get to her, and she decided that she'd better head down toward the waterfront, where it must be cooler.

All that walking in the blistering heat of the afternoon had really made her sweat, and she knew she should get something to drink lest she risk getting dehydrated. Stubbornly, she wanted to wait for Iakovos to enjoy a meal, but after wandering around trying to find a seat in the shade, or somewhere to buy a bottle of water, she gave up and headed down the hill. She'd just get something at the taverna and wait for Iakovos there.

Chapter 12

She woke up to find a circle of faces peering down at her. She felt woozy, sick to her stomach, and despite the heat of the afternoon, oddly chilled.

"Oh god," she said, pushing herself up to a sitting position. "What happened?"

The bodies attached to the faces moved back to give her room, which was a good thing considering that they spun around in a whirl that threatened to make her vomit.

She gritted her teeth and bit back the urge, her eyes squeezed shut until the feeling passed. When she opened them again, some kind old lady was offering her a bottle of tepid water. She took it gratefully, sipping at it as she looked around. She was on a sidewalk in front of a shop that featured sewing machines.

She thanked the woman in Greek, one of the few phrases she'd had time to learn, and allowed two middle-aged men to help her to her feet. The little old lady and a younger woman with a small child attached to her hip helped to brush her off.

"I'm sorry; it must have been the heat. Thank you—I'll be fine. Can I pay you for the water?"

The little old lady waved away the couple of euros Harry pulled out of her pocket.

"You are a tourist?" one of the men said to her. "American?"

"Yes, I'm American, although I'm not really a tourist. Well, I am, but I'm not. Kind of. My . . . er . . . boyfriend lives here, on an island over there." She pointed toward the water. "I'm supposed to meet him, as a matter of fact. Oh, dear god, is that the time? I should have been at the taverna half an hour ago."

"Your boyfriend?" The man had a big barrel chest, a shock of white in his dark hair, and bushy black eyebrows that he beetled at her as he looked her up and down. "Who is this boyfriend?"

"His name is Iakovos . . ." She stopped, her mind going blank on his last name. Damn him and his vowels. "Er . . . Iakovos Papa . . . er . . . he owns the island over there, the one with the big house."

"You do not know his name, this boyfriend?" the man asked, now looking at her with suspicion.

"Well, I have this problem with his name . . ." She stopped again, aware that there was no way she could admit to these people that she couldn't pronounce a Greek name without it coming across as an insult.

The water lady tugged on his arm, clearly asking for a translation. Harry just wanted to collapse in a cool, dark room, but to her dismay, the circle around her grew as a few passersby stopped to see what was going on.

"Look, I think I'll just be going on my way to find

Iakovos. Thank you again for the water, and I'm sorry if I caused any trouble."

The man grabbed her arm as she started passed him. "You do not go to bother Kyrie Papaioannou, American."

"Papaioannou," she cried with relief. "That's his name. Good on you for remembering it."

The man frowned, his bushy black brows pulling together. "He is a good man; he gives much to our town. You do not bother him."

"No, you see, I know him. We're . . . for lack of a better word, dating."

His eyes narrowed further as he rattled off something in Greek. The entire crowd of around ten people now considered her with outright hostility and suspicion.

"Honest, we are," she said, then decided it wasn't worth the trouble. "Believe what you want, but I need to go to the taverna to meet him. I'm already late."

"You call him," the man suggested. "You call and tell him you fall over from the sun, and he will come and get you."

"An excellent idea," Harry said, pulling her cell phone out of her skirt pocket. She flipped it on, and realized, to her horror, that she didn't know his cell number. "Umm . . . yeah. Why don't I just go down to the taverna."

"You do not know the number of Kyrie Papaioannou?" the man asked, triumph in his eyes.

"We just met a few days ago, and I haven't had the opportunity to get his number," she protested.

"You just met? You said you were dating him!"

He translated this to the folks who didn't speak English.

Harry ran her hand through her hair as several pointed things were said. She didn't understand the words, but she could tell from the way they were spoken that people regarded her as some lesser species of celebrity chaser.

"I'm going to the taverna," she said, pushing past the man. "You believe what you want."

"We will come with you," he said, and she'd be damned if they didn't all fall in behind her as she stumbled down the hill toward the water. The sun was glinting on the rippling water by now, gilding it orange and red and gold, but Harry had no eyes for the beauty of her surroundings.

It was at that moment that she discovered that Agios Nikos boasted not one, not two, but four tavernas along the waterfront. And Elena hadn't bothered to mention which one was Iakovos' favorite.

"Son of a bitch," she muttered as she marched toward the first one, her crowd gasping in shock as her self-appointed translator repeated her oath in Greek.

Iakovos wasn't at the taverna. She knew he wouldn't be, because that would have been just way too convenient. Neither was he at the second or the third, which were scattered along a half mile of waterfront. The fourth taverna, she could see as she stood weaving with heat exhaustion, lay even farther down the curved stretch of seafront.

"You do not find your boyfriend yet, eh, *kyria*?" the spokesman of her followers said. She turned to tell him that Iakovos was sure to be at the last taverna, but the words shriveled to nothing on her lips as at least two dozen faces glared at her. Evidently she'd picked up some bystanders at the other three tavernas.

"I'll find him," she told the crowd, and stubbornly turned on her heel to walk the five hundred miles to the next taverna.

Several people ran ahead of her as her procession made its way there. She had no idea if they ran ahead to warn Iakovos of her arrival—she rather hoped they would, so that he would come out and meet her with applications of cooling beverages and sympathy for passing out in the heat—but as it happened, he didn't.

The bastard wasn't at the taverna.

Harry stared in openmouthed dismay at the taverna full of people who weren't one of the world's sexiest, most eligible bachelors, and wanted to cry. "He's supposed to be here," she said, her gaze shifting along the long line of accusatory faces. They'd been joined now by several people from the taverna. She held out her wrist, tapping on the watch. "I was supposed to meet him at six. It's almost seven now."

No one said a word, but they didn't have to—their expressions said it all.

"Right," she said, closing her eyes for a moment. She just wanted to crawl into a hole in the ground. "To hell with this. I'll just take a boat back to the island. Either Iakovos is there, or someone will have his phone number."

"You have a boat?" her primary escort asked her.

"No, but there's bound to be one of Iakovos' . . ."

The man's expression darkened.

"Or maybe I'll just hire someone to take me out there," she amended.

"No one will take you. No one goes to Kyrie Papaioannou's island without his permission."

Harry rubbed her forehead, wondering what would happen if she collapsed right there in the middle of the taverna. Would someone find Iakovos? Or would she be handed over to the police as a potential stalker?

"Fine," she said, coming to a decision. She'd be damned if she let a lot of unfortunate circumstances keep her away from the man she loved. She looked out at the water, the dark shape of Iakovos' island visible as the last flaming rays of the sun stretched across the horizon. "It's only a couple of miles out. I'll swim to it. And the first person who tries to stop me is going to get a knuckle sandwich."

They were marching her up to the police station, two men holding either arm, half the damned town trailing behind her, when a jeep squealed to a stop a half block away.

"Harry!" a man's voice roared into the night, and she stopped, glaring furiously as Iakovos strode toward her, pulling out his cell phone as he did so.

"I found her," he snapped into the phone. "Tell the police it's all right. Where the hell have you been?" The last sentence was spoken to her, but even as the words left his lips his eyes were scanning her captors. "And what's going on?"

"I'm being taken to jail," she said, wanting to simultaneously weep with joy at seeing him and lambaste him for not being where he was supposed to be. "Evidently this town really, really likes you. And they didn't believe that we're . . . dating."

He spoke rapidly in Greek, taking her arm in one hand, the other gesturing as he no doubt explained to the people the nature of their relationship.

One of the men answered him. Harry knew what he must have said by the long look Iakovos gave her. "You broke someone *else's* nose?"

She examined her fingertips for a few seconds. "I told him that if he tried to stop me from swimming out to your island, he'd get a knuckle sandwich. He evidently didn't believe I was serious. He does now."

Iakovos took a deep breath, speaking again to the crowd, which reluctantly dispersed, before he steered her into the jeep. "That was the mayor, sweetheart."

"The man who owns the taverna where I was supposed to meet you?"

He nodded, put the car in gear, and headed down the road the way she'd just come. "Where were you, speaking of that?"

"Lost. And passed out." She explained about waking up on the sidewalk.

He glanced at her, frowning. "Where's your hat?"

"What hat?"

"You went out without a hat? That's not very bright, Harry. You're not used to the sun here yet."

"Thank you, Captain Hindsight," she said wearily.

He said nothing more, and she worried for a few minutes that she'd offended him, but if she had, he was above such things. He helped her out of the jeep and escorted her to a table, calling for water as he got her settled.

By the time she'd had three glasses of water and had eaten a little flatbread, she was feeling much more human.

Iakovos had gone to see the mayor, who had retired earlier in dignity to the back room. The two men emerged now, the mayor wreathed in smiles despite the reddish purple skin below both eyes and his swollen nose.

When Harry apologized, he said, "Is fine. My nose is broken more than once. Never has it been so happy as to be broken by the *kyria*."

"Apparently you can work miracles," Harry said a few minutes later after the mayor had toddled back off to his cronies.

He flashed her a grin as several bowls of intriguing food were set before them. "I just told him that you were a famous writer and might pick Agios Nikos as the setting for your next book. He wants you to make a character based on him."

"I just bet he does," she said, smiling as he shifted his chair over closer to her, his leg pressing with comforting solidity against hers. "Where's Elena? I thought she was going to have dinner with us."

"When you weren't here, Dmitri and Elena and I split up to find you. She's probably back home now, on the phone with her tiresome friends. Dmitri said he was going to visit a woman he sees on and off when we're here."

"So it's just you and me tonight, is it?" she asked, tracing a vein running down one of his long, sensitive hands.

"It is. Do you want to return home, or are you up to this?" he asked, nodding at the people who had gathered as music started up from a three-piece band. "They play every Monday night. I thought you might like to hear them, since they do some traditional music."

"This looks fun," she said, wanting to be alone with

him but intrigued at the same time to see this new side of him.

It was an eye-opening evening. Iakovos might have had no ear for music, but he obviously enjoyed it nonetheless, his feet tapping to the lively tunes, his fingers warm on her back and neck as he sat, relaxed, laughing and joking with the folks of the town, periodically giving her steamy looks that promised much for later activities.

She didn't know the words to any of the songs—most of them were in Greek anyway—but she hummed along as the entire taverna sang some of the numbers. A few people danced as well, but Iakovos was evidently content to just sit there with her.

It warmed her heart to know that this man who bought and sold expensive pieces of property without a second thought, had so much in common with people who worked for their daily meals. She didn't miss the byplay of a couple of older women who were clearly chaffing him, giving him little nods toward her. He laughed and answered them, his eyes amused when he turned back to her.

"Don't tell me—the ladies of the town are trying to hook you up with their unmarried daughters?" Harry asked, wanting badly to kiss him but lacking the nerve to do so in front of everyone.

"Only one of them, and she's been trying that for the last ten years. Seraphina was telling me the best way to keep you from getting sunstroke was to make sure you never left my bed."

"I *do* like Seraphina," she answered, scanning the crowd. "Which one is she?"

"To the left, in the yellow flower dress."

Harry waved at the old woman, who smiled and nodded back.

"So what do you think of the typical Greek now?" Iakovos asked, his mouth close to her ear as the music started up again.

She turned her head, her mouth almost brushing his. "I think they're all wonderful. But not as wonderful as you."

"Harry," he said on a breath, his hand in her hair, angling her head back so he could kiss her. His lips were hot on hers, his tongue hotter still as it slipped between her lips. She moaned as it twined around her tongue, the taste of him making her body feel far too hot and confined in her dress.

He was still kissing her when the music ended, the applause rippling into laughter when someone caught sight of them.

"Time to go home before I demand a room right here," Iakovos said, pulling her to her feet, making a bow when some wag called out something that she was willing to bet was risqué. She waved good-bye to them all, and was a little surprised when many of the crowd came out with them to see them into the jeep.

She glanced back as he drove off, waving to her new friends, wondering if she would ever see them again.

She would if she had anything to say about the matter.

Chapter 13

"Yacky."

"Eglantine."

Harry peeled herself off his chest and looked down at him. "We have to get out of bed."

"I don't think we do, no."

"We do. We're becoming sloths. For three days all we've done is make love, drag ourselves out to the patio to eat, take short breaks to swim, and then we're back in bed again."

His gorgeous dark eyes glittered at her with a light that never failed to make her shiver with delight. "You could be right. We should eat in bed. That would eliminate all that patio time."

She laughed. She couldn't help it—he filled her with so much joy, she felt as if it were bursting from her. She wanted badly to say it, positively ached to mention the word, but she wasn't sure if he was quite ready to hear it yet. He seemed happy, yes. He certainly had done everything possible to make the last few days filled with nothing but happy memories. He'd told Dmitri that he wasn't to be disturbed for anything short of complete economic breakdown, sent Elena off to Switzerland for her birthday trip, and rearranged his business schedule for a few days so they could stay together, alone, just the two of them and the twenty or so people he employed to maintain his island paradise.

She examined his face, his beautiful face with its long nose, straight black brows, and definitely aggressive whisker growth. She knew without looking that she sported any number of little patches of whisker burn on her neck, breasts, belly, and, she suspected, between her thighs. Iakovos offered to shave more frequently, but she had told him she didn't really mind. But it was his eyes that held her attention, those eyes that could glow with such warmth that it left her breathless.

"I love you," she said, unable to keep from saying the words.

He froze beneath her, his eyes suddenly wary.

"I'm serious. I really love you. All of you, not just your body, in case you're worried about losing the number five spot. I love your mind, and I love your mouth, and your upper lip, and your lower lip, and everything else about you, even the fact that you actually like mint toothpaste, which frankly is just beyond my understanding, but even despite that gigantic personality flaw, I love you with every little atom of my being."

He blinked at her, then smiled a slow—very slow—smile, one filled with a whole lot of male satisfaction.

"Now," she said, tapping her fingers on his breastbone, "would be a perfectly appropriate time for you to tell me that you love me as well."

"Would it?" he asked, cocking one glossy black eyebrow.

"Yes." She waited.

He just hummed softly to himself, his hands drawing lazy patterns on her naked behind.

"Yacky."

"Eglantine?"

"You're not going to say it, are you? You're going to make me beg you to say it, just because I call you Yacky, and make your life a hell, and turn things upside down, although I'm not quite sure what I'm turning upside down, but evidently I am, and for some perverse reason, you feel the need to punish me for it by not telling me you love me, when I know perfectly well that you do."

"If you know I do, then you don't need me to say it, do you?" he asked with maddening reason, giving her butt a swat as he gently pushed her off him in order to pad naked into the bathroom.

"I'm going to make you pay for that—you are aware of that, aren't you?" she called after him, unable to keep from admiring his truly spectacular butt as he strolled into the bathroom.

"I know you'll try. Can you pack your things and be ready to leave tomorrow?" he asked, pausing at the door.

She sat up, clutching his pillow because it smelled like him. "Yes. Am I going somewhere?"

"Athens, if you wish to join me."

"Your office?" she asked.

He nodded. "I've put off work as long as I could, but there are several deals that are coming to a head, and I'm needed."

"All right, but at some point I'm going to have to go home and cope with my apartment."

"I have to go to New York in two months—you can come with me when I return to the States, take care of your business in Seattle and meet me in New York, if you like."

"Do you love me?" she asked.

He grinned and went into the bathroom.

"When are you going to ask me to marry you, you annoying man?" she yelled after him.

He burst into a song. In Greek. Off-key, of course.

She wanted to scream. She wanted to throw things at him. She wanted to spend the rest of her life kissing him.

Dear god, she was in way over her head with him.

Harry in Athens for the first time was an eye-opening experience for Iakovos. He knew she had been looking forward to seeing the city, since she hadn't been to Greece before, and he had anticipated with mild pleasure showing her around the various sites. But he hadn't expected her to be so enthusiastic, or so delighted with everything historical. He had lived in Athens on and off for most of his adult life, but he felt as if he'd never really seen it until she dragged him around to every sight she could find. The time spent together as he showed her the city he loved filled him with a quiet contentment.

"You really are a lucky man to have grown up with this," she said one night at the Acropolis as she stood leaning back against him, his arms around her, her hands over his. In front of them, the Parthenon sat on its hilltop like a stately jewel, lit with soft amber lights. Above their heads, the moon was full.

He nuzzled the side of her neck. "I'm *very* lucky."

She turned in his arms, oblivious of the other tourists who had gathered with them. "This is, hands down, the most romantic night of my life."

"Is it?" He kissed her temple, smiling to himself.

"Yes. Notice that full moon."

He obligingly looked at the moon. "It's very full."

"Full moons are romantic, Yacky," she told him with slightly flared nostrils.

"So I've heard, Eglantine."

"The Parthenon, lit at night, in the company of the one you love, is also romantic."

"I'm hungry," he told her. "Shall we have dessert somewhere?"

Her teeth ground for a few seconds. "I've changed my mind. I don't want to marry you. I could never marry a man who lacks the slightest iota of romance in his soul." She slid out of his arms and started marching across the rocky ground to where his car waited.

He grinned at the back of her head, taking her hand in his as he said, "It's good, then, that I never got around to asking you to marry me, isn't it?"

She growled at him. She positively growled.

He didn't think he could possibly love her more than he did at that moment.

Unfortunately, business concerns drove him away from her side. He worried that she would be bored on her own, but he had reckoned without her ingenuity.

"I need to get this book done anyway," she told him one morning about two weeks after they arrived in Athens. "I'm behind schedule as is, and I do need quiet time to write, so stop worrying."

"Mikos will drive you anywhere you wish to go," he said, pulling out a card and jotting down a number.

"I thought he was your driver."

"He is, but I have so much work to do, I won't be going anywhere soon. Do you have a fancy dress?"

"Like the belly-dancing costume?" Her cheeks flushed as she remembered two nights past when he had convinced her to don the outfit and dance for him. He'd been right—he lasted about two seconds before he removed the outfit and made love to her all night long.

"Something suitable to wear to a reception at the archaeology museum. They're having an annual fundraising event tonight, and I should make an appearance."

"Oh. Something social?" She frowned and tapped a pen against her lips as she thought. He felt himself getting hard despite having lost himself in her just a few hours earlier. "Not really. I didn't think I'd be staying in Greece, and I didn't pack anything appropriate."

He pulled out his wallet and tossed a few bills onto the desk. "Go buy yourself something pretty."

Instantly, the tempest was upon him.

"Go buy *yourself* something pretty," she said, shoving the money back at him, her eyes flashing with ire. "I don't need your money."

"I know you don't need it, but there's no reason for you to spend your own money when you're doing something at my request." He shoved the money back toward her.

She flicked it back to him. "There's the matter of my pride. I don't want your money. I have my own. I can buy my own dress."

"Harry," he said, pulling her hand out and slapping

the money down onto her palm. "Just take the damned money and stop being so unreasonable."

She took a deep breath, jerked open his desk drawer, and dug around in it until she extracted a lighter. She held the money up, her angry gaze clashing with his as she lit the money on fire, waiting until it was two-thirds burned before dropping it into a metal wastebasket.

"That was uncalled for," he said, angry and amused at the same time. Only his storm could have that effect on him.

"I will buy a dress today. I will even go to the hairdressers and have them do something with my hair. But I will not take money from you. It's not, after all, as if you are my fiancé." She lifted her chin. "Unless you'd like to propose right now?"

He reached across the desk, tangled his hand in her hair, and pulled her forward to give her a kiss that should make it clear to her that he was not going to allow her to dictate to him. "I prefer the color green, Eglantine. Something short to show off your legs."

"Dream on, Yacky!" she yelled after him as he left the room, smiling to himself.

"Are you sure you want to get that one?"

Harry looked at her reflection and gave Elena a curt nod. "I'm not crazy wild about it, but it'll do. It has the benefit of being gold, not green as his royal highness bachelor number five commanded."

Elena giggled, her head on the side as she eyed Harry. "It's very pretty. But I don't understand why you would get a dress that Iakovos wouldn't like."

Harry turned and looked over her shoulder at the

long expanse of back that the floor-length, bias bead-encrusted gown with halter neckline showed. "I didn't say he wouldn't like it. I just said that he commanded me to get something green. And I hate to have to say this about your brother, Elena, but despite what he may have told you, he's not God's gift to the world."

Elena laughed outright. "I know he's not, but he's a love anyway."

"Yes, he is that. I'll take this one," she told the anorexically thin clerk who hovered in the background. "Do you have a bag that would match it?"

The clerk did, and after a few minutes spent in stunned silence at the price of a gown, low heels, and purse, she managed to drag Elena out of the store.

"I just don't understand how you can't like shopping," the younger woman said, reluctantly following Harry as they strolled down the sidewalk of a street filled with expensive shops. "I love it!"

Harry shrugged. "I've never really liked clothes shopping. Books, now, I can spend hours in a bookstore. But clothes? Eh. You're sure this hairdresser can get me in?"

"I told him that you're my brother's girlfriend."

"Does he know Iakovos?" Harry asked, surprised.

"Not at all."

"Then why would he fit me in?"

"Because Iakovos is Iakovos. Everyone in Athens knows who he is. If his girlfriend wants an appointment, people are going to give you one even if it means rearranging their schedule."

"Number five," Harry muttered under her breath. "Great, now I'm going to have the bad karma that comes along with taking someone's else's appointment. Thanks for your help, Elena. I knew I could count on you to steer me to suitable stores."

"My pleasure." She hesitated a minute, then put a hand on Harry's arm. "You *are* still going to marry Iakovos, aren't you?"

"I hope so. I *am* crazy wild about him."

"I know you are. And he is about you, too. I'm so happy for both of you." Elena gave her a swift hug, then, with a giggle and a wave, dashed off to meet some of her friends.

"I was never that young," she told the doorman who opened the door to the chic salon, bracing herself for a couple of hours of beautification. She just hoped it would be worth it.

Three hours later as she stood looking at herself from every possible angle in the mirror of Iakovos' bathroom, she decided that the salon owner was worth twice the sizable chunk of money she relinquished for his services.

Her hair had lightened a bit from its normal mundane brown to show a little streaking from all the time she spent out in the pool and sun. In the hands of the talented Giorgio, it had gone from sun streaked and unruly as it straggled down her back to a glossy, shining tawny brown, touched with the faintest tones of amber around her face. He'd cut off very little, but layered much of it, giving her an elegant, tousled look that she knew was much more her style than anything too fussy.

Although she didn't normally wear much makeup, she brushed her lashes with inky black mascara, and added a touch of nude lipstick.

"You're as good as you're going to get," she said, hearing voices down the hall. Iakovos must be back home. He'd be in in a minute to take a shower and shave before changing into his evening clothes. Should she wait in his bedroom in case he didn't like her dress?

"I am *so* not afraid of him," she told her reflection, tossing her tawny head and heading out of the room to find him.

He stood with his back to her in the living room, Dmitri in front of him, holding out something to be signed. She lifted her head, and slowed down from the aggressive march to a leisurely stroll, her eyes on the back of his head.

Dmitri saw her first. He was in the middle of saying something and just stopped dead, his eyes wide.

Iakovos didn't notice Dmitri's reaction right away, but when he did, he glanced over his shoulder.

The double take he did was extremely satisfying to her ego.

"Good evening, Dmitri. Are you going to the museum shindig with us?"

"Er . . . no." He cast a glance at Iakovos, who was staring at Harry as if he'd never seen her before. "I didn't think it would be interesting. I see I was wrong."

"I'm sorry to hear that. Do you like my dress, Iakovos?" she asked, sliding him a look that she hoped would steam his shorts.

His Adam's apple bobbed. Without saying a word he shoved the paper he'd been holding at Dmitri, walked over to her, and scooped her up in his arms.

"Oh, don't wrinkle me," she said, her blood catching on fire from the look in his eyes. "I have no idea how I'd go about ironing a dress covered in beads."

He was silent as he kicked the bedroom door shut and set her on her feet next to the bed.

"Turn," he finally said.

"You want to see the back? It's kind of low, but with my hair down, it doesn't make me feel quite so naked," she said, turning so he could see the plunging back.

To her surprise, he unzipped the dress, pulling it off her and laying it carefully across a chair before turning back to her.

"You don't like it?" she asked, suddenly worried. She'd thought he'd forgive her for going against his desire because the dress was, after all, rather pretty, even if she wasn't normally a gold-bead sort of person.

He slid his hands underneath the sides of her underwear, peeling it off her before pushing her back onto the bed.

"Iakovos!" she said, her eyes big as she realized what he was doing. He yanked off his suit coat, unzipped his pants, and freed himself from his underwear before spreading her legs. "You're still dressed! And I've got my shoes on! Oh my god, yes!"

He plunged into her, taking her moan into his mouth, his fingers hard on her hips as he angled her up to meet his thrusts. She twined her legs around his, still clad in his pants, and gave herself up to the pleasure that only he could give her.

Neither of them lasted long, on Harry's part because she was secretly scandalized that he would take her while they were both still partially dressed, and also flattered because the sight of her in the gown had so inflamed his passion. And inflamed he was—his mouth burned hers as he kissed her witless, his hips pounding against her, the long, lovely muscles of his back and butt moving with such grace, she just wanted to yell with the glory of it all.

When he lay heavy on her, his breath steaming a spot on her neck, she whispered in his ear, "We're going to be late."

"To hell with the fund-raiser," he said, groaning as he rolled off her. "We're staying home."

"After I went through the nightmare of shopping? I don't think so." She slid off the bed, pulling his shoes and socks off before tugging his pants all the way off. "Come on, my virile Greek stud muffin. Go take a shower so I can show you off to all the world's-sexiest-bachelor-hungry women of Athens."

He shot her a look, but got to his feet, giving her butt a squeeze as he passed her. "That dress isn't green, Eglantine," he said before going into the bathroom.

"I'm so glad to know you're not color-blind, Yacky," she yelled after him, waiting until he turned on the water to collapse on the bed and spend a few moments reliving the last ten minutes.

After a quick wash in the spare bathroom, she headed to the living room to wait. She didn't like the room, didn't like much about the apartment at all except the view. Since it was the penthouse, the patio and rooftop garden had an astounding view of Athens, especially at night. She loved the city at night, and stood staring out into the velvety blackness, wondering how she was going to address the subject of the apartment with Iakovos.

"Don't you look nice."

She turned slowly to find Theo standing next to a chaise lounge, his hair combed, his face shaved, and his body clad in a tuxedo. She frowned at this. "Evening, Theo. I didn't know you were back in town."

"Got back earlier. Did you do something to your hair? I like it."

"Thank you." She watched him warily, something he obviously noticed because he gave a wry smile and came toward her. She stood her ground, but braced herself in case she needed to deck him again.

"You don't have to look so angry—I haven't had a drink today."

"I'm glad to hear that." She hated feeling so constrained around him, but ever since the night when she broke his nose, she hadn't been comfortable alone with him.

As if reading her thoughts, he touched his nose. "I never did apologize to you for that, did I? Jake sent me off to Brazil right after Elena's party, and I didn't have the chance to tell you how much I regret what happened that night."

"Consider it forgotten," she said politely, although she had absolutely no intention of letting down her guard around him.

"I appreciate that. How about a kiss to show there are no hard feelings?"

Her mouth dropped open at his audacity, and she was about to tell him what he could do with himself when Iakovos strolled out.

"I'm joking, Harry." Theo laughed, giving her one of his charming smiles. He glanced over at his brother. "I think I scared Harry, Jake."

"I doubt that," Iakovos replied, the look in his eyes making her want to fall on him and lick every inch of him. "She doesn't scare easy. It's more likely you were just making an ass of yourself. You ready to go, sweetheart?"

"That depends. Do we have any drool cloths handy?

Because I'm going to need at least half a dozen, if not for me, then for all the other women who see you."

He rolled his eyes, holding his hand out for her. "Theo is coming with us. His mother was very big on this charity, and he likes to continue on in her name."

She slid a glance to Theo, but he really did seem to be sober tonight. She supposed that stranger things could happen than that he could see the error of his ways, so she gave him a smile and reminded herself that everyone deserved a second chance.

Besides, she had more important things to do, like stare in openmouthed wonder at Iakovos. The third time he caught her doing that on the ride to the hotel ballroom where the fund-raiser was being held, he leaned into her and whispered, "It's just me, Eglantine. The same man who was balls-deep in you half an hour ago."

"You look different when you're all dressed up. You look like you really are number five."

"Number five?" Theo asked with a puzzled frown.

Iakovos made a face. "That magazine list."

"A list? Oh, the bachelor list?" Theo grinned. "You still sore that you dropped two spots?"

"You were number three?" Harry asked, staring at the love of her life in horror.

"Last year he was," Theo told her, laughing at the expression on her face. "I keep telling him to hold out for the number one spot, but it looks like that's a moot point now."

"Three," she growled to herself, digging her fingernails into Iakovos' thigh.

He twined his fingers through hers and gave his

brother an annoyed frown. "You just had to mention that, didn't you?"

"Sorry, didn't know it was a sore topic." He tipped his head to the side and looked at them. "So, when are you two going to get married?"

Harry stopped glaring at Iakovos and turned a smile on Theo. "What an excellent question, one I'm sure Yacky is just dying to answer. Aren't you?"

Iakovos turned a smile on her that just about melted her innards. "Of course, sweetheart."

"Well?"

He answered her in Greek, kissing her fingertips. She looked from one man to the other as Theo obviously asked a question. Iakovos answered, gave her another beatific smile, patted her cheek, then leaned back against the seat of the limo and closed his eyes, his thumb rubbing little circles on the back of her hand.

"Ah," Theo said, giving her his half grin. "That should be good."

"I'm not talking to either of you," she said, and stared out the window until they arrived at the hotel, ignoring both Theo's laugh and the fire that Iakovos could start with just one brush of his thumb.

Chapter 14

The blissful routine of their life lasted for another couple of weeks until the day when Iakovos woke up to find that his body was wracked with some horrible virus that had been going around his office.

"This is what you get for going off to work the last two days. I told you that you were coming down with something," Harry told him when he struggled to get out of bed. "Honestly, men! Stay there, and I'll call the doctor."

"I don't need a doctor," he said fretfully, annoyed at her high-handed manner with him. He was a man, dammit. He had important business demands. You didn't rise to the top by lying around whenever some insidious bug invaded your body.

It took him five minutes to get himself untangled from the sheets before he could stand, and the second he did, he felt a hundred times worse.

"The doctor's on his way, and Mrs. Avrabos has made you—what are you doing out of bed?" Harry tsked, set down a mug of some steaming liquid and tried to put him back to bed.

"I have to use the toilet," he said with dignity, even though he didn't. He had an idea about taking a quick shower and escaping to the office before she noticed he was gone, but by the time he managed to get his teeth brushed, he was so exhausted and so miserable that he staggered back to the bedroom.

"Sit down for a minute and drink that flu medicine," Harry said as she stripped the sheets off the bed. "You must be running a fever, because your sheets are damp with sweat."

He groaned and leaned back in the chair, just wishing to die quietly in some dark corner.

"My poor darling." Harry's cool hands were there, helping him into bed, tucking blankets around him, and pouring an obnoxious hot liquid down his throat. He opened his eyes to stare balefully at her. She brushed the hair back off his forehead. "You don't get sick much, do you?"

"No. I don't have time for it. I don't have time for it now. We're working on a buyout. I'm going in to the office." He closed his eyes and hoped death would claim him. "I'll do that in a minute."

"Yes, you do that," she said soothingly.

He woke up an hour later, just long enough for his personal doctor to examine him and declare in a solemn voice that he had the same virus everyone else had. Iakovos muttered rude things about that, and promptly fell asleep again.

When he woke up a few hours after that, it was to find

Harry sitting on the edge of the bed next to him, speaking on the phone to Dmitri.

"No, he can't, Dmitri. He's running a fever, and he's been getting sicker and sicker, and last night I had to practically pour him into bed. The doctor says he has to rest. Just tell the board or the investors or whoever it is who is nagging you to make him come in today that he's ill, and he'll be there when he can be there."

"Eglantine, I forbid you to speak to Dmitri about me like I'm not here," he said crossly, feeling like he'd been run over by a two-ton semitruck, but irritated nonetheless that she would try to run his life like that. "If I say I have to go to work, I will go to work. Now move so I can get up and take a shower."

She pursed her lips and put one hand on his chest, holding the phone over his head with the other. "Tell you what—you get the phone, and you can go to work today."

He gave her his very best scornful look and sat up to take the phone from her. Or rather, he tried to. Somehow during the night she must have gained superhuman strength, enough to keep him pinned to the bed.

"Unhand me," he demanded, glaring at her hand on his chest.

"If you, with all those muscles and all that body mass, can't remove my hand from your chest, then you're too sick to leave the bed," she told him in that maddeningly infuriating way she had.

He shifted his glare from her hand to her face. She kissed the tip of his nose. "You go too far, woman."

"I know. It's my fatal flaw. Do you still love me despite it?"

He opened his mouth to tell her that he did, but snapped his teeth shut, smiling at her instead. That never failed to annoy her.

"Gah!" she said, and handed him the phone, storming off to the bathroom.

"How do you feel?" Dmitri asked when she was gone.

"Like hell. Worse. Can you get the meeting pushed back a day or two?"

"It won't be easy, but I think so. I'd better—I'd hate to think what Harry would do to me if she found I made you come to the office that sick."

Iakovos grunted a nonreply and hung up, wondering if he was going to have to sweeten Harry's mood, and how he could possibly do that when he just wanted to be put out of his misery.

He woke up a short while later to the bliss of a cold cloth on his face.

"Come on, bachelor number five, time for your medicine." Harry slid an arm behind him as he struggled to sit up, and held a glass to his lips.

"What is it?" he asked, frowning at the bubbling liquid.

"Flu medicine. Your doctor sent it around. Drink up. It should help with the fever."

He drank, then collapsed back onto the pillows, every bone in his body aching. "You don't have to do that," he said as she wiped his face and neck with a cold cloth.

She paused, a worried look in her eyes. "Does it feel good?"

"Yes."

"Then don't worry about it. Just rest."

He opened his mouth to tell her he didn't need her to

172 Katie MacAlister

attend to him, that the few times in the past when he'd been ill, he'd preferred to be left alone rather than fussed over, but somehow, this was different. He dozed, woke periodically to find her trying to cool him down, or tempting him with cups of tea and soup, and gradually a sense of comfort settled next to the desire to end his miserable existence. If he had to live and suffer through the horrible illness that gripped him so mercilessly, at least Harry was there to take care of him.

Three days later he emerged from the shower, feeling a little weak, but for the most part pretty damned good. As he dressed he thought with gratitude about the woman who hadn't left his side for one minute.

"If you ever want to give up writing, you could be a nurse," he told her as he entered his bedroom, looping his tie around his neck.

She raised her head from the bed, shot him a scathing look that was suddenly arrested as her eyes grew large. He only just got out of the way as she bolted for the bathroom, the sound of violent retching bringing back all too painful recent memories.

"I did point out to you that if you insisted on taking care of me, there was the likelihood that you'd end up with the same thing," he reminded her as he entered the bathroom. She was on the floor, her glorious long legs on either side of the toilet, her body hunched over the bowl. She pushed back the tangled mass of her hair, wiped her mouth, and he knew that if she had been given the means to do so, at that moment she probably would have killed him.

He loved her so much, it made his heart sing. "Eglantine."

"Yacky," she said tiredly, her cheek resting on the seat of the toilet, her expression one of utter misery.

"Marry me?"

Slowly her head rose, her eyes dark with fury. "*What* did you say?"

"I asked if you would marry me."

Her jaw worked for a few seconds. "Now you ask me?"

"Yes."

"Right now? You do see that I'm hugging the toilet, don't you? You do know that I've been vomiting for the last three hours, right?"

"I can see very well. Will you marry me?"

Her jaw worked again. "I hate you."

"I'll take that as a yes, shall I?" he said, wanting to sing and dance and quite possibly do a backflip or two.

She rested her cheek on the seat again, her eyes closing. "Go away. I never want to see you again. You are an evil, evil man."

"But you'll marry me."

"Not if you were the last world's most eligible bachelor," she said with a soft moan of revulsion.

"I'll get Dmitri working on the wedding, then. The nurse is here, by the way. I'm sorry I can't take care of you the way you did me, but I'm told she's very good."

Harry told him, in exquisite detail, what he could do with himself. He left the apartment whistling a cheerful tune.

Six weeks to the day after Iakovos finally got around to asking her to marry him, Harry sat in a doctor's office in Seattle, completely speechless.

"You're sure?" she finally got out, her whole body in shock as she searched the face of the woman who stood in front of her.

"Quite sure. I take it this isn't something you were expecting?"

She looked from the woman to the computer screen that showed the test results. A surge of pure emotion shot through her. "You're really, really sure? There hasn't been some sort of a mix-up in tests?"

"No, no mix-up." Her doctor gave her a little pat on the shoulder. "Harry, I've known you for what, fifteen years? I know you said you were getting married, but is there a reason you *don't* want to be pregnant right now?"

"No. Other than . . . well . . . I just wasn't really thinking along those lines yet. Iakovos and I haven't talked about kids. And, to be honest, I'm almost thirty-four, Bess. That's kind of pushing it for babies, isn't it?"

"Pah. You're in good health, the babies are fine, and there's no reason you shouldn't be able to present your handsome Greek with two beautiful children."

Twins. She was going to have twins. She looked at the screen again, at the results of the blood test and scan that had been done when she'd come to Bess complaining of feeling punky. She left the doctor's office walking a good foot off the ground, and barely made it back to her apartment before she sat down on one of the packing boxes holding her possessions and dialed his number.

His voice was clipped as he said his name.

"Hi. Am I bothering you?"

"We're about to go into a meeting. Can I call you later?"

"Sure. It's just . . . Iakovos . . . there's something . . . important I have to tell you."

"Are you coming to New York earlier than you thought?" he asked, his voice sending little warm skitters down her back. They'd been apart for ten days while she wrapped up her life in Seattle and he worked on the pressing business in his New York office. "No. Yes. Oh, I don't know. Listen, call me as soon as you can. But, Iakovos?"

"Yes?"

"Make sure you're alone when you call."

"Phone sex is no substitution for the real thing," he told her sternly before ringing off.

It seemed like an eternity before he called that night, and she had a hard time actually accomplishing anything but wandering around her half-empty apartment, taking a few calls from friends who knew she was moving to Greece; one from her publisher, who called to congratulate her on her upcoming marriage; and a visit from Tim with an invitation to come over for dinner to see the new baby.

Through it all she smiled and chatted, all the while secretly hugging herself with her news, hardly able to contain herself until she could share her excitement with the man whose life was now inexorably bound to hers.

"All right, my wild sea nymph, I am back at the hotel, and alone, as you requested," Iakovos said a few hours later, his voice warm and comforting in her ear. "You may now proceed to torment me with sexual talk, but be warned I will have my revenge when you come to New York. I plan on taking out all my frustrations on your delicious body."

"You're more than welcome to. But before we get to the smutty talk, I have something to tell you."

"Oh?" He sounded politely interested.

She smiled at nothing, knowing she was about to knock his socks off. "I really wish I could tell you this in person, but since I won't be in New York for another ten days, I'm just going to have to do it this way. I'm pregnant."

Silence met her ears. A stunned, disbelieving sort of silence. A silence that Harry suddenly felt went on for far too long.

"Iakovos? Did you hear me?"

He was silent for a few more seconds, and when he spoke, his voice sounded hoarse, as if it were the voice of a stranger. "I heard."

Her stomach dropped to her feet. "You're not happy? I know we haven't talked about kids, but . . . well, somehow, it happened. It must have been when I ran out of birth control pills before we went to Athens. I'm sorry that I couldn't prepare you for the news better, but—"

"You can tell me just one thing," he interrupted with cold calculation. "You can tell me who the father is."

Harry stared at the floor with disbelief. "You didn't just say that. No, you couldn't just say that. You couldn't in a million years say something as crass as that."

"Crass it may be, but I want to know, Harry. Who is the father?"

She took a deep breath. Was she hallucinating? Was this a nightmare? It couldn't be real, could it? "You are the father, you insensitive ass. How dare you think I would screw around on you? More to the point, *why* would you think that? Why wouldn't you think the babies are yours?"

"Babies?"

"Twins, actually. Answer my question, please."

He was silent for a good ten seconds, making Harry wonder if the cell connection had been lost. "I know because I'm unable to have children. I'm sterile, Harry."

"I don't know who told you that," she said, wanting nothing more than to curl up in a ball and cry. "But they were wrong, and I have the scans to prove it."

Iakovos said nothing, but she could sense his fury. "We'll talk tomorrow about this. It's late. I'm tired."

She hung up without saying another word, stared at the phone for a moment, then around at the apartment. It was real. It wasn't a nightmare. He actually asked her who the father was. He wasn't happy.

Sterile?

She shook her head, wanting to cry. Everything had been so wonderful up to now. She loved him, he loved her, they loved each other. . . . Where the hell had it suddenly gone wrong?

She sat in her silent, dark apartment for two hours, her mind going round and round. How could he say that to her?

Her books, her most precious possessions, were all packed up and ready for the shipping company to pick them up and send them to Greece. Her furniture was marked to be given away to friends and local charity shops. Her knickknacks and other everyday things were mostly boxed, some going to storage, more-cherished items also marked to go to Greece.

"I'm going to have twins," she told the boxes. "And

Iakovos doesn't think he's the father. He can be incredibly stupid sometimes."

Her voice echoed hollowly in the room. She closed her eyes for a moment, swamped with the pain of his accusation, then leaped to her feet and pulled her laptop out of the suitcase that she had been slowly filling for her trip to New York City. If she was hurting this much when she knew the truth, how bad must he be feeling?

The next day she called him again. His voice was abrupt when he said hello.

"Do you have a pen? Good. Take this down." She recited an address to him. "They're expecting you sometime today. Please be there before nine p.m."

"Be where?" he asked, the chill seeping off his voice, through the phone, and straight to her heart. "Your lawyer's office?"

"No, a doctor's office. They need your blood for the paternity test."

"Harry—"

"Before nine." She hung up, turning with a grim expression as a medically garbed technician gave her a little smile.

"Ready?" the tech asked.

"Not really. It's going to hurt, isn't it?"

"I'm told it's . . . uncomfortable," the woman admitted, escorting Harry to a room in the medical office, located within a mile of Iakovos' New York office.

"It's going to hurt," Harry said, thinking of him. She just hoped he appreciated what she was about to do for him.

*   *   *

His life really had become a hell, a nightmare that he couldn't seem to escape from. The moment Harry had announced her pregnancy, he felt like someone had kicked him in the belly. She couldn't be pregnant, at least not by him. But that meant she had to be sleeping with someone else, and he couldn't believe that, either. Oh, there was a nasty five minutes when he did just that, called her every foul name he could as he envisioned how she was laughing behind his back for fooling him. But the moment he remembered how her eyes glowed when she looked at him, he knew it wasn't true. She loved him, and when Harry loved, she loved with her whole heart.

He was going to tell her that when she called, her voice so thin and unhappy, and politely requested him to have a blood test. He wanted to tell her that he was wrong for doubting her, to explain the situation, but she had rung off, and he spent a hellish half hour trying to decide if he should do what she wanted, or if he should just fly out to Seattle and tell her in person that he was wrong.

In the end, the demands of his business made the decision for him. He wanted to take time off to spend on a honeymoon with Harry, and that meant he had to get through as much business as he could beforehand. He did the paternity test just to make her happy, even though he knew it wasn't really needed.

She didn't answer her phone that night, nor the following morning, either. He was trying to get through the most pressing business so he could fly to Seattle and see her when the storm broke in his office. He was in the boardroom, meeting with a West Coast rival developer whose business was going under and whose concerns Iakovos was trying to buy, when a commotion from outside the room made itself known.

He signaled to Dmitri to see what the problem was, but before his cousin could rise, the door to the boardroom was thrown open, and his own personal tempest stood in glorious fury, her hair as wild and untamed as her spirit.

"Hello," she said, tearing her gaze from his to smile at the four other men in the room. "I'm so sorry to interrupt, but I really have to speak with Iakovos for about five minutes. Who needs a potty break?"

Iakovos rose as she marched over to him, taking him by the arm, still talking as she urged him toward the door. "I'll have him back with you before you know it. Oh, hi, Dmitri. Long time no see."

The door closed behind them. He stared down at her, annoyance at the interruption fading to concern about the faint purple shadows beneath her eyes, but most of all, it was joy that filled him as he beheld her fury.

"Here," she said, shoving a piece of paper at him. "Read the bottom part. I highlighted the important bits."

He glanced at the heading. "I don't need to see the results of the test," he told her.

"Yes, you do!" She looked like she was going to explode, her eyes blazing with righteous indignation, her hair wild around her head, her body language aggressive. Why wasn't she in his arms kissing him? Why wasn't she murmuring words of love to him, words of happiness at seeing him? Didn't she feel the same sense of bliss that he felt when she was near?

A horrible thought occurred to him. What if he had killed her love for him? What if his temporary idiocy had ruined everything? How was he going to live without his beautiful wild goddess?

He took her by the arm and hustled her down the hallway to his office.

"Iakovos, please, read it. I know you think the worst of me—" she started to say once he closed the door.

"I don't need to read it. I know you're telling the truth. I know I'm the father. I don't know how I am, but I accept that if you're pregnant, I'm the father."

She stared at him with surprise all over her face, her shoulders slumping as she tossed her bag onto his desk. He paced over to the window, then suddenly exhausted, sat down in his chair. He was going to have to explain. He didn't want to, but after causing her pain, he was going to have to. He just needed to say the words quickly. He opened his mouth to say them, but what came out wasn't at all what he expected. "Do you still love me?"

"Do I still . . . You're serious, aren't you?"

He nodded, unwilling to speak. He needed to know he hadn't screwed things up past fixing. He needed her.

She looked like she was going to say something very cutting, but then she slowly walked over to him and put her hands on his shoulders as she sat on his lap facing him, her heels tucked alongside his legs. "Love doesn't work that way, Yacky. I can't turn my love for you on and off whenever I like. So, yes, I still love you. You drive me insane sometimes, but I love you despite that."

He relaxed into his chair, his hands sliding up her waist to her hips, and higher to where her breasts were contained in a sea green mohair sweater. The color of the sea for his storm. "You drive me insane, too, sweetheart."

"Yes, but you love that about me." She kissed him, a sweet, slow kiss that she didn't want to end, but there were people waiting for him. "Why do you believe you're sterile?"

His face adopted a shuttered expression for a moment, but she wasn't going to back away. This was important. "When I was seventeen, I was in a car accident. I lost . . . a piece of metal pierced my groin, and destroyed a testicle. It was too damaged to repair. The doctor told my father that although I could have children via artificial insemination, it was highly unlikely that I could impregnate a woman by natural methods."

"The doctor was wrong," she told him, taking his face into her hands and kissing him again. "You may have just one, but it sure did the job. Only . . ." She frowned, concentrating. "You have two testicles, Iakovos. I know; I've seen them. They're right where they should be."

"One is a prosthetic."

"Really? They have prosthetic balls? Who'd have thought?" She was amazed by that fact, unable to keep from glancing down at his lap. "Er . . . which is the pretender?"

"The right," he said with a twist to his lips. She kissed the twist.

"So . . . if you thought you couldn't have children, why did you ask me if I was on birth control? I mean, that explains why you weren't overly panicked when I ran out, but earlier, when we first went to bed, you asked."

"I asked because I always ask. The first time I slept

with a woman after the accident, I didn't ask, and she thought it was strange. After that, I made sure to inquire."

She stroked a hand down his cheek. "You could have told me, you know."

"I was going to, as soon as we got back home." He gave a little shrug. "You never mentioned children, so I didn't think they were high on your priority list at the moment."

"They weren't, but you are." She smiled at him, wishing he knew just how much she loved him.

"Harry . . ." He hesitated, looking incredibly uncomfortable.

"Oh, no, you're not going to make me feel guilty and let you off the hook. You have to apologize. You put me through a hellish two days, you know."

He took a deep breath, his big chest rising, almost enough to distract her. "I'm sorry. I knew as soon as I hung up that you would never betray me. I know you love me, and yes, to answer your question, I'm very happy with the news, although not at all surprised that you're giving me twins. I should have expected you wouldn't follow convention even with that."

"Twins are quite conventional," she protested, and let him kiss the breath out of her. By the time he was beginning to make noises about making love to her on the couch, she knew that everything was good again.

"Go on and do businessy things," she said, shooing him from the desk, smiling when she saw that the picture on it was one he'd taken of her and Elena the day after the birthday party. "You have two children to support now."

He grinned and started to leave, pausing when she called his name. A beautiful teal blue glass mug was on his desk, empty but for half an inch of coffee. She ran her fingers idly around the rim. "You could do one thing for me."

"I intend to do a great many things for you, many of which will require you to be naked." He thought a moment. "No, I lie—all of them will require you to be naked."

"Now would be the absolutely most perfect time ever to tell me you loved me."

"Yes, it would, wouldn't it?" he said with a grin, and left the room.

The sound of glass splintering against the wall was loud, but not so loud as to drown out the sound of his whistling as he returned to the boardroom.

Four days later, he was in his office when his New York secretary, a middle-aged woman named Nanna, entered his office with a stack of mail, most of which she handed to Dmitri. Her lips pursed as she handed Iakovos a large square envelope. "I assume this is meant for you."

He looked at the envelope. It was addressed to Yackynos Papamaumau. "Yes," he said without the slightest quiver of his lips. "It is from my fiancée."

"Hrmph." Nanna snorted her opinion of women who didn't take a man's heritage seriously, and left the office, Dmitri on her heels. Iakovos opened the envelope to find a handmade card inside.

On the front, someone had drawn a stick figure of a man with a sad face, standing in front of a plaque with a crossed-out number three, below which the numeral five had been written. Across the top were the words "Sorry to hear you only have one testicle." He opened the card to find another stick figure, this time of a woman with a huge stomach. Beneath it Harry had written, "On the other hand, if you had two, I'd probably be having quadruplets."

Chapter 15

She had to return to Seattle, of course. She didn't want to leave New York, and it was true that Iakovos offered to get someone to pack up the remainder of her belongings so she could stay there with him, but she told herself she wasn't so clingy that she couldn't be away from him for a few days now and again.

"How are you feeling?" he asked when she'd been back in Seattle for two days.

"Horrible. I'm moping. I barf all day long, and picture myself as big as a house, and you standing around in a tuxedo at cocktail parties with all sorts of skinny, beautiful women slinking their way around you. I hate them. I don't even know them, and I hate them. How are you doing? Are you doing anything interesting?"

"I'm fine, and about to meet with a woman, as a matter of fact."

"I bet she's svelte and beautiful, and wants your number five perfect body." Honestly, could she be any more miserable? Just the thought of him meeting with women made her furious. Oh, she trusted Iakovos, but if she wasn't there to guard him, all sorts of women would annoy him with their unwanted attentions.

"She's beautiful, yes. She's not particularly svelte, though."

Well, that, at least, was something. "Is this for a meeting?" she asked him, trying very hard not to pout, wishing a magic genie would just pick her up and plop her down in New York City.

"Lunch," he answered.

She looked up as someone knocked on her door. It was probably Tim coming to invite her over to see more baby pictures. She didn't want to see more baby pictures, cute as he was. She wanted Iakovos. "Someone's at my door. Have a nice lunch. I love you. This would be a good time for you to tell me how much you love me, too, not that I expect you will because that would improve my day too much, and evidently I'm not allowed to be happy anymore."

"I have to go, sweetheart. Enjoy your moping."

She swore as he hung up, stomping over to the front door, intending to take out her horrible mood on whoever it was who had the nerve to interrupt her misery.

Iakovos leaned against the doorframe, a smile on his face. "Hello, Eglantine. Would you like to have lunch?"

She shrieked and threw herself on him, kissing every part of his face that she could reach.

"Why didn't you tell me you were coming out here?" she asked some time later, when she was sitting on his lap, unable to keep from touching him.

"I didn't know if I was going to be able to make it until the last minute. And then I figured I'd just tell you when I saw you. I missed you, my round little tempest."

"I am not round!" she protested, her hands on one of his where it rested on her belly.

His eyebrows rose.

"All right, just a little round, but Bess says that's normal at this point if you're carrying twins. Did you get the pictures of the scans that I sent you?"

"Yes. They don't look like babies. Are you sure you're not having meerkats or frogs?"

She straightened up and gave him a quelling look. "I will thank you not to refer to our progeny in that manner. They will be perfectly baby-like babies later on. How long are you staying?"

"Two days if we're lucky. Can you be ready to go by then?"

She thought of all the things still left to do, all the packing, all the managing of business affairs, all the leave-taking of friends, and licked his upper lip. "Piece of cake."

Harry came to a sad conclusion the following day. "You don't fit in my life, Yacky. I'm sorry, but it's the truth."

Iakovos looked up from where he was sprawled naked on her bed, his laptop on his bare thighs as he tapped industriously away on the keyboard. "This is about the incident last night, isn't it, Eglantine? I apologized, if you recall, and I will do so again if it will make you feel better."

"I have forgiven you for the fact that you pushed me out of my own bed last night," she said, giving up trying to pack her entire wardrobe tidily. She'd long since gotten past the point where she gave a damn if all her clothes came out of the boxes wrinkled and twisted into blobs. She dumped the armload of clothes unceremoniously into the box and turned to face him. "I'm willing to admit that my bed, while perfectly sized for a normal person, is not meant for a normal person who is possessed of a six-and-a-half-foot-tall former number three most-lusted-after man in the world. I also know you were sound asleep and you aren't aware that when you sleep, you spread."

"I'm aware of it," he said, his eyes once again on the laptop screen. "That's why I have big beds. And I didn't push you out. You fell out."

"I fell because I, as a nurturing woman who loves the aforementioned six-and-a-half-foot-tall former number three most ogled man in the world, accommodate you at night."

His grin warmed her. "You certainly do."

"That is not what I meant, and you know it. I'm simply trying to absolve you of guilt for spreading out over the entire surface of my bed so that I ended falling off the edge. No, my darling number five, what I meant about you not fitting in has nothing to do with my bed. I meant that you don't fit in here. Into my life here."

He looked up again, and her heart squeezed at the flash of uncertainty in his beautiful dark eyes. "What are you trying to say, Harry? You don't want to come home with me?"

She shoved the box aside, picked up his laptop and set it on the nightstand, swinging a leg over his as she sat on his thighs facing him. She took his face in her hands. "The day will never dawn in which I don't want to spend every single moment with you."

He relaxed against the pillows, his hands sliding under the gauzy skirt that was one of the few things she found would still fit her. "In what way, then, do I not fit in your life?"

"You're too handsome. No, don't give me that look; I know you can't do anything about your appearance any more than I can, but, Iakovos, there is a big difference between you looking like a fashion model when you're at gala events in Athens with ambassadors and movie stars, and even-richer-than-you oil billionaires, and you wandering down the aisle of the local grocery store buying toilet paper. I cannot in a million years conceive of you popping down to the local store to pick up toilet paper, my darling. I just can't."

"Do we need toilet paper?" he asked, looking confused.

She kissed his upper lip dip. "No."

"Then why are you upset about this?"

She was silent for a moment, trying to figure out how to explain her tangled emotions without hurting him. "I love you, Iakovos. I'm going to marry you. I want to have your babies and spend every day of the rest of my life with you. But your life isn't my life, and although I'm happy to live yours, it's just kind of a rude shock to see how different our lives really are."

"Is it because of my money?" he asked after a few seconds.

"No. Yes. Not really. It's just more of a lifestyle thing. You own your own friggin' island, for god's sake."

"You like my island," he pointed out.

"I love your island. I love you! It's just . . . oh, never mind. It doesn't really matter, because I'm going to live with you."

He looked thoughtful. "Are you saying you want me

to live here with you, in your apartment? And do things that you do, like buying toilet paper?"

She brushed a strand of hair back off his brow. "Would you live here if I said yes?"

He looked around her bedroom, which at that moment resembled a war zone. "Would you let me get a bigger bed?"

"Yes," she said gravely. "You could have a bigger bed."

"Then I would live here with you."

She leaned down to kiss him. "You are so adorable when you think you can fool me. No, don't tell me you meant it. I know if I suddenly lost all my marbles and demanded that we not live in your fabulous house and beautiful, if a little sterile, penthouse apartment, that you would agree to it, because underneath all that handsomeness that makes women want to rip off their underwear and fling themselves on you, there's a truly wonderful man, but you don't have to worry; I'm not going to do any such thing."

"You forgot the villa in the Bahamas," he said, his hands moving up to cup her breasts.

"I don't know why I brought it up. Just, I guess, to point out that unlike you, I'm not used to a life of glamour, and . . . you have a villa in the Bahamas?"

His teeth flashed white against his lovely olive brown skin. "Two, actually, although I was thinking of selling one."

She stared at him for a second, then slowly climbed off, putting the laptop back on his lap. "Do your work," she said in a voice that even to her ears sounded strangled. "I have to go say good-bye to the morning group."

"Morning group?" he asked, his attention once again on his laptop.

"It's a group of ladies I exercise with three times a week." She glanced at the clock balanced rather precariously on a stack of books that hadn't yet been packed. "In fact, I need to hustle if I want to get there."

He turned off the laptop and stood up, stretching. Harry stopped in the middle of changing her clothes, unable to take her eyes off him. Really, you'd think after living with him for more than three months, she'd be used to seeing him naked, but there she was, standing there with her mind squirreling around, and all she could think of was pouncing on him.

"I'll come with you," he said, and went into her little bathroom.

"You will?"

"Yes. You're absolutely right in that I haven't made much of an effort to fit into your life, while you've done everything to fit into mine. I would be honored to meet your friends."

She stared into space, trying to imagine the effect he was going to have on the ladies' gym where the group met.

He popped his head around the door. "Unless you don't want me to go with you."

She looked at his drop-dead-gorgeous face. He would have the same sort of an impact as if someone had set off an atomic bomb in their midst. All would be chaos and havoc and utter confusion.

There was no way on this green earth that she was going to miss it.

"I'd be delighted to have you go with me. I think the

ladies would ... *enjoy* ... meeting you." Honestly, she
deserved an Oscar for being able to deliver that last sentence without bursting into hysterical laughter.

"Good," he said with a nod. "I'll just take a quick
shower. I'd invite you to take it with me, but your bed
isn't the only thing not big enough for us both."

Her lips quivered as he returned to the bathroom, his
voice raised as he sang loudly over the sound of the water.

Oh, this was promising to be one of the most entertaining mornings of her entire life.

Half an hour later, all hell broke loose at the women's
gym. Men weren't forbidden to enter the august confines of the gym, but Harry knew that never in the memory of the ladies who utilized the facilities had a man
been entertained who wasn't of the delivery persuasion.

As Iakovos strolled in next to her, she adopted an
expression of mild surprise when all the women in the
place froze like so many deer caught in an abnormal
number of headlights.

The woman nearest her, a plump brunette, literally
fell off her elliptical at the sight of him standing there,
one hand on Harry's back as he looked around with interest, clad in black jeans and a white shirt that Harry
had made sure was open to show a bit more of his manly
chest than was normal.

"Harry!" the woman said, rubbing at the shin she had
whacked when she fell off the machine, her eyes never
leaving Iakovos as she spoke. "Nice to see you again.
We've missed you. You look great. Who is your ... uh ...
friend?"

"Harry!" A woman emerged from the bathroom, a

bottle of water in her hand, a towel around her neck. "Come to say good-bye to us at . . . holy Mary, mother of god!"

"Hello, ladies," Harry said, enjoying herself hugely as eight women descended upon them. "How's everyone doing?"

"Fine, just fine. Who . . . er . . ." The sore-shinned woman gave Iakovos a sharky smile. "Aren't you going to introduce us?"

"Introduce you?" Harry looked confused. "To who? Oh, this man?" She gestured toward Iakovos. "I have no idea who he is. We just happened to come in at the same time."

The bottle of water being held by Carrie, one of Harry's oldest friends, dropped to the floor.

Iakovos slid Harry a look before turning to the group of ladies surrounding them. He gave them all a smile that Harry knew could cause palpitations a hundred paces away, and she wasn't at all disappointed with their gasps in reaction to it.

"I am delighted to meet all of you," he told them. "I am Iakovos Papaioannou, Harry's fiancé."

"Fiancé!" One of the ladies gasped again. "Good lord, he's going to *marry* you, Harry?"

"I had to beg her to accept me," he told the ladies, and she honestly thought that Sue Ann, a sixty-something grandmother, might swoon right there and then.

It took only two minutes before Harry found herself pushed to the outside of the crowd as the ladies crushed in around Iakovos, asking him a hundred and one questions about Greece, his work, his personal likes and dislikes, previous girlfriends, and pretty much anything they could think of to keep him talking.

Harry was content to lean against the door, watching the love of her life handily deal with eight googly-eyed women. Most men might have run screaming from the room, but not her Yacky. He was simmering sensuality personified, and she could see why Theo had once told her that Iakovos had yet to meet a woman he couldn't charm.

"Why, if it isn't Harry," came a cool voice from behind her. "We haven't seen you in weeks."

Harry turned, her smile growing when she realized that her day really was going to be the best ever. "Hello, Tess."

Tess Hayerson, it was whispered around the gym, was a woman who chewed men up and spat them out, usually after marrying them. Rumor had it that her third ex-husband had agreed to a divorce settlement that paid her in enhancement surgery, rather than money. In her early thirties, with long auburn hair, and an eye for the male of the species, she was the sexpot of their little group.

"Been putting on a bit of weight, sweetie?" Tess asked, giving her a scathing once-over. "I think a little extra time at the gym and a little less sitting around eating bonbons is in order, don't you?"

"I can honestly say that I've never had a bonbon in my life," Harry said. "Nice to see you, too."

Tess opened her mouth to make a response, but at that moment she caught sight of Iakovos and his swarm of ladies. "*What* do we have here?" Tess asked, her voice a purr. "My god, he's gorgeous. Just look at those legs! And that chest."

"He's something, isn't he?" Harry asked, fighting to keep her lips from betraying her. She leaned closer and said softly, "Rumor has it that he's packing, too."

"A man that big? I wouldn't doubt it at all. I bet he's a handful in bed. Or should I say, two handfuls."

"Two, definitely," Harry said, pretending her nose itched so she could cover her mouth.

"He looks familiar. What is he doing here?" Tess asked, her gaze all but eating Iakovos up. "Is he a vendor or something? No matter, I don't care if he's here to fix the toilets, it's clearly time to separate the girls from the women!"

She oiled her way forward, all sinuous hips and outthrust breasts. Iakovos had evidently reached the saturation point of female adulation, for he managed to extricate himself from the gaggle of ladies and headed straight for Harry. Tess stopped in front of him, cooing, "Hello there."

"Hello," he said politely, not pausing until he reached Harry.

"I love you," she told him before she leaped on him, wrapping her legs around his hips. He chuckled as he hoisted her up, kissing her with the passion that never failed to flare between them.

She heard more gasps behind him, followed by a smattering of applause.

"Are you ready to go?" he asked as she lowered her legs to the ground.

"In just one sec." She turned back to the ladies, her hand on his arm. "Tess, I don't think you got to meet my fiancé, Iakovos. If he looks familiar, it's probably because you've seen him in magazines. I'll miss you all, but you know you're welcome to visit if any of you ever come to Greece." She hugged each one of her friends, Tess included, accepting their best wishes and promises to stay in touch.

As they left the building and headed for Harry's car, Iakovos slid her a glance and asked in a misleadingly bland tone, "Was it everything you hoped it would be?"

"Oh, that and so much more. I particularly liked it when Ruthie had to sit down with her head between her knees because you kissed her hand."

He stopped her as she was about to get into the car. "Are you sure you're not going to miss this?" he asked, nodding toward the gym. Harry couldn't help but notice that the entrance was a solid mass of women plastered against the glass watching them.

"I'll miss it, but it's not a vital part of my life. You are."

"As you are to me, sweetheart."

"You know," she told him as he slid behind the wheel, "this is exactly the sort of moment when a person might declare his love to the woman who is giving up her entire way of life just so she can be with him. Don't you think this is that sort of a moment?"

"I do," he agreed, pulling out of the parking lot. "The next time such a moment comes up, I count on you to remind me."

Chapter 16

Iakovos was anxious to get back to New York so he could wrap up his pressing business there. He wanted to be back in Greece with Harry—no, not wanted, he *needed* to bring her home so he could finally relax.

He didn't understand just why he felt uneasy about her being in the States; he knew only that he wanted her where she belonged. He wasn't going to be happy until he had her home.

There was one last task she had to perform before they could leave, however, and he bit back his impatience, determined to give her the time she needed to wrap up her business and social affairs.

"You sure about this?"

Iakovos' gaze settled on the man who was speaking quietly with Harry in the hallway. Even though he was seated in a minute living room of the apartment next to Harry's, he could hear every word the neighbor spoke to her. "Greece is an awful long way away."

"It is a long way, but I'm more than sure it's the right thing, Tim. Iakovos makes me deliriously happy, happier than is right for any one person to be. Besides, you can visit us, and I'm sure we'll be back in the U.S. frequently. Iakovos has business concerns everywhere, and he says he visits New York a couple of times a year."

"That's still a long way away," the man protested. Iakovos wanted to grab him by the collar and shake him.

"Then you'll just have to get that European tour for the kids set up that you keep talking about." Harry entered the room, taking a seat next to him, her hand going to his leg. He liked her little shows of possession. Normally such things in his lovers irritated him, but Harry always seemed to turn his feelings upside down.

Tim rolled his eyes as a woman entered the room.

"Baby's down at last," she said, giving him a smile. Iakovos approved of Jill, although he thought her husband was out of line in trying to convince Harry to stay in Seattle. "What are we talking about?"

"A European tour for the kids," Harry said, her hand stroking his thigh. She did it without being aware of the effect she had on him, he knew. Despite her propensity for flinging herself on him in public, she wasn't the type of woman to tease him physically when others were around. That didn't change the fact that if she stroked his leg two inches to the left, she'd be brushing his growing erection, and then he'd be forced to pick her up, make their excuses, and take her back to her almost empty apartment to show her that there were limits to what he could endure.

Jill snorted. "With little miss prima donna Cynthia? I think Tim would prefer keeping them in a country where she's not likely to cause so much trouble."

"Cynthia? What happened to *Cyndi*?" Harry asked.

"Oh, she's determined to remake herself. She's Cynthia now . . . and she's tried to break the contract and grab a bigger percentage," Jill answered.

That didn't surprise Iakovos in the least. She'd always struck him as being wholly concerned with her own well-being regardless of who was inconvenienced.

"Ugh. Well, you guys know you're welcome to visit us, with or without them."

Harry glanced at him. "Certainly," he agreed, his fingers tangled in her hair. "We would enjoy having you as our guests."

"Maybe when John is a little older," Jill said, and to his relief, Harry indicated it was time to leave.

He watched her as Tim gave her hands a squeeze and told her to be happy. Her gaze met his for a moment, and he was reassured to see the love in them.

"I will be. I am," she told Tim.

"Let us know about the wedding," Jill said from behind her husband.

"Will do, but don't hold your breath."

"Despite asking me to marry her, Harry seems to have trouble actually picking a date to do so," he told them, his arm around her.

"I like that! You asked me after I asked you, so that's the one that counts." She glared at him until he was forced to kiss her. "And I can't help it if I've never been a big wedding sort of person. Besides, we have plenty of time."

He would prefer to be married sooner than later, but he was determined not to force her into a date. He knew how touchy she was about being perceived as being interested only in his wealth, and rather than get into an argument about it, he left the decision of a date to her. He just hoped she'd get over her reluctance soon.

Business demands took him back to New York, this time with Harry at his side. They settled into a relatively calm existence while he dealt with a couple of complicated situations regarding a land dispute in New Zealand, but life, he decided one evening when he lay with Harry snoring softly in his arms, was strangely free of storms. He stroked his hands over the little bump that was her belly, some primitive need inside him to reproduce well pleased with the knowledge that it was his children who grew there. He'd long since come to terms with the fact that he would never be able to have children. A man, he had once thought, didn't need children. He had been perfectly happy without the possibility of them, or so he'd told himself for all those years.

But now . . . He gently rubbed her belly, picturing a life he hadn't thought possible. Trust his wild child of the sea to turn everything in his life upside down. He went to sleep with her held tight, happier than he had ever remembered being.

Harry was seriously unhappy. She glared at the message on her cell phone.

Delayed getting out of Ottawa. Theo arriving early. If not back in time, go to dinner with him.

Can't believe you're telling me to go to dinner w. another man, she texted back. *What's next? Breakfast w. Chippendales dancer? Lunch w. male model?*

Smart-ass, was his answer, but the follow-up text made her smile. *Miss you.*

She climbed into the car waiting for her. "Home, Mikos."

"Something wrong, Harry?"

"Yes. Your boss is driving me nuts."

"So, business as usual, then?" Mikos smiled at her. She liked him—he had a breezy manner and a wicked sense of humor that appealed to her. He was also a womanizer, but she turned a blind eye to the fact that he was always juggling at least three different women at any one time. He seemed to have that Greek charm that had so many women panting.

Herself included, she thought, rubbing her expanding belly at the thought of seeing Iakovos after a five-day absence. She went over the many and varied things she planned to do to him when she got him alone. Originally she'd wanted to meet him at the airport, but that plan was now revised to simply waiting until she was back from the publishing industry dinner at which she'd been asked to speak.

And Iakovos wasn't going to be there to be shown off, dammit. She debated making an excuse and just staying home, but that wasn't fair to the people who'd invited her to participate. "Poor souls, they'll just have to survive the evening with a non-listworthy handsome Greek."

"You talking about me, Harry? Because if you are, I'm going to have to break your heart. No, no, don't beg me to go with you to your party tonight—it won't do any good. Mr. Papaioannou is a good employer, and much as I would like to do as you ask, I couldn't betray his confidence."

"Darn," she said, making a face at him as he laughed

at her in the rearview mirror. "And here I was ready to throw Iakovos over just so I could sit next to you when you drive him around places."

"Life is hard, but we do the best we can," he said with a grin.

"Uh-huh."

"Theo going with you tonight, then?"

"Sounds like it." Harry mused sourly on that, told herself to stop acting so immature, and instead made some plans for Iakovos when he did, eventually, arrive home.

Iakovos didn't have an apartment in New York, since he wasn't normally in the U.S. long enough to justify one, he had told her when he showed her around the hotel suite where he stayed when in town. The fact that the suite was at least five times the size of the apartment she had just left was neither here nor there, she guessed. At least not to a man like Iakovos, who liked room to spread out.

She greeted the concierge, Marcel, who dealt with the rich people living in the suites, exchanging pleasantries for a few minutes before proceeding on to the four-bedroom suite.

"Oh, you are here. Hello, Theo," she said as she dropped her bag and laptop onto the couch in the living room. "I understand Iakovos has called you in to pinch-hit for him tonight—oh, bloody hell, Theo!"

She'd thought he had been watching TV, since a large flat screen was blaring away, but as he slowly rotated his head to look at her, she saw the familiar expression of incomprehension.

"'Lo, Harry," he said, struggling to get to his feet. "Jake isn't here."

"I know. He's on his way home, though." She looked at the young man who was soon to be her brother-in-law. He made an effort to pull himself together, brushing the shoulder-length black hair off his face, rubbing his whiskery chin, and giving her a smile that she knew would probably melt the underwear off a nun.

"I'm so tempted to just leave you like this so your brother can see for himself that you have a serious problem, but I don't suppose that would do much but make him furious." She took his arm and steered him toward the small kitchen portion of the suite. "Come on, let's get some coffee into you. Iakovos is going to be seriously annoyed if you don't take me to that dinner to-night."

"You're not so bad after all," Theo told her as he stumbled alongside her, shaking his head somewhat groggily as he almost tripped on an ottoman. "Not a gold-digging bitch like Patricia says. I'm going to tell her that, too, the next time I see her."

Harry blinked at him in surprise, grabbing him when he veered off course and was about to fall over a bar-stool. "Sit," she ordered, pushing him onto the high-backed stool before pulling out a couple of bags of sealed beans and a coffee grinder.

Theo watched silently as she set up the grinder and poured beans into it. "You can stop looking at me like that," she told him. "I'm from Seattle. We take our coffee very seriously there. I'm having a case of the coffee shipped straight to Iakovos' former palace of sin."

"We're Greek," he told her with yet another sloppy smile. "We know how to do strong coffee."

"Oh, yes, strong enough to strip paint off a wall as

well, but thank you, I prefer to keep my stomach lining. All right, you've dropped your bombshell. Who is Patricia, why were you talking about me to her, and why do I care if she thinks I'm a gold-digging bitch? No, wait—" Harry held up her hand. "I'm having a premonition. She's one of Iakovos' ex-girlfriends, someone who he still sees, and who you probably expect me to get quite jealous over."

"It's like you're psychic," he said, laughing as she poured him the first few inches of coffee without waiting for the rest of the water to work through the coffeemaker. She knew it was bound to be hideously strong. He drank it and smacked his lips. "Just like my mother used to make."

"You're impossible," Harry told him with a shake of her head.

"Yeah, but you love my big brother, so you have to put up with me. Besides, I'm a Papaioannou. Women can't resist us."

"Uh-huh." She hoisted herself up beside him. "Go on, tell me the worst. Is this Patricia monster someone Iakovos still works with?"

"She runs a decorating business, so the answer to that is yes."

"I might have figured," Harry said, sighing dramatically. "There just had to be at least one jealous ex-girlfriend on the scene bent on making my life a misery. You don't get to number five without that. Is she pretty?"

"Gorgeous," he said, trying to wink at her, but failing. She shoved the coffee cup closer to him. "Legs up to her armpits. Tits that make your mouth water. Cute little ass. Great in bed."

"You've slept with her?" she couldn't help but ask.

"First. Then she caught sight of Iakovos, and that was all she wrote. I was forgotten until they broke up."

I'm not going to ask, I'm not going to ask, Harry told herself. It doesn't matter. I know he loves me. I see it in his eyes. I see it in his face. I feel it when he touches me. His past with this woman has absolutely nothing to do with me. Besides, they probably broke up years and years ago.

"When did they break up?"

"I mean, really nice tits . . . Huh?" He weaved in the seat as he thought. "Must have been four . . . no five . . ."

Four or five years. That wasn't so bad, Harry thought, relaxing against the back of the barstool.

"No, it was four months. Right before Elena's party. I remember thinking it was funny that Iakovos hooked up with you so quickly after Patricia. Usually he takes a few months off between women."

"There are times," Harry told him with great dignity as she climbed off the barstool, "when I am convinced fate has determined I should live my life as if it were a soap opera. I won't have it, do you hear me? I won't be jealous! I will not be jealous of this ex-girlfriend!"

"That's good, because you're probably going to see her soon. She's been out of the country working on that hotel reconstruction in Buenos Aires, but now she's back in town. I ran into her today."

Harry took a deep, calming breath but said nothing.

"Want to see a picture of her?" Theo said, pulling his cell phone out of his pocket. It took him a few minutes of poking around, but at last he smiled and held the phone up for her to see.

She looked at the blond woman, petite, thin, dressed in a gauzy evening gown that seemed to float around her and heighten her elfin appearance. But it was the man next to her that held her attention, the tall, broad-shouldered man whose head was dipped down to the blonde's, a smile on his delicious lips.

"Not . . . jealous . . ." she ground out between clenched teeth, and marched off to the bedroom, where she took great pleasure in destroying the pillow that bore Iako-vos' scent.

Theo managed to sober himself up by the time she was ready to leave. She wore a black knee-length cock-tail dress with a crimson satin sash that tied under her breasts, a dress she was barely able to get into. That was just one more thing to annoy her—she'd have to go shopping at some point to buy maternity clothes.

"You have a feather in your hair," Theo said as they met in the living room.

"You want to make something of it?" she snapped, and refused to notice that he looked very nice in his tux-edo. Damn those Papaioannou genes.

"You spoiling for a fight, Harry?" he asked, holding the door open for her.

"No. Yes. I just really wish you wouldn't drink when you go somewhere with us."

"That coffee you gave me sobered me right up," he said, taking her by the elbow.

She watched him from the corner of her eye as Mar-cel called an elevator up for them. She had to admit that a shower and copious amounts of coffee had seemed to do wonders for Theo. His face had lost that slack look, and his eyes looked unglazed, if a little bloodshot.

"Why do you drink so much?" She asked him when they were in the car, heading across town to the banquet.

"Why do you love Iakovos?" he shot back.

She was a little taken aback. "I love him because he's . . . well . . . I just do."

"Exactly. I drink because I do."

"Yes, but—"

"Harry." He gave her knee a little squeeze, then immediately removed his hand. "I don't even have a little buzz now, OK? So stop fussing, and tell me about this dinner we're going to. All Jake said was that it was important to you, and he didn't want you going to it alone."

"It's just a publishing dinner, but it's being held as part of a big multigenre readers' conference where there'll be a lot of women, so I expect you to be on your best behavior. Although I suppose really the dinner we're going to will be pretty boring for you. I'm going to give a short speech, and then my publisher will give a speech, and so on. I just want you to promise that you're not going to hit the bar or go into the main ballroom."

"Come on, Harry. I know there's been some bad blood between us, but I'm here for you now, and I'm not going to let you down. What's in this ballroom you don't want me to see?"

She sighed, her shoulders drooping. Why, oh why couldn't Iakovos have been here? "That's where the erotica readers are having their . . . dinner."

"So?"

"I just don't want you going there, OK? We'll be in an auxiliary meeting room, so don't wander around."

"Whatever you like," he said, giving her another smile

to which she had a hard time not responding. "I won't even look at another woman."

It wasn't his behavior with women that worried her. It was what the ladies in that ballroom would think if they got a look at him.

"So long as you keep your nose clean, no one will notice us," she said, and prayed that was true.

It wasn't, of course. The second she showed up in the room set aside for her publisher's dinner, every female eye was on Theo. By now, she was used to what she mentally termed the Papaioannou Effect, but it still irked her to see her own editor rush over to Theo and start cooing and flirting shamelessly.

"Isn't he gorgeous!" Carmel said an hour later, having managed to tear herself away from Theo only when Harry reminded her that she was married with grandchildren. "And you're marrying his brother?"

"A brother who is even better-looking," she said, nodding.

Carmel looked at her with awe. "I can't even begin to imagine. How do you keep your hands off him?"

"I don't," she said, patting her stomach. "Luckily, he doesn't seem to mind."

"Well, better you than me. I don't know if I could cope with having a man who every woman lusted after. Oh, dear god, look at those interns! They're practically shoving Theo's hands down their dresses! I'd better go intervene before one of them starts molesting him."

Things settled down once the younger female members of the publishing staff were dissuaded from fawning over Theo, and Harry was able to give her speech with a modicum of calm. But it was a short-lived calm,

one completely shattered when she returned to the
room from a visit to the bathroom.

Not many guests remained as the dinner concluded,
just a few of the older publishing house employees chatting in groups. None of the younger women remained,
however. Nor was Theo in sight.

Harry asked the few people remaining in the room,
but they hadn't seen Theo leave. She went first to the
hotel's bar, but he wasn't there. It wasn't until she passed
the ballroom and heard screams and whoops of joy that
a truly horrible thought occurred to her.

Chapter 17

Iakovos sighed with relief at the sight of the bags, towels, and various items of clothing strewn around the living room of his suite. Not a terribly fastidious man himself, he was amused that Harry couldn't be in a room for more than five minutes without making it look as if a whirlwind had hit it.

A glance at his watch told him that she was probably off having dinner with Theo, but soon she would be back, and then he would be able to give himself up to all the pleasures to be found in reacquainting himself with his delicious, delectable, wonderfully wild goddess.

He pulled out his phone and dialed her number as he peeled off his suit coat and tie, heading for the shower. "Hello, sweetheart. Enjoying your dinner?" he asked when she answered.

"I did, until I lost Theo."

"Lost him? How did you lose him?"

"I don't know. He's just gone, and no, he's not in the bar. I checked. I was just going to see if he'd gone outside for a breath of air."

"Did you call him?"

"Yes. He's not answering his phone."

"Well, he's probably—" Iakovos stepped into the room that served as his bedroom and stopped, unable to believe what he was seeing.

"There's one place he could be, but I'm praying he isn't there, because if he is . . . lord. He's not outside. I'll have to check the ballroom after all."

"Eglantine," he said, breathing heavily through his nose.

"Not now, Yacky, I have to start praying really fast that Theo isn't where I think he is."

"Why," he said, enunciating each word very carefully, "is our bedroom covered in feathers?"

Silence filled his ears.

"Oh, I don't know," she said, a dangerous note in her voice. "Why didn't you tell me that you broke up with your last girlfriend mere days before we met?"

For a few seconds he couldn't see what the one had to do with the other. Then he realized that she was jealous. He almost laughed out loud at the thought. "I don't know. It didn't seem to be important."

"Well, it is."

"Is it?"

"Yes. Very."

"Why?"

She sputtered for a few seconds. "I don't know why! It just is!" she yelled into his ear.

He chuckled to himself. Could this woman be any more wonderful? "Eglantine, have I mentioned that my previous lover and I broke up a week before you arrived on my island?"

"No, Yacky, you didn't. Have I mentioned that I am going to hang up this phone and kiss the very first male I see? In fact, I see one right now, a gorgeous specimen, too, with curly blond hair and brilliant blue eyes, and just as soon as I'm done giving you a piece of my mind, I'm going right over to him, and I'm going to plant one on his lips. What do you think about that, Mr. I Didn't Think It Was Important?"

"Would the male that you happen to be looking at be under the age of five?" he asked, stripping off his trousers, ignoring the feathers as he made his way to the bathroom.

"Damn you!" she snarled, and hung up the phone.

It didn't take him long to dress—in Theo's feather-free room—and take a cab down to the hotel to find Harry. He didn't like the idea of Theo giving her any grief, not when she had been so wary around him since that night at his house.

He found the banquet room where her dinner had been held, but it was empty, and there was no sign of where she'd gotten to.

He was about to text her when a group of three women emerged from an elevator, screamed, and rushed over to him. "It's another one! Oh my god, you're even better than the other model!"

"Pardon?" he asked in his most austere voice, removing the hand that one of the women had clamped on his arm.

"You're here for the model competition, right? Oh my god, I'm totally voting for you," the grabby woman said, all but swooning at his feet.

"I'm not here for any competition. I'm here to find—

Another one?" A nasty suspicion began to grow. "Is there a man who looks similar to me at this competition?"

"Oh, is there ever. He's winning, too," a second woman said, fluttering her lashes at him. "Or he was until his wife came in and made him stop dancing. But day-am, you can dance for me any day."

He swore under his breath, promising Theo retribution that would make the heavens quake as he demanded to be shown where the "competition" was being held.

The ballroom was filled with women in various stages of intoxication, cheering and screaming as a man in a G-string strutted down a makeshift runway, while loud, pulsing music blared from a sound system.

Lights flashed, momentarily dazzling him as a photographer standing at the back noticed him. He swore again, detached the fawning woman from his arm, and marched into the room, searching for Harry or Theo.

"That's contestant number twelve, ladies," a woman at a podium announced as the music came to an end and the male dancer sauntered off the stage. "And now, good news—contestant number twenty-two has graciously agreed to do an encore!"

A woman's voice screeched, "Over my dead body he has!"

His head lifted. He knew that screech. The curtains to a flimsy backstage area fluttered and Theo strolled out, thankfully wearing his pants, but his tie was hanging loose around his neck, his shirt open to the waist, and he struck a pose as more music started. Lipstick marks were scattered across his chest, neck, and face like some sort of horrible pox. Just as Iakovos reached the stage, a fury burst out from behind it in the form of Harry, who threw herself in front of Theo, her arms spread wide as if to protect him. The two photographers in the back of the room started snapping pictures.

"Back off, ladies!" Harry yelled. "Theo, for the love of god, get off the stage!"

"Yes, Theo, get off the stage," Iakovos shouted over the pulse of the music.

Harry's head snapped around, her mouth an O of surprise for a few seconds before she hurried over to him, relief filling her face. He lifted her down to the floor, keeping one arm around her as the women crowded the stage, still cheering and hooting.

Theo's face was flushed beneath the lipstick, but he was too involved with grinding his way down the runway to notice when a large male hand reached up, grabbed the back of his shirt, and pulled him off it.

"Hey, Jake," Theo said, his eyes far too bright and his words not quite slurred, but too liquid for Iakovos' peace of mind. "You want a turn, too? The ladies are having some sort of a contest, and the winner gets to be on a book cover."

"We're going home," Iakovos said, mindful of the photographers who were trying to get closer to them. "Now!"

"God, you're no fun now that you have a woman," Theo muttered, but he gave in to the hold Iakovos had on his shirt and allowed himself to be pushed out of the room. Harry clutched Theo's jacket, which she silently handed to them once they were past the gauntlet of women, most of whom were now booing.

"Iakovos—" she started to say.

"Not here." He inclined his head toward the photographers. "Later."

She was a smart girl, his tempest. She gave him one worried look, then slapped a smile on her face and halted when the photographers called for her to stop. "Let's have a few pictures of the Papaioannou brothers!"

"Put your jacket on and wipe your damned face," Iakovos snarled in Greek to Theo. Harry, obviously trying to give him a moment to put Theo to rights, moved in front of them and asked the photographers if they were enjoying the competition.

"Parts of it, yes," the male photographer said, winking at her. "What's your name, darling? And which brother are you with?"

"Well, I'm sure as hell not with Theo," Harry said indignantly, taking Iakovos' arm.

As she turned in profile the photographers' eyes widened, and they took several more shots. "You going to be a father, Iakovos?"

"When's the happy event?"

"Who's the lady?"

"Theo taking up modeling?"

The questions were shot at him with the force of a cannon. He had long familiarity with the press, however, so he simply posed with a tight-lipped Harry and said, "The lady is my fiancée, and yes, she's expecting. She's also very tired, and I'd like to get her home, so if you're through, we'll be on our way."

They weren't through, of course; their sort never was. He ignored them, however, making a fast call to alert

Mikos to be ready for them, after which he shoved Theo out the door and put his arm firmly around Harry in an attempt to protect her.

Harry was mortified and furious at the same time. She waited until they were safely inside the car before collapsing against Iakovos' chest, fighting to keep back tears of shame. "I'm so sorry," she told him, breathing in his wonderful scent. "I'm so, so sorry."

"Sorry for what?" he asked, his hand rubbing her back. "Unless you poured liquor down Theo's throat and pushed him onto that stage, you don't have anything to apologize for."

"No, of course I didn't do either, but he was here because of me, and I feel horribly responsible." She suddenly sat up straight, indignation filling her as she glared at the privacy window. Iakovos had Mikos dump Theo on the front seat, rather than in the back with them. "Although for the love of god, how did Theo get drunk in the time it took me to pee?"

"What happened, exactly?" Iakovos asked, his voice calm, but that muscle in his jaw that liked to jump around when he was controlling his anger was leaping as if it were on a trampoline.

She gave a succinct account of the evening. "I swear I don't know how he got from the room we were in to the ballroom so quickly, but judging by the way some of those ladies were lit up, I suspect that once they got a look at his face, they just swept him along."

"Giving him drinks as they did so." The muscle jumped again as Iakovos glanced at the front window.

"He's an alcoholic, Iakovos. He needs help," she said, taking his hand and rubbing his knuckles on her cheek.

"He's uncontrolled. He just needs to stop screwing around and start taking life seriously."

She opened her mouth to argue the point, but his jaw muscle was going into overtime, so instead she relaxed against him, gently stroking his thigh. "I'm glad you're back. I missed you."

"You did that time, but if you move your fingers half an inch, you won't miss me at all."

What on earth was he talking about? She looked down to his thigh, which she was alternately squeezing and stroking. He was obviously aroused. She pursed her lips as she glanced first out the window, then again at the privacy window between the back of the car and the driver's area.

She looked at Iakovos again, who was watching her with a little smile teasing his lips.

"Well?" he said, obviously leaving the decision to her.

"You have no idea how tempted I am, but Theo could wake up at any moment and decide he wants to sit back here with us. Besides, I have an entire list of things I want to do to you, and I couldn't possibly work my way through it before we got back to the hotel."

"That's a shame," he said, his fingers stroking down her arm in a touch so erotic that a little buzz of electricity ran through her groin. "I've always wanted to do it in a car."

"You've never made love in a car?" She couldn't believe it.

He shook his head, his eyes smoldering.

"Me, either, but that is totally going to the top of my fantasy list," she told him with a kiss, moving her hand that half inch.

He shifted in the seat, giving her better access, his hand now stroking her back.

"Jacket," she told him, moving away.

Without a word, he peeled off his tuxedo jacket. She tossed it on the other seat, then moved to kneel on the floor in front of Iakovos. She spread his knees, reaching for his belt, pausing to ask, "You're sure Mikos can't see?"

"I'm sure."

"And people outside?"

"Neither can they."

She glanced over her shoulder, but the black privacy window did indeed appear to do exactly what its name implied.

He was watching her with a half smile on his lips, his gaze burning her, his hands open and relaxed on the seat.

"Well, then, I believe I need to welcome you home properly."

"You don't have to," he said.

"I want to." She loosened his belt buckle, feeling very wicked, very worldly. He was hard, and growing harder with each brush of her hand against his fly. She slid the zipper down, reveling in the heat of his erection behind the silk of his underwear. She slid it down for better access, admiring the pure male length of him, bending to press little kisses to his testicles. She always made sure she paid equal attention to the prosthetic one, because she didn't want Iakovos believing that she found anything about it repugnant, and, to be honest, she wouldn't have known it wasn't real if he hadn't shown her the little scars on the underside.

"Let's see . . . I don't believe I ever did get that constructive criticism I asked for in Greece," she said, giving the tip of him a little swirl of her tongue.

He groaned, his eyelids drooping. "I had none to give. Your technique is excellent."

"I don't know, if you can still talk, then it must be lacking somehow." She bent her head to her task, and soon had him swearing under his breath, his hands fisted on his legs as his hips rose to meet her.

"Sweetheart, I can't . . . god, this is going to be close." He grabbed her under her armpits, pulling her over him, his fingers moving under her dress to find her underwear. With a little grunt he snapped the thin satin straps, pulling the panties off her.

"Theo!" she whispered, glancing over her shoulder.

"Sleeping. Now, sweetheart, now."

He thrust upward to meet her as she lowered herself onto him, his penis a hard intrusion into her sensitized flesh.

"Tell me you're ready," he murmured into her mouth, his fingers stroking her core.

"I'm always ready where you're concerned," she gasped, her body tightening around him as his touch pushed her over the edge. She caught his moan in her mouth, his fingers tight on her hips as he jerked inside her, the sudden deceleration of the car as Mikos slammed on the brakes serving to drive him deeper into her. She glanced out of the window to search through the darkened glass for signs of where they were, but Iakovos murmured, "It's all right—we're not home yet. Did I hurt you?"

"No." She bit his lower lip, her body trembling with

little aftershocks of pleasure. "But we shouldn't stay like this. Sleeping Beauty might wake up and want to join us."

"That's a shame. I was going to tell Mikos to drive us through the park. Slowly," he said, smiling as she rose off him, using the remains of her underwear to tidy them up.

She snuggled against him when they were both once again decent. "That does bring up a question, though, Yacky."

"What question is that, Eglantine?"

His mouth was warm on her neck, his fingers gently stroking one breast.

She turned her head to press a kiss to the spot above his upper lip. "This fantasy is now crossed off the list. So what's next? We've done your boat, and already joined the mile-high club in your jet. . . . Hmm, I wonder. Do you own any horses? I've heard that if you have really good balance—"

Chapter 18

Iakovos was having a trying day, and it didn't look like it was going to get better anytime soon.

"What the hell were you thinking?" he roared at his brother, who was slumped on the couch in his office. Because he knew how upset Harry became when Theo drank, he'd held off tearing into Theo until they were at the office, but now he was going to say everything he'd been saving up. "I asked you to do one simple thing for me, one bloody simple thing, to escort Harry, and you end up half-naked and stinking drunk. You embarrassed her, dragged her name into the papers, and made Papaioannou International look like fools."

"Jesus, Jake, I don't know what came over me," Theo said, his head in his hands as he hunched over his knees. "Everything was fine until those women started shoving drinks at me and trying to get me out of my clothes."

"You could have walked away. You could have said no." Iakovos was so angry he was pacing back and forth, and lord knew, he never paced. "It's not that hard, Theo. Just open your damned mouth and say no."

"Like you ever said no to a woman." Theo groaned and lay back on the couch, one hand over his forehead.

"I've said no plenty of times, but we are not talking about me. Listen to me closely, Theo. Harry thinks you need to be sent away to some clinic to dry out, and I'm starting to think that she's right."

"Harry thinks, Harry thinks." Theo mimicked him, his eyes so bloodshot he looked demonic. "Christ, Jake, you're not even married yet and already you're so whipped you're letting that bitch think for you."

Iakovos had never struck his brother in anger, but he was about ready to throw caution to the winds. He grabbed Theo by his collar and jerked him to his feet, snarling in his face, "You ever speak of her that way, again, and I'll grind you into the ground."

"You don't own me," Theo snarled back, shoving Iakovos away. "I work for you because I want to, not because I have to. And I'm damned good at what I do, so the next time you get on your fucking high horse, you remember who's bringing in all the money."

"Get out," Iakovos said, so furious he almost couldn't speak. "Just get the hell out of here. Go back to Brazil. Go to Australia. Just don't show your face again until you're ready to apologize to Harry for what you put her through."

Theo stalked out covered in injured pride. Iakovos sat down heavily, his eyes on the picture of Harry and Elena, unseeing as he remembered his father's drunken rages that eventually led to depression, followed by suicide.

Dammit, he didn't want Theo going down that same path.

The intercom buzzed. His head was beginning to pound, but he kept his temper in check as he said, "What is it, Nanna?"

"Security in the lobby called to tell me there's a person there who is raising a ruckus. Evidently she wants to see you, but she doesn't have an appointment."

It was probably another damned journalist. They'd been waiting for him earlier, both when he left the hotel and when he entered his own building. "Tell them to escort her out and call the police if she won't leave. And get me some pain tablets. A lot of them."

He rubbed his temples for a minute, then pulled his laptop over, determined to get some work done.

The mobile phone in his pocket buzzed. He pulled it out, intending to turn it off, but then he noticed the caller's name. "What is it, sweetheart?"

"What is it? What is it? I'll tell you what it is, Yacky! You threw me out of your building, that's what it is!"

"I what—oh, hell."

"Hell indeed!"

He rubbed his forehead. "I thought you were a journalist. Why didn't you tell Nanna who you were?"

"I did. I told her I was your girlfriend and that I wanted to see you. She said all sorts of rude things about women saying that every day, and then told me that if I couldn't even say your name right, I must not know you, and the next thing I knew, two giant bulls in human skins hustled me out of the building saying Mr. Papanono said that he'd call the cops if I tried coming back." She took a deep breath. "I do not find this amusing, Iakovos."

"Neither do I. Just a minute." He pressed the speaker button. "Nanna, please go downstairs and apologize to

my fiancée for refusing to let her see me, and then escort
her up here."

"I don't know what you're talking—"

"Do it," he said, struggling to hold on to the shreds of
his temper. "Harry, one of the secretaries will be right
down."

"Thank you. You're not going to believe what I have
to show you."

Oh, he had a very good idea what it was. He ended
the call and looked up as Dmitri entered. "Got rid of the
journalists for you by promising an interview with you
and Harry."

Iakovos grimaced.

"I know, but it was the best I could do. I pointed out
that because of her pregnancy, if they hounded Harry,
we'd have grounds to slap a restraining order on them.
Then I offered the interview. It seemed to do the trick.
You look like hell."

"I feel like hell," Iakovos said, running his hand
through his hair.

"Theo?"

"I told him to get out of my way."

"Probably best for a while. Harry's out for his blood
anyway. What do you want me to do about Meriton?"

They discussed business briefly before Dmitri disappeared to his own office. A few minutes later, Harry entered Iakovos' office, bringing her storm with her.

"Here is the person you requested," Nanna said, gesturing abruptly toward Harry. "I have apologized to her.
I did not recognize her with that . . . outfit. Here are your
aspirin."

Harry, he had to admit, was almost unrecognizably

clad in a bizarre outfit consisting of a knitted cap pulled down over her hair, a pair of sunglasses, a faded pink T-shirt that proclaimed she was a proud reader of banned books, which didn't quite fit over her growing belly, a navy pea jacket, a long purple knitted scarf, and a pair of what appeared to be his sweatpants, the waistband and ankles of which were rolled up to accommodate her shorter height. A three-inch swath of her belly showed between the waistband and her T-shirt.

She tugged at the T-shirt, giving Nanna an angry look before slamming the newspaper she held down onto the desk in front of him. He winced at the noise.

"Just look at this! Just look!"

He looked. It was as bad as he'd expected. "Yes?"

"That's all you have to say? 'Yes'?" She started pacing the same path he'd taken a short while before.

Nanna, with a stiff back and a righteous air, left the room.

"It's not as bad as you are making it out to be, Harry. I admit it's not pleasant, but no real harm is done."

She was livid—he could see that. She stomped back and forth, and he seriously thought she was going to burst a blood vessel when she saw the captions.

"*Greek playboys times two, and the woman who came between them!* My god, the nerve of those bastards! And this! *Noted author and her three-way love fest! Baby on board . . . but whose is it?* That's it! That's just it, Iakovos!"

"It is?"

"Yes, it is. I demand you do something. Sue them and make them take it all back."

"Why would I do that?"

"Because they're telling lies about us! About you and Theo and me!"

"If I sued every publication that printed an untruth about me, I'd be a gazillionaire," he told her wearily.

"Yes, but—" She stopped, suddenly, frowning at the aspirin. "Are you not feeling well?"

"Just a headache."

Her gaze narrowed on him. "Theo?"

"That was part of it, yes," he said, taking a few aspirin with a swig of cold coffee.

"And here I am yelling and screaming at you. Up."

He frowned at the imperious hand she was using to gesture to him. "I don't have time to make love to you, Harry."

"As if I would seduce you at your office." She paused in thought. "Well, all right, I would, but not right now. Come on, I'll make you feel better."

"It's just a headache," he protested, but he did as she ordered and was soon shirtless, on his belly on the couch, with her sitting on his ass. He groaned in mingled plea-sure and pain as she rubbed hand lotion into his shoul-ders, her fingers working deep into muscles he hadn't realized were so tense and tight.

"Is that newspaper thing going to hurt your busi-ness?" she asked, shifting higher on his back so she could massage his neck.

"No. What will it do to your books?"

"Oh, probably make them sell like hotcakes. Who wouldn't want to read a book by a woman who's having a threesome with two incredibly hot Greek playboys?"

"You're angry, though— Right there." He moaned as she hit a particularly sore tendon on the side of his neck.

"Well, of course I'm angry, but if you say it's not a big deal, then I won't worry about it."

"Mm-hmm." The tension and pain seemed to leach out of his body with every stroke of her fingers.

"Better?" she asked a few minutes later.

"Much."

"Headache gone?"

"Yes."

She leaned down and kissed his ear. "Are you aroused?"

"Hell, yes."

She laughed and got off him, handing him his shirt and tie as he sat upright on the couch. "It sounds like you've had a horrible day."

"It has had its moments." He looped the tie around his neck and took her into his arms, breathing in the wonderful sun-warmed woman scent of her, his lips caressing her temple. "But you have made it all worthwhile."

"That is just about the sweetest thing you've ever said to me," she said, offering him her lips. He didn't hesitate, taking into himself all her sweetness and warmth. "It's almost as nice as saying, oh, I don't know, that you love me."

He smiled down at her, wondering how he'd ever been so lucky as to have this particular woman come storming into his life. "You're going to have to go shopping, Eglantine."

She made a face. "Says who, Yacky?"

He rubbed a finger across the bared stripe of her belly. "When you can't fit into your own clothes and start poaching mine, it's time to go shopping."

"I hate it when you're logical," she said, pulling down

the T-shirt with a sniff. "As it happens, I was going to ask if I could borrow Mikos today so I could pick up a few things."

"You may have him with my blessing. I'll be trapped here all day." He glanced at his watch. "In fact, I have a videoconference due to start shortly. Buy something for a cocktail party, Harry. Something green. I like green."

She looked startled. "Just on a whim, or are we going to one?"

"We're going if you want to come with me. Tonight. I've turned down the previous three invitations from a contractor's wife, and one more would be considered an insult."

"Well, if you don't mind people looking at us and wondering if you or Theo is the father of the twins, then I'm happy to go."

"I don't particularly care what anyone but you thinks, sweetheart."

She stood at the door and looked at him with so much love in her beautiful face, he felt blessed. "Man, they were so wrong to bump you down from three to five."

She was gone before he could respond.

Nine hours later he arrived home, exhausted and desirous of nothing more than for Harry to comfort him. His heart stopped when he walked into the bedroom. A woman stood there, a woman with glossy, tawny brown hair that spilled down her back like skeins of silk, little amber-gold highlights catching the subdued overhead lighting. She turned to face him and his breath caught in his throat. She was so beautiful, it was all he could do to keep from carrying her to the bed and burying himself to the hilt in her warm, welcoming body.

She froze, as elegant as a gazelle, her eyes watchful as he examined her from the top of her gleaming hair to the face that he knew as well as his own, down to breasts that made his scrotum tighten just thinking about them. She was wearing a scarlet dress that was gathered and draped across her breasts, flowing down to a skirt that fluttered slightly as she moved. She was getting bigger now, a fact that filled him with a deep sense of satisfaction. The dress stopped a few inches above her knees, those long, elegant legs of hers shamelessly bare of stockings, ending in little rose-pink toenails that peeked from the toes of her sandals. She was a goddess come to earth, and he would be damned if he wasted one single moment of time.

"To hell with the party," he said, reaching for his tie.

She laughed, the rich, throaty laugh that seemed to resonate within him. "After I went through the hell of shopping for a dress that didn't make me look like I was eight months pregnant instead of four? No, sir. I have a new dress to show off. You like it, don't you? I think it hides my stomach pretty well."

"Why would you want to hide your belly?" he asked, shaking his head. He took her hands in his and stood back, his head to the side as he gave her another once-over, just because he liked looking at her. "You are carrying my twins. There is nothing to be ashamed of."

She gave him an odd look. "I want to hide it because everyone else at this party is going to be skinny and beautiful."

"Who said that?"

"Dmitri." He frowned until she explained. "He said that your ex was going to be there. So in other words, in the midst of all those little petite blond elfin fairy-type creatures who are too ethereal for words, I'll be lumbering around like a giant ox."

How it amused him when she couldn't fight being jealous. "I never thought you'd fish for a compliment, sweetheart, but if you want one, I'm happy to reassure you that you're utterly ravishing, even if that dress isn't green."

"You have to say that," she said, her nostrils flaring. "It's in our contract. You are legally obligated to say nice things to me when I'm as big as a house, and I can't tell everyone in the delivery room that your parents weren't married, or that you have an unnatural passion for sheep."

He had a feeling that if he laughed, he'd just hurt her feelings. He kept his face sober as he kissed first the fingers of one hand, then those of the second, never taking his eyes off her. "Of course my parents were married. And how did you find out about the sheep?"

Her eyes widened and he couldn't do it any longer. He couldn't keep a straight face. He laughed, kissed her with the passion that he'd been saving up all day, and some minutes later, when he retrieved his tongue from her mouth, he took her hand and placed it on his crotch. "Tell me I don't think you're the most beautiful goddess who ever walked the earth."

She stroked the hard length of him until he groaned and caught her hand. "I wasn't fishing for a compliment, you know. I just feel. . . . Oh, hell, I guess I was fishing. It's my boobs." Harry adjusted the chiffon material that was gathered and tastefully draped across her breasts, showing a bit of cleavage but not so much that it would give everyone the idea she was a great big milk cow.

"I love your boobs," Iakovos said, dipping his head to press kisses to the exposed flesh.

"Well, that's good, because they're growing."

He rubbed his hands together, a wicked smile matching the glint in his eyes. "It's all going according to my plans, then. Come along, my beautiful tempest. Since you suffered for your vanity, the least I can do is show you off to the very boring and not at all elflike Tobias Johnson and his stout wife."

Harry hummed to herself as he took a quick shower and shaved, secretly smiling at the looks he shot her way as he dressed in a very handsome blue suit. It was worth every agonizing hour she had spent trying to find a maternity cocktail dress that didn't make her look like a hooker or a dowd. And Iakovos really did seem to be pleased with the pregnancy, insisting on feeling her belly while they were driven across town to a very chic neighborhood.

"You will tell me when I must change how I do things," he murmured in her ear as he kissed her neck.

"Change what things?"

One side of his mouth quirked up. "My preference for being on top."

"Oh." She glanced at Mikos. The privacy window was down between front and back, so she contented herself with saying in a soft voice, "My friend Bess is a doctor. She said so long as I was comfortable, we were fine, but if it started to get uncomfortable, then to stop. But right now all I can think about is jumping your bones, so I suspect stopping isn't going to be on the plate for a while."

"I'm going to risk sounding like a boorish sensualist, but I'm glad to hear that." His breath was hot in her ear as he spoke. She shivered at the promise in his voice, holding on to the warm sense of pleasure until she stepped into the apartment of the rich contractor. At first the gathering looked like a typical party, with clumps of people mingling, chatting, and laughing. Cocktails and little plates bearing expensive snacks were brandished, but as Iakovos introduced Harry to the host and hostess, she realized that there was one giant difference between this party and every other cocktail party: every woman here turned to look at Iakovos when he entered the room.

She thought at first that she was seeing things, but as she smiled at the balding middle-aged man whom Iakovos had said he was trying to sweeten, her eyes scanned the room, and she'd be damned if every single woman there—old, young, and everyone in between—hadn't turned to look at the stunningly handsome man at her side.

And he was stunning. In that perfectly cut suit, Iakovos looked every inch the world's fifth most eligible bachelor. Hell, he looked like the first most eligible bachelor to her, and evidently the women in the room weren't about to disagree with that assessment.

"Just so you know," she whispered to him as he escorted her across the room to meet one of the people who worked for him, "if you were suddenly to get leprosy and lose your nose, an ear, and most of your fingers, I'd still love you."

"You don't know what a relief it is to hear you say that," he said, the quirking side of his mouth doing just that. "I lay sleepless the last few nights worrying about just that very thing."

"I'm also not the teeniest bit jealous of the fact that every single woman here wants you. And yes, I mean that in a biblical sense." She smiled brightly at the man who came up to greet Iakovos.

And she kept her word, at least until there was a flutter at the door and several people she'd met, but whose names had blurred in her mind, turned to look at her with knowing smiles that raised the hackles on her neck.

Slowly she turned around to see an elfin blonde greet the hostess, size up the room with a quick emerald-eyed glance that sharpened on Iakovos where he stood in conversation with the contractor, and shimmy her way over to them, putting a possessive hand on Iakovos' arm.

"She's very beautiful," a soft voice said at Harry's shoulder.

She turned to smile at the man who stood there. "Good evening, Dmitri. I didn't know you were in New York. I thought Iakovos said you were taking care of some business in Greece."

"I was. Got in this morning, just in time to make the party. Iakovos said he might give it a miss if you needed him, so I showed up since it was important that someone from the firm make an appearance."

Harry was touched at the thought of Iakovos dragging his cousin all the way over from Greece. "I'm sorry you had to fly all the way for nothing."

"It wasn't for nothing. I was coming out anyway. Jake told me your good news, by the way. I hope you don't mind, but I wanted to tell you how happy I am for you both."

"Thank you," she said, warmed by the genuine emotion evident in his smile. "It wasn't quite what we planned, but I think it'll be pretty wonderful nonetheless."

He tipped his head toward where Iakovos was leaning down to hear something the ethereal Patricia was saying. "You're not going to let that bother you, I hope?"

"Bother me? No, not unless she steps over the line. Then I'll make it my business to straighten her out on a few things."

He grinned, and slid a hand behind her, giving her a little squeeze. "You know, I almost wish she would, just so I could see that, but I suppose it's better for the business if it doesn't happen. Have you met everyone? Do you need something to drink?"

She held up her glass of tonic water. "I'm fine, thanks, and I think I've met everyone. Do you think it would look very jealous of me if I was to stroll over there and *accidentally* spill my drink down the front of that dress she's almost wearing?"

His laughter was loud enough that it caught the attention of several people, one of whom was Iakovos, who turned to smile at her. The smile faded from his face when he realized that Dmitri's arm was still around her.

Harry watched with delighted amazement as Iakovos' expression turned black. He shook off the hold tiny little Patricia had on his arm, snapping something to her as he strode toward them.

"Tell me you didn't do that on purpose," Harry said out of the side of her mouth.

"Of course I did. If he gives me a black eye, I expect you to get me some ice," Dmitri answered, turning to face the wrath of Iakovos.

Harry didn't know what Iakovos said because it was in Greek, but the look on his face had her making two mental promises—the first was that she was going to learn Greek just as soon as possible, and the second was that somehow she was going to convince him to give his cousin a raise.

"What the hell do you think you're doing?" Iakovos snarled to her in an undertone when Dmitri, with a little bow and a wink to her, took himself off.

"Standing here talking to your cousin. Did you have a nice chat with Patricia?"

"Not particularly. I want her to do the decorations on a hotel we're planning to buy and remodel in the Azores. She is being difficult about it."

"Difficult how?"

He didn't have a chance to answer before the woman in question wiggled her way over to them. Honestly, Harry thought to herself, with that dress, and the slinky way she headed straight for Iakovos, she might just as well have stripped naked and put an OPEN FOR BUSINESS sign on her boobs.

"Iakovos, darling, is this your little wife-to-be?" The minute little blonde subjected Harry to a detailed scrutiny, making her feel the size of a linebacker. The blue gaze looked with speculation at her belly before flashing her a wholly shallow smile. "Or should I make that mother-to-be?"

"She's both. Harry, this is Patricia. She's worked with me for several years decorating my renovations."

"Oh, I've certainly done more than just *decorate* your renovations," Patricia cooed with an obvious meaning that you'd have to have been a Martian to miss. She made a little kissy face at him and ran her thumb next to his lip, murmuring, "Oh, I left a little lipstick there, darling."

Harry had to bite her lip to keep from laughing, but she did, knowing that if she said what she wanted to say, it would just make Patricia worse.

Iakovos' dark eyes met hers, a question in them. She kept her lips straight, but she knew he saw the smile in her eyes when he relaxed, and allowed Patricia to pull him back to the conversation with their host.

"I'm under strict instructions not ever to touch you unless you're in danger of hurting yourself in some manner, or giving birth," Dmitri said, returning to her side. "But he didn't say I couldn't talk to you. I take it you met the bane of the Papaioannou brothers? What did you think?"

"I think—" Her eyes grew wide with disbelief as she watched Patricia wrap her arms around Iakovos and pull his head down for a kiss. "Oh, it's on now!"

"Yes, I can see that it is," he said as she strode away from him.

"Hi," Harry said as Iakovos forcibly detached Patricia from his person. She smiled first at him, then at the smaller woman, whom she took by the arm, and with an even brighter smile scattered around to everyone near them, she said through her teeth, "We need to have a little chat, you and I."

"Delighted," Patricia said, a look of venomous pleasure in her eyes as she jerked her arm out of Harry's grasp. They moved to an empty corner of the room where Patricia spun around, her arms crossed, giving Harry a sickeningly sweet smile. "Hormones making you jealous?"

"No, my hormones make me barf right up to noon. My jealousy is reserved for people who deserve it. You aren't one of them."

"Miaow," Patricia said, her face filled with scorn. "You do know that he's not going to stick with you."

"I beg your pardon?" She couldn't be serious, could she? Was Patricia really that stupid that she believed Harry was so jealous she had lost all ability to reason?

"Iakovos. He's not the domesticated type, darling; he's just not. I don't know why he's suddenly pretending he is, but I've known him for years and years and I can assure you that I've seen women come and go. The longest they lasted was a year . . . until he met me." She smirked. "You obviously aren't aware of the fact that we were an item for two years."

"Wow," Harry said, looking at the smaller woman with wonder in her eyes. "Two years?"

Patricia's smirk lost a bit of wattage. "Yes."

"So you really screwed up big time, huh?" Harry tipped her head to the side as she studied the woman.

"I—what?" Patricia straightened up, indignation making her color rise.

"Well, you must have screwed it up somehow," Harry pointed out. "Do you know what you did to ruin everything between you? Or did you just start to bore him?"

"I didn't bore him, and I certainly didn't screw things up! We just decided, mutually, I'll have you know, to take a little break from our relationship and see other people."

Harry thought about that for a few seconds, then shook her head. "No, sorry, that just doesn't sound like Iakovos."

"What do you know? You've just been around for a few months," Patricia snapped, her expression turning sour.

"Yes, but when I decided that I was going to spend my life with one of the world's most eligible bachelors, I came to a few realizations. One was that he had a past that featured pretty heavily in the public eye, but that didn't mean anything to us. I also took a look at all of the women he'd been linked with, and you know what I found out? They were all cookie cutters."

"Cookie cutters!" Patricia sputtered.

"Yup. Every single one of them was small, blond, and had either been a model, was a model, or quite easily could have been a model." Harry paused for a moment. "I believe you've done some modeling yourself?"

"Yes, but that means nothing—"

"More importantly, though, I took a good long look at Iakovos, and do you know what I found?"

"I'm sure you're going to tell me whether I want to hear it or not," Patricia said with a toss of her head.

"I found that he's a man who may give the appearance of being a playboy with nothing more on his mind than having a good time with as many tiny little blondes as he can humanly bed, but in reality he's a man who values his family. He faces his responsibilities whether he wants to or not. He cares about other people. He has a sense of humor that he hides from most people, but that is the most irresistible of all his charms." Harry felt a little brush of air at her back. "Mind you, he's not without his flaws. He likes mint toothpaste, for one, and he sings off-key Abba tunes in the shower, and cheats at Mario Kart."

"I have never cheated at Mario Kart," Iakovos said behind her as his arm slid around her waist. "You simply have no control of your car and you always end up crashing into cows."

She turned to smile up at him.

"Having a nice time, sweetheart?" he asked her.

"Just getting to know Patricia. I think we're done, aren't we?" Harry asked the other woman.

She seethed and managed to snarl, "We certainly are."

"Good," Iakovos said, steering her toward the door. "It's time I put you to bed."

"You didn't just say that," Harry laughed as he escorted her to the door.

"I don't know what you're talking about," Iakovos said, bidding farewell to his hostess before leading Harry to the elevator.

"Oh, don't you. Have I told you today how much I love you, Yackados Papandromeda?"

"As a matter of fact, you haven't, Eglantine Amaranthe Knight."

Harry smacked him on the arm as the elevator door opened. "Low blow, Yacky. Very low blow."

Chapter 19

It took longer than Iakovos had hoped to return to Greece. The original estimate of two weeks in New York stretched to four weeks, then six, and by the time two months had passed, the weather had turned cold, and he was anxious to get Harry back to the warmth of Athens.

He did manage to do one thing while he was in New York. Two days before they were set to leave, he cornered Harry in the room in their hotel suite that she'd taken as her office.

"Eglantine," he said, strolling into the room, purpose and determination his new bywords.

"Not now, Yacky," she said, her fingers flying over the keyboard of her laptop. "I'm writing."

"You're always writing lately," he said, frowning down at her, his eyes feasting on her beautiful face, her mane of hair pulled back in the ponytail she always wore when writing, her breasts lovely round pillows atop her swelling belly. He couldn't help feeling a certain amount of pride at that belly. He loved it. He loved that nestled inside it were his twins, his children, the children who would be the best of them both. He loved the way she held herself now that she was so large, as if she was aware of the precious burden she carried, her wildness tamed only so long as it took to deliver them into his arms. He loved the fact that he could give her something that he'd thought was impossible outside of a lab. But most of all, he just loved her.

"That's because I have a deadline coming up, and as usual, I'm behind." She glanced up, giving him a narrow-lipped look. "Mostly because you keep distracting me with your thin man's body."

He looked down at himself. "I'm hardly thin, sweetheart. In fact, I've been thinking I'm going to have to go to the gym soon."

"Oh, please. You're just as ripped as you ever were," she said with a disgusted curl of her lip.

"Ripped . . ." He frowned.

"It means buff. Toned. In such fabulous shape that I just want to stop writing this book that's due in three weeks and lick every square inch of you. Besides, why would you want to go to the gym? You never did so when we were in Athens."

"That's because I swam every day," he said, feeling oddly pleased by her comments. "I'm a big man, Harry. If I didn't swim a few miles every day, I'd get fat."

"No," she said, pushing herself back from the desk, and coming around it with a look in her eyes that warned she was itching for an argument. She waved at her belly. "This is fat. What you are is ready for the cover of *Playgirl*. Not that I would let you do that, but you're certainly prime material for it. And if you had a decent bone in your body, you'd get fat so I wouldn't feel so huge in comparison to your buffedness."

"If I did that, I wouldn't be able to keep up with your sexual demands," he said, pulling her into his arms, her hard belly pressed against him. "And that would be a shame. When are you going to marry me?"

"Before the babies are born," she said, letting him kiss her out of her sullen mood. "But after the book is done."

"That leaves us with two months. Are you sure you want to cut it that close?"

"Worried that we'll have illegitimate children?" she asked, giving him an odd look.

He hesitated, not wanting to pressure her into doing something she wasn't comfortable doing, but at the same time, needing to think of the future. "Such things are not unknown in Greece, but they are not as commonplace as here. I would not like our children to be treated with contempt because we were slow in marrying."

She slanted a look up at him, smiled, and bit his lower lip. "All right. As soon as we get back to Athens, OK? But I don't want a wedding. Just a civil ceremony with your close family."

"You're the bride," he said, relieved she had agreed so easily.

"You sure you don't want a big wedding?" she asked.

"I would be pleased to give you one if you wanted it, but I am perfectly happy with a civil ceremony."

"Good." She slipped out of his arms and returned to her chair and laptop.

"There's just one more thing," he said, turning her so she faced him. "The ring."

She made a face. "I told you I don't usually wear jewelry, and don't need an engagement ring."

"I know what you said, but if you recall, I pointed out that it's my prerogative to give you one if it so pleases me, and it does."

"I don't like diamonds," she said, waving her hand dismissively.

What a delight she was. He'd never known a woman who was so obstinately determined *not* to receive gifts of jewelry. He had practically had to get down on his knees to get her to accept a jade necklace that reminded him of the sea when it crashed on the rocks on the north side of his island. "And I have promised not to give you a diamond. How about an emerald?"

She made a face.

"Sapphire?"

"Meh."

He kept his expression bland as he pulled a small box from his pocket. "How about this?"

She looked at the ring sitting inside the box, her eyes showing her interest. "That's lovely. Is it a ruby?"

"Yes. It was my mother's." He took the ring out of the box and held out his hand. She put hers in it, smiling as he slid the ring onto her finger. "It's a bit old-fashioned, and not nearly as big as I'd like you to have, but I thought you might prefer this one over others."

"Oh, Iakovos. It's beautiful," she said, her eyes brightening with unshed tears. "It means so much more than something you found in a store. Thank you."

Her kisses were sweet, but sweeter still was the knowledge that they would soon be home, and he could relax.

*   *   *

The first day back in Athens, Harry realized there were two problems. The first was the fact that she really did not like the penthouse apartment that was Iakovos' home when he was in Athens, as he was for much of the year.

"The city itself, I like," she told Elena the following day as they sat on the sun-drenched patio, sipping tea and looking over the city. "I like the noise, I like the busyness, I love the sights. . . . no, Athens isn't the problem."

"If you don't like the apartment, just tell Iakovos. I'm sure he won't mind if you redecorate it," the younger woman said with a shrug.

"It's not a matter of making a few changes," Harry said slowly, finding it difficult to put into words what it was she objected to in the apartment. "It's just so . . . cold. Impersonal. Everything is chrome and glass and cool lighting, and nothing says *home*. Surely you must have felt that? You've lived here most of your life, haven't you?"

"On and off, yes. When I was small, my mother preferred to live at the house in Corinth, but after she died, Papa wouldn't ever stay there, so we lived mostly here, or later at Iakovos' island. I think you're nesting," Elena said with a wise nod. "I heard pregnant ladies do that."

"Possibly." Harry patted her large belly. "Or it could just be me being silly. Don't say anything to Iakovos, will you? I don't want him to think I don't like his home."

Elena murmured her agreement, and Harry put away the problem of the impersonal feeling of the apartment for something much more worrisome.

Iakovos had a small office in the apartment that he used when he was overloaded with work and wanted to get away from the downtown office. He'd given over one of the bigger rooms to Harry, saying that since it was her primary work space, she should have more room. She sat behind her desk a few days after her conversation with Elena, staring at the paper that Dmitri had dropped onto it.

"What is this?" she asked.

He cleared his throat and looked over her shoulder. "I believe it's a prenuptial agreement."

She took a deep breath. "If he thinks he's going to do this to me, he's nuts."

Dmitri looked uncomfortable. "This really isn't any of my business, Harry."

"It is, too," she said, snatching the paper and slapping it against his chest. "You're his assistant. You can just take this right back in to him and tell him I'm not signing it."

"Harry—"

"Not. Signing. It," she repeated, her gaze sharp enough to cut glass.

Dmitri sighed and left her office.

She glared at the computer screen for a minute, and made a note to add in a character named Jacob whom the heroine of the book accidentally ran over with a forklift.

Dmitri was back after a few minutes. "I'm sorry. He says you have to sign it."

"No."

"Harry, please, just sign it," he pleaded. "He's already annoyed about the whole thing. Don't make it worse."

"You can tell Mr. High and Mighty Number Five Most Friggin' Fabulous Bachelor in the Whole Friggin' Universe that I will not sign that monstrosity. He has to change it."

"Change what?" Dmitri asked, looking resigned. "Show me what you want changed."

She tapped a line. "That."

"The amount of money you are entitled to should you decide to separate or divorce?"

"Yes. That . . . that . . . gah! Tell him to change it, or else."

Dmitri sighed again, and left the room. He was back almost immediately. The figure that was previously written had been scratched off, a new one scrawled in its place, initialed by Iakovos.

"That bastard!" she yelled, not even bothering to read the figure before snatching up the paper and marching down the hall to his office.

"Yacky!" she snarled as she flung open the door.

"Why, Eglantine, what an unexpected pleasure," he said smoothly, leaning back in his chair, his fingertips steepled. "What brings your bright and cheering self to my humble presence?"

"You gigantic rat! How dare you do this to me!" She slammed down the paper and glared at him.

"What's this?" he said, just as if he didn't know, damn his adorable hide. "It looks like a prenuptial agreement."

"It's a travesty!"

"A generous prenuptial agreement!"

"It's barbaric! I won't have it!"

"Really?" He put his feet up on the desk and surveyed her down the long length of his body. "I do believe that I offered to forgo the prenup altogether. Would you care to go back to that?"

"No, I will not! Dammit, you are going to be protected whether you like it or not."

"As a matter of fact . . ." he began, bringing his feet down and standing just so he could tower over her. She hated it when he used his height to his advantage. "I don't like it. I didn't like it when you first insisted on having a prenup, and I don't like it now. I mistrusted you once, Harry, for five whole minutes, and I'm not going through that hell again. I know you don't want my money. I know you're not going to take me for all I'm worth. I trust you with everything I have. I don't want or need a prenuptial agreement."

"I will not marry you without one!"

"And I gave you one," he said, shoving the paper toward her.

"Yes, you're giving me half of everything you own!"

"Seventy percent, I think you'll find," he said, smiling.

She looked back at it, her fury rising at the sight of the scrawled number. "You son of a bitch! I won't sign it! You'll give me one percent, or nothing, do you hear me?"

"Forty," he said, narrowing his eyes at her.

"Two percent!"

"Forty-five. And that, my little storm cloud, is my final offer."

"Well, it's not mine," she spat, snatching up the paper and stalking off.

"Where are you going?"

"To find a lawyer and get him to draw up a real agreement! One that gives me nothing, the way it should be!"

She slammed the door, muttering rude things to herself when his laughter rolled out of the room.

"Yacky," she said that night as she emerged from the bathroom.

"Eglantine," he said, hastily trying to hide something under a pillow.

Harry smiled to herself, amused by the fact that Iakovos didn't want her to know that he read her books. More than once she'd caught him reading the latest release, but for some reason she couldn't figure out, he liked to pretend he had no interest in them. She wondered if it was a matter of male pride, since her books had quite a bit of romantic elements mingled with the suspense. "My lawyer says your lawyer has to stop being mean to me."

"How is he being mean?"

"He says he will personally call you to escort me from his office if I go in there to yell at him again. My lawyer says that's harassment. Or something." She took a deep breath. "It could also have been happiness. I don't quite know because Panoush's accent is very thick."

"I would be happy to tell my lawyer to leave you alone, but you are being unreasonable about this whole thing."

She waddled around the bed that was every bit as big as the one in his palace on the sea. "I just want you to be protected."

"I know you do, sweetheart. I want the same thing for you."

"Then you'll let me have one percent?"

"No." He pulled her close to him. "I've changed my mind. I'm not giving you a damned prenup at all."

"But—"

"No. It's not going to matter, because we're never getting divorced. We're going to grow old together and you're going to make me crazy, and I'll do my best to keep up with you. That's all."

"But—"

"No!"

There was something in his eyes that warned her he was at the end of his patience with regard to the subject.

"What if I suddenly decide I want a sex change, and become a man? You'd be stuck being married to a man, and people would think you were gay."

"Then they would think I was gay. We're still not getting a divorce, and I am through discussing the matter."

"All right, then." She climbed into bed. "If you insist on being completely unreasonable—"

"I insist."

"—then I want to talk about this wedding."

"What about it? I thought you were happy with the civil ceremony."

"I was. I am. But somehow, it's gone from just being you and me and Elena, to everyone in the Eastern Hemisphere wondering where their invite is."

"Tell them the wedding is private."

"I have been, but there's still a couple of people who I think would be hurt if they weren't there."

"Sweetheart, you're the bride. The only person I want to be there is you. Everyone else is optional."

"Well," she said, fluffing the pillows behind her. "We have to have Elena, and Dmitri. They'd be very hurt if we didn't have them. And then there's your friend Peter and his wife. I liked them."

"Good. They liked you."

"It sounds like he'd be hurt if they didn't get to come. You went to school with him, didn't you?"

"Yes."

"So he's your oldest non-family friend. And then there's Theo."

She looked at him out of the corner of his eye.

"Theo can come if he wants," he said, his voice flat.

"Is he even in Greece?"

"No."

"I think we should give him the date, don't you? In case he wants to come back for it?"

"I'll give him the date."

Something was wrong. There was something in his voice that wasn't at all like Iakovos, but she knew he wouldn't tell her what it was until he was ready to do so. At least she'd gotten him to promise to tell Theo the date. "Have you ever thought about giving him something . . ." She hesitated, not sure how best to put her concerns. "Something a little less stressful to work on?"

"Stressful?"

"Well . . ." She made a vague gesture. " 'Delicate,' perhaps is a better word."

"What are you trying to say, Harry? You don't think my brother should be working for me?"

"No, I—"

"You're the one who told me I need to learn to delegate more, and I agreed. I put Theo in charge of the Brazilian project because it's exactly the sort of thing he's perfect at—wining and dining the Brazilian consortium, charming the wives and being the perfect host."

"Yes, but—"

"I don't tell you how to write your books," he said with stony finality. "I would hope you'd give me the same consideration. Now, do you want me to rub your back?"

She looked at the closed expression on his face, and knew that the discussion was over, at least for that moment. After having lived with Iakovos for seven months, she had learned that there were subjects he was willing to let her probe, and others about which he simply wouldn't entertain discussion. The subject of Theo's drinking, and the potentially devastating effect it could have on his life, was one of those subjects.

Harry slid onto her side, going through the nightly tussle when Iakovos wanted her to remove her nightgown, and she refused on the grounds that she was as big as a tanker. By the time he wrestled the nightgown off her, and started stroking her lower back, she decided she'd simply have to tackle the issue of Theo a different way.

"Now would be the perfect time for you to tell me just how much you love me," she cooed as he rubbed away all the aches in her lower back, his big hands making long, sweeping strokes that worked magic on the tightness that seemed to spasm after too long on her feet.

He nuzzled her neck, his chest hair tickling her back as his hands began to roam. One hand cupped her behind, slipping down between her legs while the other slid under her until he found a breast. Gently, because he knew she was sensitive, he caressed it, sending waves of languid pleasure rippling through Harry's body.

"Are you up to this tonight?" he murmured, kissing

her ear and neck and shoulders, his magical fingers sliding between her thighs to find sensitive flesh.

"Oh, yes, please," she said on a sigh, squirming as his fingers danced in her warmth. He rolled her over onto her back, his hair brushing her chin as he kissed a path across her collarbone, dipping even lower to catch a nipple in his mouth and gently, ever so gently, rolling his tongue around the tip.

She moaned with the feel of his mouth, her hands tracing the muscles of his arms and shoulders as he moved over to pay tribute to her other breast. She felt a momentary qualm as he moved lower, kissing his way down her big belly.

"I'm as big as a house," she said, moving restlessly when he rubbed his cheek against the side of her stomach.

"Yes, you are."

She propped herself up on her elbows to glare at him. He crawled up her body with a wicked look in his eye as he lay next to her, one arm around her belly. "Do you have any idea how erotic it is for me to see you lying there, swollen with my children? Do you know what it does to me, here?" He caught her hand and pressed it to his chest, where his heart beat so strong and true. "I know you feel ungainly and awkward, but to my eyes, you are a goddess, a vision of beauty that will give me something I never expected to have, and the only thought that consumes me is to be a part of this miracle the only way I know how."

"Oh god, they really need to move you up to the number one spot, because there isn't a woman in the world who wouldn't sell her soul to have you," Harry told him as he rolled her onto her side again, and pulled her leg back a little until it lay over his.

"Didn't I tell you?" he whispered into her ear as he slid slowly, oh, so very slowly into her body. "I resigned my spot on the list. I told them my wife wouldn't let me remain on it any longer."

Her body tightened around him as his fingers gently stroked her. He was so tender with her, so gentle it brought tears to her eyes. The last month or so, when she had started to feel so unwieldy, she had offered to give him pleasure with her mouth and hands, but he had gravely declined the offer, saying he preferred to wait until such times as she was ready to receive his attentions, no matter how long that might be.

She moaned her release as he moved against her, the feeling of his warmth behind her sending her spiraling into a well of absolute pleasure that was made perfect when his voice turned hoarse with his own climax.

Chapter 20

Harry ran into Patricia the following day at an afternoon tea given by one of the leading socialites in Athens, in aid of a children's charity. Harry had let herself be talked into attending by Elena, who told her that it was a cause that Iakovos had long supported.

"Well, if it isn't the happy homemaker," Patricia said when she spotted Harry, standing somewhat awkwardly on the fringe of a group of chattering women. Patricia stopped, her face a picture of horror as she gazed at Harry's belly. "Good god, are you having a *litter*?"

Harry was too uncomfortable to put up with any crap from the infinitesimally small blonde. "Thus speaks the woman who doesn't have a child," she snapped.

Patricia's face froze. "You inhuman bitch," she growled before pushing past Harry and quickly leaving the tea.

Harry had a horrible feeling that she'd said something wrong, but she had no idea what. When she returned home shortly thereafter, pleading a very real headache as her excuse to leave, she tackled Elena, who was out next to the pool sunning herself.

"How'd the tea go?" she asked, looking up from a stack of fashion magazines.

"It was fine. What do you know about Patricia?" Harry asked, getting right to the point.

"Patricia? You mean Iakovos' Patricia?"

Harry grimaced. "Iakovos' previous girlfriend, yes. Do you know if she has any children?"

Elena frowned, slowly shaking her head. "I don't think she does, no. She never mentioned a child, but I didn't see her much. She and Iakovos were only together for a little while, you know."

"Two years," Harry said grimly.

"Well . . . yes, but that's really not very long."

"If she doesn't have children, why did she get so . . . oh, lord." She must be infertile. Perhaps she'd been trying to get pregnant and couldn't, and then the very pregnant Harry waddled up and snapped at her. "Nice job, Harry."

"Are you talking to yourself?" Elena asked, sitting up.

"No. Yes. Oh, hell." She went back into the coolness of the apartment, feeling horrible. "Dammit, I'm going to have to apologize."

She called Dmitri, being too embarrassed by her bad behavior to admit it to Iakovos. "Dmitri, I'm going to ask you to do something and not only not ask questions about it, but also don't mention it to Iakovos."

"Is it anything illegal?" he asked, the hint of a smile in his voice.

"No."

"Then I'll do it. What do you need?"

"I want Patricia's phone number and the hotel she's staying at in Athens."

"She has an apartment here, actually, assuming you're talking about the Patricia who does design work for Iakovos."

"That's the one."

"All right. Here's the address." Harry wrote down the information, thanking him for not telling Iakovos. "I don't normally like keeping secrets from him, but so long as you're willing to take responsibility for this, I'll keep quiet."

"I'm not going to do anything to hurt her," Harry reassured him. "Quite the opposite, as a matter of fact. Not only am I going to apologize, I'm going to give her some work."

She could have sworn Dmitri choked at that news, but as he didn't say anything more, she hung up, gathered together her purse and her digital camera, and called a cab.

Forty minutes later she pressed the buzzer outside Patricia's door, clutching a bottle of local wine.

Patricia's expression upon seeing her when she opened the door was not pleasant, but Harry had never shirked a duty when it was necessary.

"What are you doing here?" Patricia asked.

"I'm here to apologize."

"You can't come in," Patricia said stubbornly.

Harry held out the bottle. "I brought booze."

"All right, you can come in, but you can't stay long." Patricia snatched the bottle and turned on her heel. Harry followed her into the apartment. "I assume you're not going to have any of this wine."

"You would assume correctly."

Patricia's mouth twisted as she brought the opened bottle and a glass into a sunny living room. Harry looked around and acknowledged that she was right to do what she was about to do.

"You have a cute apartment. Did you decorate it yourself?"

Patricia shot her a glare that should have at least stunned Harry. "Of course I did. Look, I don't know what you want from me, but I really am not in the mood to play nice, so why don't you get off your chest whatever you came to say, and we'll move on."

"I came to apologize for what I said at the tea. I don't know why it upset you so much, but it did, and I feel bad about that. So I'm sorry."

Patricia sat down, taking a big swig of the wine while Harry stood awkwardly, unsure whether she should sit or just leave.

"So you say you're sorry, and it's supposed to make it all good again?"

"I don't know what else I can do," Harry said, feeling at a loss. "Obviously, I touched on a sensitive area."

Patricia closed her eyes for a moment, then poured herself another glass of wine, and gestured toward the door. "All right, you apologized. Now get the hell out of here."

Harry was silent for a moment, then nodded and started for the door.

"No, wait a minute. Oh, Christ, this is ridiculous. I don't want to talk to you. I don't want you in my house. I don't want to see you in that stupid dress, standing there feeling sorry for me."

Harry turned around slowly. She knew the sound of pain when she heard it, and although she had no love for this woman, she would never forgive herself if she just walked off and left another person in pain that had its origins in her actions.

"My dress," she said, smoothing a hand down over her giant belly, "is extremely cute. I ordered it online. It's from New York." The dress *was* cute—the empire bodice was navy blue and white stripe, while the flowing skirt was in matching navy. It was very sailor-like, and Harry had fallen in love with it when she saw it online. "And as for feeling sorry for you, I'm not, but mostly because I have no idea why you were so upset about what I said, unless you're infertile, and thus my comment was unusually cruel."

Patricia swore, standing up, the wineglass still in her hands. "I loved Iakovos, you know."

Harry stood very still. "Then I do feel sorry for you. I can't imagine anything worse than loving him, but not being loved in return."

Patricia's face twisted into a cruel mask. "You think you're so different from me, don't you? You think he won't get tired of you, too, in the end? Oh yes, you were right there, damn you. He got tired of me; he said that we no longer had anything to offer each other. God damn it, I was going to dump him, and he dumped me first." She sat back down, poured more wine, and tossed it back.

"If you loved him, why did you want to break up with him?" Harry asked slowly.

"Because I didn't love him." She ran her hand through her perfect blond hair. "Oh god, just shut up and sit down. I can't stand looking at you."

Harry sat down in a straight-backed chair as Patricia stomped off to the kitchen. She returned in a minute with a tall glass of orange juice that she shoved into Harry's hands. She wasn't terribly fond of orange juice, but sipped at it to be polite as Patricia poured herself another glass of wine.

"Just so we understand each other," Harry said after a minute of silence, "you're not going to make me jealous of your previous relationship with Iakovos."

"Because you're so perfect for him?" Patricia sneered. "Because you think he won't get tired of you like he did me?"

"Yes," Harry said. "Because he loves me, and I believe that love is not just infatuation."

"Maybe you are perfect," Patricia said, her face twisting again. "Maybe he is. I hope he is."

"You hope he's happy with me?"

"Yes. Because then when I take him away from you, it'll be that much more satisfying." Her smile was glittering, as cruel as the sun is bright. "You don't think I can do it, do you? I can. I know what he likes. I know what drives him wild. I know what he wants from a woman, and I can give it to him. I *have* given it to him. I kept him by my side for two years, longer than any other woman, longer than you. If I wanted him again, I could take him away from you. And do you know what? I've just decided I want him again."

Harry stood up slowly, looking down at the beautiful, bitter blond woman. "I don't play games when it comes to Iakovos," she finally said, her heart heavy. "So I'm not going to tell you to go ahead and try. I love him. I know he loves me. We're getting married in three days, and having twins in less than two months. If you want to spend your time and energy trying to destroy that, then that's what you'll do. But you have to ask yourself if what you'll destroy is my relationship with him, or your own soul."

Patricia swore, and Harry went to the front door again, intending to wash her hands of the woman. As she reached for the door, Patricia made a horrible moaning, gasping noise. "I'm not infertile. I had a daughter. She was killed."

Goose bumps crawled up Harry's back as she turned around. Patricia's face was a mask of indifference, but her fingers were white around the stem of the wineglass.

"I'm sorry."

Patricia made a gesture with the glass, then splashed more wine into it, her hand shaking. "It was six years ago. She would have been ten this year."

Harry returned to her chair, not wanting to ask what had happened, but curious nonetheless.

Patricia took a long, shuddering breath. "My husband fought me for custody when we divorced. He told the judge that a workaholic wasn't any sort of mother for Penny. When the judge didn't agree and gave me custody, my husband . . ."

Harry had a horrible feeling of what was coming. She wanted to comfort Patricia, but there was an air of tense fragility about her.

"He grabbed her and ran. Right into the side of a commuter train. The bastard."

The last word was spat out as Patricia's face crumpled.

Harry moved awkwardly to the couch, her arms

around the now sobbing Patricia, her own eyes streaming in sympathy.

"I'm sorry. I'm so sorry," she kept saying, wishing there was something she could do.

In time Patricia pulled away, mopping at her face with a couple of tissues.

"Don't think this changes anything," she said in a low, ugly voice. "I don't like you. I plan on taking Iakovos from you."

"No, you won't," Harry said, sliding forward on the couch so she could hoist herself up.

"Shows what you know," Patricia said, blowing her nose with more tissues.

"You won't because you know how precious life is, and you would never take away my babies' father."

Patricia's jaw worked, but she said nothing, just looked away. "Leave me alone. Just take your fat body away and leave me alone."

Harry went to the door for a third time, looking back to say slowly, "I want to hire you. I want you to redecorate our apartment before my babies come. I know you're expensive, and busy, but I want you to do this. I think you are very talented, and I know that you'll help me transform our apartment into a home."

"You just don't hear anything I say, do you?" Patricia said, her face red.

"I hear what you're saying," Harry said, giving her a long look. "I also hear what you're not saying. If you can come to lunch tomorrow, I'll show you around the apartment and we can talk about redecorating."

"I'm very familiar with the apartment," Patricia threw at her head as she pulled open the door and walked through it. "And there's no way in hell I'm going to do anything but take from you the man I once loved."

Harry stopped by Iakovos' office on the way home. He was standing in the hall outside his office, talking with Dmitri. She walked up to him and wrapped her arms around him, burying her face in his neck to breathe in his scent.

"Hold me," she said.

He did.

Dmitri made an excuse and left. Harry stood holding on to Iakovos, allowing his love to wash away all the pain that seemed to cover her in sorrow. After a few minutes, she looked up at him. "I've asked Patricia to redecorate our apartment."

His eyebrows rose.

"She said she's going to take you from me. I told her I trusted you. Don't prove me wrong."

He said nothing as she left.

The following day, promptly at noon, the doorman buzzed to say that Patricia was waiting downstairs.

"All right, let's get this done as quickly as possible," Patricia said a few minutes later as Harry held open the door for her.

"Lunch on the patio in ten minutes, please, Mrs. Avrabos," Harry told the housekeeper.

"Yes, *kyria*," the woman said, her eyes flicking between Harry and Patricia.

"This is the living room, as you probably remember," Harry said, waving toward the room in question. Patricia whipped out both a digital camera and a notepad. She took a few pictures, then made a few quick notes.

"The bedrooms are down this way. Elena's you won't

need to touch—she's happy with it. Theo's should probably be left alone, as well. This is our room."

"I remember that one, darling," Patricia said with a
toss of her head as she entered the room. "Hmm. I see
not much has changed. Iakovos still favors the right side
of the bed."

Harry was determined to keep her temper. "You'll
have to work around the bed. It's custom-made to Iakovos' specifications. But other than that, I'm open to
change. The dressing room could use some freshening
up as well. I really do not like the bathroom at all—it's
too grimly modern, so if you could warm that up, I'd be
grateful."

Patricia snorted.

"The room next to ours will be the nursery. I don't
have anything in there yet, so I'd like it to be one of the
first rooms you work on."

"You don't have your nursery in order?" Patricia
looked like she couldn't believe her ears.

"It's not that I don't want to—I just hate shopping. I
was going to order everything online, but it's kind of difficult to navigate through online Greek stores. And I
have a book due, and . . . well, it's just been delayed."

Patricia made a disgusted sound.

"The offices are down this hall," Harry said, walking
back through the living room to the other side of the
apartment. "My office needs work. It's too dark. This is
Iakovos' office, but he said he'd like it left the way it is.
This one next to it is Dmitri's. He's willing to have you
make changes, so long as you let him see the desk first.
He evidently is quite picky about desks. Oh, and he said
no floral designs. Over here is the theater. The electron-

ics are fine, but if you could find more comfortable seating, I'd be grateful. The two guest rooms need full makeovers. The kitchen is this way."

Patricia continued to take pictures and make notes. By the time they were done touring the kitchen, formal dining room, and housekeeper's rooms, Harry was more than ready to sit down.

"I see Mrs. Avrabos has lunch ready. Shall we?"

"But of course, Lady Bountiful."

Harry bit her tongue, determined to get through this if it killed her. As she took her seat, however, she couldn't help but notice the housekeeper's glare pointed at Patricia.

"Old biddy," Patricia muttered as the housekeeper served lunch and left.

"I take it you don't like her?" Harry asked as she helped herself to salad and moussaka, unable to keep from adding, "She doesn't seem very happy to have you here."

"No, I'm sure she's not." Patricia smiled, and Harry knew a big zinger was coming. "Not since she caught Iakovos and me making love in the kitchen that time."

Harry looked at her. "I give that about a six-point-five. Not enough to really piss me off, but adequate enough that I will think about it the next time I'm in the kitchen."

To her surprise, Patricia gave a bark of laughter. "All right, since you are so determined to do this, let us play designer and client. What do you want me to make of this place?"

"I want it to be a home."

Patricia shot her a fiery look.

"Have you seen Iakovos' house? Oh, I'm sure you have."

"Yes, I have," Patricia responded with a tight smile.

"Well, that's what I mean by a home. That house is beautifully decorated. It feels warm, and real, like people live there, not automatons."

"I'm glad you think so. I worked hard on that house."

Harry bit back an exclamation. "You decorated it? The house on the island?"

"Yes. It's how Iakovos and I met."

She digested this information. "Well, you did a beautiful job ... er ... you didn't do this apartment, did you?"

"No." Patricia's lip curled. "You can't blame me for this place."

"Well, then you must know the sort of thing I want. You know the colors Iakovos likes—those are fine with me. And you know the style of what I want."

"Yes, I think I know what you want. You want me to make a home for you and your children, so you can be happy here with the man I love."

Harry just wanted to throw the pitcher of lemonade at her. "Oh, for god's sake, Patricia! Can't we be civilized about this?"

"By all means, let's be civilized," Patricia snarled. "We're two women who are both intent on having the same man, but that doesn't mean we can't be pals."

Harry had had enough; finally she'd had enough. "Stop it, Patricia, just stop it!" She slammed down her glass of lemonade. "You don't want Iakovos!"

"Who says I don't?"

"I say you don't. Do you know what I'd do if Iakovos told me he didn't think our relationship had anything to offer either of us anymore? I'd fight, Patricia. I'd fight like hell to make sure that it did. I'd fight to keep his love, and I'd fight and fight, and go on fighting until I had his love again. I sure as hell wouldn't walk away from him. You don't do that to someone you love."

Patricia sat stiff as a board, her face red, her gaze on the distance.

"So let's have a little understanding, you and me," Harry continued. "You can pretend whatever you want. You can tell me about every single one of your intimate moments with Iakovos. You can threaten me and do your damnedest to piss me off, but if you do, it'll only be to make yourself feel better. It won't have *any* effect on me."

Patricia got up and walked away without another word.

Harry stood up slowly, catching the eye of Mrs. Avrabos, who stood in the living room, looking out onto the patio.

"Oh, that went well, don't you think?" she said, wanting to cry.

Mrs. Avrabos nodded her head. "Yes, *kyria*, that went well. It went very well."

Chapter 21

His wedding day dawned stormy, dark, and with the threat of oversetting the entire event. He should have known that such an important event would never go the way it should when it concerned his turbulent sea goddess.

"Sweetheart, you're going to have to get up or you won't make it to the wedding," he told Harry two hours after he had risen to see what sort of wind damage had been done to his house. The waves pounded with ferocity on his little island, spray flying up from the rocks to splatter against the windows.

Harry rolled over from where she'd finally gotten comfortable on a number of pillows. "Oh, stuff the wedding."

"Is it too much for you?" he asked, wondering if he'd pushed her into something she wasn't ready for yet.

"Is what too much for me? Help me up." He put an arm around her and helped her to her feet. She wore that damned nightgown again, the one he hated, but she had, the last few weeks, been overcome with shyness around him, and had insisted on wearing it to bed.

"The wedding?"

She paused on the way to the bathroom, tossing him a smile over her shoulder. "No, I'm just being cranky. Although, good god, look at those storm clouds. I just hope the boat from town can make it over, or we won't have Elena and the mayor."

"They'll be here."

An hour later the boat did make it over, but he had been watching the skies, worried that perhaps the sea was celebrating their marriage a little too vigorously. He went down to meet the launch expecting to see Dmitri, Elena, and the mayor—who would be performing the ceremony—but the two additional people huddled into the cabin gave him a moment's pause.

"Theo," he said as the other three made a dash for the house.

His brother stood before him for a moment before turning around and holding out his hand.

"You didn't think I'd miss your wedding, did you, darling?"

Iakovos swore under his breath as Patricia emerged from the cabin to give him an arch smile. "Did Harry invite you?"

"She's here as my guest," Theo said, with a challenging look.

Just what he needed—something to upset his bride on the day that was supposed to be one of her best.

"You're both welcome, then," he said through his teeth, glancing up in surprise at the sky as lightning flashed across the clouds, followed by a rumble of thunder.

"Looks like you're having all sorts of bad omens. Doesn't a storm for a wedding mean it's doomed?" Patricia asked as she hurried with them to the house.

"Perhaps for anyone else it might, but not for us," Iakovos said, feeling cheerful about that at least. Harry, he knew, loved storms almost as much as he did. "The ceremony will be in half an hour in the music room."

"Should I go offer my help to the bride?" Patricia asked, a thin smile on her face.

Iakovos knew what was going on between Harry and her, and had enough sense to stay out of their battle to establish a working relationship. Unless Patricia gave him reason to, he wouldn't interfere. "If you think she would benefit from it, then by all means, do so. She's in our bedroom."

He went off to greet the mayor properly before tending to his other duties. After getting a report about a few windows broken in one of the bungalows, checking with Spyros regarding the house, and listening to Rosalia complain about Patricia's presence, he spent a few minutes alone with an excited Elena, who had just come from seeing Harry.

"I'm so happy," Elena cried, hugging him a third time. "I just know you will be, too."

"I will—" They both looked up when something struck the house.

Iakovos went out with Spyros to evaluate the damage, returning to the house soaking wet. He took the stairs three at a time, heading for his dressing room since Harry had claimed their bedroom for the day. He changed into his wedding clothes, then paused outside the door, listening for voices. There were none. He stuck his head in to make sure everything was all right.

"You're not supposed to see the bride before the wedding, you know," Harry said, looking at her reflection as she stood in front of the mirror on the bureau. "It's bad luck. Not that I believe that, because honestly, how is that supposed to be bad? You saw me a little bit ago, and you didn't run screaming from the room declaring you had changed your mind and that you wanted to stay number five and not be stricken off the list. So really, if you didn't run away then, how can seeing me now be bad?" She turned to look at him as she spoke the last words, her eyes opening wide as she took in his appearance.

He would have been pleased by her reaction, since he'd ordered the tuxedo from his favorite tailor just for the wedding, but he was too busy staring at her to be able to think.

The dress she wore was floor length, a mottled green that started at her shoulders in a pale jade color, flowing down in elegant, rippling lines over her breasts, flaring out with her belly, and falling to gentle folds, the color of the fabric changing from jade to a deep, dark forest green at her feet. Her hair had been swept back off her face, but tumbled down her back in a riotous mass that he longed to touch.

But it was her eyes that made him feel like someone had just punched him in the chest. They glowed with so much love, he wanted to go down on his knees and thank god for her.

"I suppose it's expected that a bride in my condition

should say something about wishing she was thinner and able to wear white on her wedding day, but somehow, I don't seem to care about that," she told him.

"You take my breath away, you're so beautiful," he said.

She actually blushed, which delighted him beyond understanding. "You take my breath away, too, you know. That tux is gorgeous. I like the white tie. I like the way the pants cling to your thighs. I like the fact that beneath it, you're naked."

He pulled a long, slim box from the inner pocket. "I know you don't want this, and I know you'll give me hell for it, but I have to do this, Eglantine. I have to give you this."

"What is it, Yacky?" She looked suspicious as he opened the box. She gave a little shake of her head as she reached out to touch it. "It's beautiful."

"Not even remotely close to your beauty. Will you wear it?"

Her fingers ran down the curling gold wire that twisted around and above and below the thick emeralds. He'd asked the designer for something that would mimic the waves of her hair as it lay spread out on his bed, and he was pleased with the results. "Yes, I'll wear it. Thank you, Iakovos."

He moved around behind her to drape it around her neck. In her hair were shining gold leaves, twined through the tumbled curls. He brushed aside the heavy fall of hair, pressing a kiss to the back of her neck. She gave a little shiver and looked over her shoulder at him, the fingers of one hand touching the emeralds reverentially.

"How did you know I was going to pick a green dress?" she asked.

He smiled and backed away from her, lest he damn everything but his own need to claim her. "I know how you think, sweetheart. You didn't do as I asked for the last few dresses, so I knew this one would be green."

She sighed mournfully. "Well, now all the magic's gone, and you'll get tired of me, and then Patricia will be right and I'll have to eat crow."

"I am walking away from you," he said, doing exactly that. "But only because if I stay here with you, I'll end up stripping that very pretty dress from your magnificent body and spending the rest of the day making love to you."

"I love you, too," she called after him, making him smile.

The wedding ceremony was short, sweet, and just exactly how Harry wanted it to be. The wedding night, she mused several hours later as she sat huddled under a blanket in a small sitting room, could have been better.

"If I'd have known I was going to be held prisoner here, I would have brought something to read, at least," Patricia complained as she paced past where Harry sat.

Elena looked up from one of her magazines. "You can have one of mine."

A blast of wind hit the side of the house, making the windows shudder. All three women looked silently at the windows for a few seconds before returning to their previous occupations.

"We have books," Harry said slowly.

"I don't want your books. Where's Theo? The least he

could do is distract me with sex, so I don't have to sit here and watch you gestate."

"Well, if it makes you feel any better," Harry said, suddenly too tired to care, "I don't particularly want to spend the evening with you, either."

Patricia glared at her for a moment, then stomped out of the room, only to return a short while later with a stack of catalogs and fabric samples.

"Go through these and tell me what you like," she said, throwing them down on the couch next to Harry.

"Fabric samples?" Harry asked as she touched them. "You brought fabric samples to my wedding?"

"Is there any other reason I would be here?" Patricia snarled. "You want me to redecorate; I'm redecorating. Now which of the blues do you like for the nursery? And do you want a mural on the wall or stenciling?"

A surprisingly enjoyable half hour was spent sorting through the paint chips, rug samples, and little swatches of fabric, as well as perusing a couple of fixture catalogs. Elena abandoned her fashion magazine to peer over Harry's shoulder, offering advice and announcing that she wanted her room redone in the style of a harem.

"I suspect your brother will have something to say about that," Harry said, handing back to Patricia the last of the samples. "And I don't imagine it'll be anything positive. Thank you, by the way."

Patricia gave her a wary look. "For doing my job?"

"For being human." She struggled to her feet. "I'm sure today couldn't have been easy for you. Ugh. Must pee or burst."

She tended to her bladder, braving the journey upstairs to remove her wedding finery, touching once again the lovely gems at her neck. She knew it frustrated Iakovos that she wasn't much for bling, but she wouldn't have been female if she didn't appreciate the necklace he'd picked out for her. It was just the sort of thing she could see herself wearing on those occasions when she had to dress up.

Honestly, could there be a man any more perfect? There couldn't. He was everything she could ever have wanted in a man.

She gave his pillow a fond pat and started back downstairs. As she approached the stairs, footsteps from below caught her ear. She glanced over the banister to see Iakovos, Patricia at his side. He'd removed his tuxedo jacket and tie, and wore only the shirt, open partway, the white material stark against his darker skin as it molded to the thick muscles of his chest dampened by the rain and spray of the sea.

"Does she know?" Patricia asked, sliding Iakovos an unreadable look.

"No," he answered, and with a nod, he strode to the bottom of the stairs.

"You *are* going to tell her soon, I hope," Patricia called after him.

"Yes."

Harry hurriedly backpedaled, spinning around to run somewhere, anywhere. The sound of him coming up the stairs sent her into a fast waddle to Elena's room, where she closed the door and leaned against it, her heart beating wildly.

Perfect man, her ass! That bastard was two-timing her!

The second the thought emerged, she realized just

how stupid it was. The look on Iakovos' face was not
even remotely lover-like; in fact, he looked more tired
than anything. And there she was, hiding from him, the
man she loved with her whole being, and he was tired
and could probably use a bit of comfort on a day that
he'd done his best to make special for her.

She flung open the door and marched into their bedroom, but it was empty except for a damp shirt lying on
the floor.

"I will not do this!" she declared, kicking the shirt
because she couldn't bend down to pick it up and stran-
gle it, as she would have liked. "I will not play this
game!"

She marched back downstairs, searching the rooms
until she found Patricia standing near the kitchen, talking on the phone.

"I know something is up between you and Iakovos,"
she announced, tapping Patricia on the shoulder.

She took great satisfaction in the fact that Patricia
looked startled for a moment. Good. If that little blond
elfette thought she could drive a wedge between Iakovos and her, she had just better start thinking again.

"I'll call you back, Leo. One of my clients is having a
hissy. Of course there is something between Iakovos and
me, darling. I believe I did warn you about that," Patricia
said with a smile that made Harry's palm itch.

"I don't care if there's something between you. I absolutely don't care. I don't even want to know what it is,
because I trust him."

"That makes it all so much easier," Patricia said with
a smirk. That smirk did it. It pushed her over the edge.

"You want me to play the jealous wife?" Harry shrugged.

"Sure. I can do that." She reached out and slapped that smug face.

Patricia's jaw dropped open for the count of three. "You *slapped* me?"

"Yes," Harry said, feeling a whole lot better.

Patricia sputtered something rude, and after a moment's pause, slapped Harry across the left cheek.

"I am *pregnant*," Harry roared, slapping the little twit again. "You don't hit pregnant ladies!"

"I'm half your size," Patricia snarled, slapping her a second time. "You outweigh me by at least a hundred pounds! That's just as bad as hitting a pregnant person!"

"Oh!" Harry said, outraged, her cheek stinging.

"Harry, I— Uh . . ." Elena emerged from the kitchen, eyeing the two women. "Is something wrong?"

"I told you before that you're not going to make me jealous," Harry said, ignoring Elena.

"That's why you hauled off and decked me, is it?" Patricia taunted.

"Uh . . ." Elena looked from Harry to Patricia and back.

"If I had decked you, you'd be out cold, you insipid little midget!"

"I am not a midget!" Patricia said, bristling with indignation. "And that is completely non–politically correct! It's little people, not midgets! Not that I am one!"

"I am not going to go speak with my husband about what it is you two are plotting." Harry pulled her dignity around herself. "Because I just don't care. But I am going to have him throw your minute little body off this island."

"Harry, I don't think—" Elena started to say.

"Shut up, you," Patricia snarled at Elena, shoving her face into Harry's. "You just go right ahead and do what you want. Ruin what you have. See if I care. I'm so sick of you right now, I couldn't care less what you do."

Harry opened her mouth to tell her exactly what she thought, but a sudden pain bit hard across her belly. She gasped and doubled over, grabbing her stomach with both hands, tears springing to her eyes.

"Oh my god!" Elena said, staring in horror at her.

"What is it? Pain?" Patricia asked.

Harry nodded, unable to catch her breath, the pain was so bad. She thought for a moment that she was going to collapse.

"Get Iakovos," Patricia ordered Elena, gripping Harry's arms and guiding her to a bench that sat against a wall. "Breathe, Harry. Is the pain in front or back?"

"Front," Harry said, gasping for air.

"Could be a Braxton Hicks. I got them a lot toward the end of my pregnancy. It should ease up in a minute. I know this sounds ridiculous, but if you can relax, it'll get better."

It did, just as Iakovos burst into the hallway, skidding to a stop in front of her, kneeling as she rocked with the effort to relax her muscles.

"Are you in labor?" he asked, his hands on her legs.

"No. I don't think so."

"I'll call the doctor," he said, rising. Then he obviously realized the storm was still raging, and no one would be coming to or leaving the island until it passed. He swore.

"It's most likely a non-labor contraction," Patricia told him. "She needs to relax, though. Why don't you take her upstairs, and we'll get her into a bath. Those always helped me."

Iakovos didn't at all seem to notice the irony of following his ex-lover's orders, but Harry appreciated it, almost as much as she appreciated the fact that he carefully picked her up and carried her up the long flight of stairs.

"OK, this is way beyond weird," she said as both Iakovos and Patricia stripped her down, Patricia running a warm but not too hot bath in the big marble tub. "I feel like we're about to have some sort of bizarre pregnancy fetish threesome."

"My god, you are huge," was Patricia's only comment when she got a look at Harry's naked belly.

"Iakovos!" Harry gave him a look to let him know she'd reached her limit.

"Out," he said to Patricia.

"Fine. I didn't want to be part of your pregnancy fetish threesome anyway," Patricia snorted, head high as she stalked to the door.

Harry had a long bath, and was relieved that she had no further painful contractions. She had a harder time convincing Iakovos that she was fine and didn't need to be airlifted to the nearest hospital.

An hour later she wandered back downstairs. "Thank you for your help," she told Patricia when she found her and Elena back in the sitting room. "I've had those little contractions before, but never like that."

"Sometimes if you move wrong, they can zap you," was all Patricia said, clearly bored with her presence.

Harry fussed around the room for a few minutes before finally saying, "Oh, this is ridiculous. I'm going to find Iakovos."

"I'll come with you," Elena said quickly, throwing down her magazine.

"I'll be damned if I'll be left here by myself!" Patricia added, and hurried after them.

Harry found the men nailing boards across the west side of the long sitting room that had witnessed such spectacular sunsets. There was no sun to be seen now, just broken glass, water, and some branches that had been whipped up by the storm and slammed into the French doors.

"Have you had more pains?"

"Not a one," she reassured Iakovos when he hurried over to take her hands. She examined his face. He still looked tired but not, she noted with relief, overly worried. "Are we in trouble?"

"From the storm? No. This house is built to withstand it, and I think it's about to blow itself out anyway. I'm sorry it's ruined your wedding day, though."

"Nothing could ruin the day on which I yanked you off that damned list once and for all," she said, licking his lower lip. "How does it feel to be a former world's most sexy pants bachelor?"

"Like I've been saved from ever answering another question about what I'm looking for in a woman," he answered, humor lighting his eyes.

"I love you, Mr. Papamoussaka," she murmured against his mouth.

"And I—"

Glass exploded on the other side of the room, making Harry jump. Iakovos ran to help as Theo, Dmitri, and the mayor pulled aside a small lemon tree that had been lifted, pot and all, and smashed into one of the big windows.

"That doesn't count, Yacky! You still have to say it!" Harry yelled after him, glaring out at the stormy night sky. "Man, I just can*not* get a break!"

Iakovos was right. The storm, obviously satisfied that it had made its point, faded to just periodic winds not long after the last of the glass was swept up. A few hours later, the mayor and Patricia returned to the mainland.

"It's not that I haven't had a perfectly wonderful time, darlings," she drawled, shooting Harry a sly look. "But I draw the line at having to play marriage witness and midwife on the same day."

Harry watched the boat as it disappeared over choppy water to the town before turning to Iakovos. "How on earth did you ever stay with her for two years?"

"It wasn't easy," he said with a little grimace, and once again Harry was filled with love.

"I think, my handsome Greek, that you deserve a wedding night." She nuzzled her face in his neck, her belly keeping her from pressing herself against him as she'd like.

"I can think of nothing I'd like more," he answered, swinging her up in his arms and carrying her up the path to the house. "But we're not having one."

"We aren't?"

"No," he said firmly, coming to a swift decision. "You're too close to birth, and with that contraction you had earlier, it could be dangerous."

She brushed the hair back from one of his ears. "Oh, so now you're an expert on pregnancy?"

"That's exactly what I am." One of them had to think about the consequences, although he'd be damned if he could think at all with her so soft and warm in his arms, her scent wrapping itself around him.

She put her mouth to his ear and whispered, "But there are so many things I want to do to you tonight. And want you to do to me."

He groaned, thinking of any number of things he'd like to indulge in, as well. "Stop trying to seduce me, Eglantine. I told you I don't like aggressive women."

"And I told you that I don't like men who shove their tongues down my throat without permission," she said, slipping one hand into his shirt to stroke his nipple.

Blood instantly raced to his sex, and he was aware once again of that primal need to have her, possess her, tame the storm that lived within her.

"I haven't shoved my tongue down your throat," he said, his voice thick with want and desire. He entered their bedroom and set her on her feet.

"Not yet, but you're about to," she said, wiggling against him, her hands in his hair as she pulled him down.

She was right. He couldn't kiss her without tasting her, reveling in the sweetness of her mouth.

"Make love to me," she purred, and he couldn't resist her.

"I don't want to hurt you."

"You won't." Her hands stroked him through the material of his trousers, her mouth warm on his as she released him into her hands. "I want to watch you, though. I want you on top."

He looked down at her big belly even as he stripped her of the soft dress she'd put on after her bath. He looked at the bed, taking a quick visual measurement, then scanned the room before reaching behind her to get a couple of pillows and the body pillow she used when she didn't have him to rest her belly on, arranging them on the desk that sat in the corner. "You will tell me if anything hurts. You will tell me if anything is even vaguely uncomfortable."

"Oooh," she said, looking interested as he dragged a blanket over and laid it on top of the pillow nest. "Kinky! I like how you think."

"Hardly kinky, but if you want me on top, this is the best I can do." He removed the rest of his clothing, helping her up onto the desk. "Are you comfortable? Does that hurt your back? Is the table too close to the wall?"

"Yacky," she said, grabbing him by his hips and pulling her toward him. "Too much talking, not enough making your wife wild with pleasure."

He was hot and hard and just wanted to lose himself in her heat, but now was not the time for that. He slid his hands up her thighs until she opened for him, his penis rubbing against her belly as he braced his hands on either side of her, leaning down to swirl his tongue over one nipple.

"Oh god," she moaned, relaxing against the wedge of pillows he'd created for her. Her legs slid along his as she dug her fingers into the muscles of his shoulders, her touch sending little rivulets of fire straight to his groin. He wanted her ready for him, so he set about driving her wild, using his hands and mouth to stir her passions until her body was writhing on the pillows and she demanded that he take care of her right that moment before she died of frustration.

He kept his stroke shallow, the sensation of her full womb almost driving him past the bearing point as he moved slowly, watching her eyes go all dewy and soft when she pulled him down for a kiss even as her muscles tightened around him, sending a shudder of exquisite pleasure through him.

"Now that," she told him later as she snuggled into bed and settled herself against and on him, "was one hell of a wedding night, and well worth all the waiting."

He lay awake late into the night, just listening to her breathing, stroking the warm flesh of her body that he knew as well as his own.

Chapter 22

The problem of Theo niggled at Harry's mind, and she never was one to tolerate a niggle for long.

Something was up with him and Iakovos. Theo's return for their wedding apparently signaled some sort of a change in the brothers' relationship. Theo seemed to lose his lighthearted, semi-flirtatious self to a darker, more somber version who spent his time casting sour looks at both her and Iakovos.

"I'm glad you're home again," Harry had told him two days after she and Iakovos had returned to Athens following a honeymoon spent in blissful happiness on the island. "Did you have a good time in Brazil?"

"Don't you mean am I drinking again?" he asked, his eyes angry.

"That isn't what I meant at all. I was just inquiring if you had a good time while you were wheeling and dealing in São Paolo. Theo . . ." She hated to be the cause of any sort of strife between him and Iakovos. "I worry about you. I know you think you're perfectly in control, but sometimes people need a little help with . . . things."

"You'd like that, wouldn't you? To see me shut away in some clinic?" He started to turn away from her, but stopped when she put her hand on his arm.

"No, of course I don't want that. I really don't want you unhappy, you know."

He swung around, his eyes blazing, and she knew real fear a second before he shoved her against the wall, his fingers biting into her shoulders as he ground his mouth against hers.

She tried to shift so she could get her knee up, but her body was slow and awkward these days. It was all she could do to wrestle one arm free to grab his hair, and try to yank his horrible mouth off hers.

Suddenly he was gone, and she gasped for air, wiping her mouth with her sleeve, shaking with horror as Dmitri stood with his back to her, shielding her from Theo.

Theo's lip was split, blood dripping down onto his shirtfront.

"I don't have an issue with you, Dmitri," he snarled. "Stay the hell out of my business."

"I sure as hell have one with you," Dmitri answered, and nailed Theo with a punishing right.

Theo looked surprised for a half second before collapsing.

"Man, I wish I could have done that," Harry said, more than a little shaky. She rubbed her arms as Dmitri turned back to her, his face black with anger.

"Did he hurt you?"

"No. Just scared the crap out of me. He's been drinking again, Dmitri. I could . . . taste it." She shuddered at the memory of his hard mouth on hers. "Oh god, Iakovos is going to kill him."

Dmitri looked grim as he bent down, hoisting his cousin over his shoulder. "It'll serve him right for going after you that way."

"It's not me he's trying to hurt." Harry tried to get a grip on herself. "He's just using me to strike out at Iakovos."

"This can't go on," Dmitri said, gesturing toward the fallen Theo. "I'll tell Iakovos."

"No." She came to a decision. "I will. You get him out of the way. Hopefully he'll have enough sense to lay low for a bit."

"He's not to be trusted, Harry."

"I know. But he needs help, Dmitri, not banishment or worse. I'll talk to Iakovos. I'll get him to see reason."

She spent the rest of the day online, doing some shopping for much-needed baby furniture and accoutrements but spending the bulk of her time using a translating service to read about various alcoholic treatment centers in Greece.

By the time she climbed into bed, she'd come to a decision. Iakovos held a book on his lap, obviously having just stuffed one of hers under the pillow.

"Enjoying that?" she asked, nodding at the book.

"It's excellent," he said, glancing at the book, then sliding her a look out of the corner of his eye as he turned it right side up.

"I'm so glad. That's one of my favorite authors, too. Have you ever heard of a place called the Neo Center?"

He started to answer, but stopped when his gaze narrowed on her shoulders. "You hurt yourself?" he asked, nodding toward them.

She looked down and realized that Theo's grip had given her little bruises on either arm. "Uh . . . yeah."

"What did you do?"

"Um . . . I don't really remember," she said, miserable. She hated lying, and especially hated doing it to Iakovos.

"Eglantine," he said, setting the book down and turning to face her. "You will cease lying to me. What happened to your arms?"

"Yacky—" she began, trying to think of something she might have done.

"No, Harry," he said, lifting her chin so he could stare into her eyes. "The truth."

She took a long, sorrowful breath. "Theo—"

That was all she got out. He snarled in Greek what she knew was a really rude word, then snatched up a silk bathrobe and headed straight to Theo's bedroom.

"Wait!" Harry yelled, fighting to get out of bed. "It takes me longer to get up, damn you! Iakovos! Don't you do anything until I get there!"

She struggled into her own bathrobe as she followed, running barefoot after him. Theo wasn't in his room, and for a moment she thought perhaps he'd gone, but a roar of anger from the living room told her that Iakovos had found his brother.

She got to them just as Iakovos ripped a bottle of vodka from Theo's hand and smashed it against the wall opposite. Harry stared in shock; she'd never seen Iakovos so angry before. He snarled something in Greek to Theo, who answered in kind, shoving his brother away and stalking toward the bar.

Iakovos yelled again, and the two started going at it hammer and tongs. Harry stood in the hallway, one hand clutching the neck of her bathrobe as the two brothers screamed at each other. She didn't need to speak the language to know that Iakovos was furious and telling Theo that his drinking days were over.

Theo made the mistake of yelling something at the same time he reached across the bar for a bottle. Iakovos roared in fury, shoving him aside to snatch up the bottles that sat in a tidy row, hurling accusations as he threw each bottle against the stone wall.

Mrs. Avrabos appeared in the door that led to the kitchen and her own rooms. Her eyes were huge as she watched Iakovos destroy every bottle of liquor in the house. Her gaze slipped back to Harry, who said quietly, "I'm sorry you have to see this."

"It is time," the older woman said with a nod toward Iakovos before silently slipping back into the kitchen.

Theo stumbled away from Iakovos as the last bottle shattered against the wall. The brown and white stones were stained with every color possible, greens and reds of liquors mingling garishly with wine, rum, and even beer, the whole dripping into a huge, muddy pool on the floor. Glass lay splintered everywhere, an ugly, stark reminder of Iakovos' fury in the middle of an otherwise pristine room.

Iakovos turned toward her, his face hard, his eyes glittering as if lit from deep within. He caught sight of her and yelled at Theo, "If you lay so much as one finger on my wife again, I'll kill you myself!"

She didn't say a word when he put his hand on her

back and gently pushed her toward their room. She did glance back to see Theo standing in the middle of the room, his pants splattered with alcohol, his head down.

She wanted to talk to Iakovos, to reassure him that she was fine, that Theo could be helped, but one look at his tight jaw told her that talk was not going to happen. She let him help her into bed, then lay with him curled behind her, his hand protectively over her belly.

She'd wait until the morning, and then she would try to reason with both men.

"Well, this is a surprise," she said eight hours later, when she staggered out to the kitchen in search of a hot cup of tea.

Iakovos stood at one counter, a mug in one hand, a breakfast roll in the other as he eyed the financial pages of a newspaper spread out before him. Mrs. Avrabos bustled around looking happy, the smell of cinnamon and orange filling the kitchen. On the other side of Iakovos, Dmitri stood with his laptop propped up on a stack of newspapers, a cinnamon roll hanging from his mouth as he typed furiously.

"What's a surprise?" Iakovos asked, glancing up and giving her a little waggle of his eyebrows.

She tried not to grin. She'd woken up early in a strange mood, half aroused but feeling too heavy and awkward to benefit from any attentions Iakovos would pay her. So instead, she saw to it that he started his morning in a way guaranteed to put him in a good mood.

"Well, for one, you're in a suit, and I thought you were going to take me shopping today because you secretly fear our babies will be sleeping in drawers because we have no furniture for them—not, I'd like to

point out, that it's all my fault, since Patricia is dragging
her feet with her decorating bit, but still, you're in the
suit that makes you look like your name should be
Adonis Adonisopolis, and back on the bachelor list.
Which means you've got meetings on your agenda today, and not baby shopping. And for another, there's
him." She nodded to where Theo sat at the small kitchen
table, sipping coffee.

"What about him?" Iakovos asked.

"I assumed after the row last night that you guys
weren't speaking to each other."

All three men looked surprised. Mrs. Avrabos shook
her head, and offered her a freshly made orange roll
from a plate piled high with them. Harry, feeling it was a
sin against nature to turn down any fresh-baked item,
took the entire plate and sat down with it.

"Of course we're speaking," Iakovos said, giving her
an odd look.

"Yeah, but you were yelling at each other. You trashed
all the booze in the house."

"We're Greek, sweetheart. We yell when we get angry," Iakovos said, turning his attention back to the
newspaper.

"You know, if I said something that stereotypical,
you'd never let me hear the end of it," she said, glancing
at Theo.

He gave her a long look, then put down his mug, and
got to his knees, taking her hand in his. "I'm very sorry
about yesterday, Harry. Jake was right—I was out of
control, and I feel awful that you got the brunt of that. I
swear to you that it won't happen again. Forgive me?"

He smiled up at her with the old Theo charm, and although she couldn't help but feel that alcoholics did not reform so quickly as that, she was so relieved to see the return of his normal self that she didn't quibble. "Of course I will, although you don't have to be on your knees. You look like you're going to propose to me."

He laughed and kissed the back of her hand, his eyes dancing as he said, "Maybe I should. Would you leave that old man for me, hmm?"

"Not in a million years. I happen to be madly in love with that old man."

Iakovos shot her an indignant look.

"That incredibly sexy, devastatingly handsome, formerly ranked five most hunkalicious man of the year, I should say."

Iakovos nodded, setting down his coffee mug, and before Harry could say anything more, he swooped down on her, making her giggle as he snogged her neck.

"I do have meetings today, my tempestuous beauty, but I have not forgotten your doctor's appointment this afternoon. In addition, I am happy to lend you Mikos to take you around to the shops so my poor children don't have to sleep in cardboard boxes."

"What you could do is prod Patricia. I've left her three voice mails in the last few days, and she's not answering any of them. I think she's deliberately trying to punish us."

"I'm sure she'll get to it," was all he said before heading to the living room. "I'll tell Mikos to come back here after he drops us off."

"You don't need to do that," she answered, feeling restless for some reason.

"I don't, but I am."

Harry watched as he stuffed his laptop into a bag, shuffled through a few papers and tossed them into his briefcase. He looked every inch a billionaire business-man, ready to make deals that would boggle the mortal mind. Who would he be meeting with today? Some equally rich Arab looking for a new real estate invest-ment? An Asian conglomerate that wanted a new re-sort? Or perhaps some überskinny, nonpregnant blond heiress who saw him in a magazine and instantly desired his manly body? "I just bet she does," she muttered.

He gave her a knowing eye. "You're writing dialogue in your head again, aren't you?"

"Yes."

"I liked it better when your mouth told me what you were thinking," he grumbled.

"Oh, trust me, my love," she said, slipping her arm through his. "In this case, you really don't. Would it do any good to point out that I'm perfectly able to drive myself now that I have a driver's license here?"

"Would that be the same driver's license that you couldn't obtain until you called me up to ask how to spell your last name?"

She flared her nostrils at him. "The clerk was being obnoxious about it. And besides, I don't know why I have to be able to spell everything! I'm a writer! Spell-check is my best friend!"

"The answer is no, Harry," he said with a pointed look at her massive stomach.

"Pregnant women can drive," she pointed out.

"Not *my* pregnant woman," he said, and patted her on the butt as he left, Dmitri following with a wink at her.

Theo was a few steps behind them, pausing as he glanced back at Harry. "Friends again?"

"Of course," she said, telling herself she was an idiot to be uneasy.

"If there's one thing I've learned over the years," Harry told Mikos a couple of hours later, "it's to pick my battles. There's simply no sense in making a big deal over the fact that your boss wants me to be driven everywhere."

"I hope not," Mikos said as he gestured toward the waiting limo. "Good jobs are hard to find these days."

"It's just that I feel so . . . ugh . . . movie star in a limo. Can we take that other car, the smaller one?"

"The BMW?" Mikos shrugged. "It's up to you."

She was soon settled in the much more—to her mind anyway—reasonable car, and consulting a list she had printed the day before, she spent the morning crossing off a significant number of items before deciding she had earned a little reward for such hard work. "What do you think, Mikos? Lunch at the café next to the Archaeological Museum? The one on Patission Street? We can grab a quick lunch there before tackling the last few things on the list."

"Whatever you like, pretty lady." Mikos hummed along to a song on the radio. She had to admit that she was grateful Iakovos had insisted she take Mikos for the day—not only had it been less stressful to be driven than to cope with the noise and traffic of Athens, but he'd served as an excellent translator when needed.

All in all, she was pleased with herself. That feeling stayed with her until Mikos announced that there was no parking near the café. "I will drop you off in front of it and find somewhere else to park."

"Sounds good. I am feeling the heat a bit today, so I really don't relish the thought of walking out in that sun too long."

He dropped her off about half a block from the café, reminding her to take her sun hat.

"Yes, Mother," she said, smiling at him as she jammed the straw hat on her head. "Don't be long. I'm starved."

She strolled down the block, glancing at a few windows, but more interested in the people than anything else. As she approached the café, she knew she'd have to use the bathroom, so she stepped around the tables into the cooler interior. As she was about to ask a waitress where the bathroom was, she caught sight of a familiar shape leaning over one of the small tables . . . and a tiny little blond bit of fluff with her head so close to his, they were touching.

"OK, Harry," she said out loud, ignoring the waitress as she stared at the couple. "This isn't the end of the world. They work together. There's no reason they shouldn't be here having lunch. Just because he's married and about to become the father to twins doesn't mean he can't have lunch with a former girlfriend."

Brave words, a little voice in her head said as she watched them, hurt pricking the edges of her heart, those cryptic words spoken on the day of her wedding coming back to her.

Does she know?

No.

You are going to tell her soon, I hope.

Dear god, could she have been wrong all along about

Iakovos? No, that was insane. She wasn't wrong. She felt it in her bones. But something was up, and dammit, she wanted to know what. Should I go over and say hi, she thought to herself, and ask Iakovos what the hell he's doing? Or pass by with a friendly wave, as if it's nothing to me that they're here, practically kissing, right in front of everyone? Or, she thought with a sigh, simply go home and remind myself that I trust him.

"God, I hate being adult sometimes," she snarled as she turned on her heel and went to find Mikos.

Chapter 23

"Change of plans," Harry told Mikos with a smile that she knew was too bright to be convincing. She took his arm and steered him in the opposite direction. "Let's go to that other place, the one with the yummy calamari."

He seemed surprised by her change of heart, especially since all she did was pick at the food, but Harry was too angry with herself to eat.

She finished her shopping with grim efficiency and returned home for a short rest. As she entered the apartment, she found Mrs. Avrabos scrubbing the stone wall. The glass and pool of liquor had long since been cleaned up, but a faint pink still stained the stone, which evidently insulted Mrs. Avrabos' sensibilities.

"You don't have to do that," Harry said with an indignant look at the wall, as if it personally offended her. And why shouldn't it? she thought to herself. The whole apartment offended her. Damn that Patricia! Damn Iakovos!

Harry closed her eyes for a minute, suddenly so tired

she felt as if she could sleep for a solid month. Just exactly what *was* Iakovos doing having an intimate lunch with Patricia? Unable to keep the little spike of jealousy from pricking at her despite her promise to the contrary, she pulled out her phone and dialed a familiar number.

"Hi," she said, when Iakovos answered. "I don't suppose you're free for lunch today?"

"I'm sorry, sweetheart, but I've got solid meetings all day. Speaking of that—would you be angry with me if I couldn't go to the doctor with you this afternoon?"

"You don't want to go see the scan?"

"Of course I want to, but things are insane here today. Bring me the pictures, and I'll look at them tonight, all right?"

"Sure," she said, not liking the emotions that were roiling around inside her. "I'll see you later."

"All right. Harry?"

"Yes?"

"Are you well? Your voice sounds strained. You're not trying to do too much, are you?"

Would a man who was out having a sneaky lunch with an ex-lover ask if you were doing too much, the voice in her head asked her. No, he would not. "I'm fine. Just a little grouchy. You know shopping makes me cranky."

Harry hung up the phone, out of the blue wondering why he couldn't tell her he loved her. At first she had assumed it was a little game he was playing, his way of getting back at her when she teased him mercilessly about something or other.

But all of a sudden, his inability to say it took on huge

importance. "How dare he?" she yelled once she got to the privacy of their bedroom, and promptly hit the RE-DIAL button.

"What is it, Harry?" he asked, his voice tinged with the tiniest bit of annoyance.

"Why the hell can't you tell me you love me?" she shouted into the phone. "What's wrong with you that you can't say the words?"

Silence was the answer for a good ten seconds. "You want me to tell you that I love you right now?"

"Yes!" she said, brushing away a couple of errant tears. "Yes, I do. I think you should tell me right this very second that you love me, because frankly, I'm tired of waiting for you to get around to remembering it."

More silence. "Are you angry with me about something?"

"Say the words!" she demanded, tears streaming down her face now.

"All right. Harry, I—"

"No!" she shrieked, interrupting him. "Don't you say it! Not like that! Never mind. Just ignore me. The pregnancy hormones are making me insane. Good-bye. Have a good . . . meeting."

She hung up before he could say anything more, then turned off her phone in case he tried to call her.

"Well, as long as I'm making a mess of my life, I might as well go share my gloom," she said, a sense of righteousness filling her as she stomped out to the living room. She glared at all the offending pieces of furniture made of leather, black glass, and gleaming silver.

"Mrs. Avrabos?" she yelled, her hands on her hips as she stood in the center of the room.

"Yes? You wish something?" the housekeeper emerged from the kitchen, wiping her hands on a little towel.

"I want movers in here this afternoon. Tell them to take everything out of here, every single piece of furniture, every lamp, every picture, every postmodernistic piece of crap artwork."

The housekeeper gave a confused look around the room. "You want the things . . . removed?"

"Yes, I do. Each and every item here offends me on a personal level that I can't begin to describe. They blight my existence. I want them gone in the next three hours. I am going to take a bath and then see the doctor, and when I get back, this room had better be empty."

Mrs. Avrabos nodded, watching with an open mouth as Harry charged down the hall toward the bedroom, pausing at Theo's room to yell, "You'd better be sober when you get home, Theo, because if you get drunk again, I'll lay you out so you won't ever get up."

Mrs. Avrabos wondered to herself if the *kyria* knew Theo had left, then decided that it really didn't matter. She would enjoy seeing the Kyrie's face when he came home to find his living room gone.

"He loves me, dammit!" she heard Harry yelling from the bedroom. "I know he does! He can just bloody well get with the program and tell me!"

Mrs. Avrabos smiled. She remembered the first few months of her marriage. She recalled doing a little shouting of her own, then. It was the way of things.

Harry said several rude things to no one in particular as she stripped off her clothes and turned on the tub with the wonderful jets that would help relax some of the tension she felt simmering along her skin like electricity.

Mikos was waiting for her when she was once again dressed. She nodded to the three men in overalls who were in the process of moving furniture out of the living room, saying nothing to Mrs. Avrabos but that she wanted pizza for dinner, and she didn't particularly give a damn if Iakovos didn't like it.

Her scan was amazing. She could actually see the twins as individual babies now, tucked away safe as they waited in her belly. She was overwhelmed by the thought of them, overjoyed that they were healthy, and furious at the man who had given them to her because he wasn't there to see them.

She had the technician save a copy of the video for her on a DVD, which she asked Mikos to drop off at the office after he took her home.

She ate her pizza in solitary grandeur, occasionally glancing at the text from Iakovos. *Late meeting. Don't wait dinner.* The bastard.

She fell asleep immediately after eating, and was only dimly aware of Iakovos stroking her back later, asking her if she was hungry.

"Just tired," she said, trying to find a position that was comfortable. He helped adjust pillows under and around her belly until she could relax again. She woke up in the middle of the night, her bladder about ready to burst, Iakovos sound asleep next to her.

She stared at his face for a minute, wondering if she would ever get tired of looking at him. He was so beautiful—how could any woman resist him? And did she really want to spend the rest of her life worrying about what woman was sharpening her claws in an attempt to get them into him?

"Yes," she said, brushing a bit of hair back off his brow. "But you could be a little less perfect, you know. You could get a beer belly. You could grow a wart on the end of your nose. You could snore."

He didn't wake up, just made a comfy noise when he turned his face into where her hand was stroking his hair. It was a little noise, a wordless, brief expression of comfort, something he probably never in a million years knew he was making, but it went straight to her heart. No man could make that noise and not mean it.

"You love me," she said, pressing a little kiss to his head before sliding carefully off the bed so as not to wake him. She visited the bathroom, then suddenly hungry, went out to the kitchen and made herself three sandwiches, all of which she ate while sitting on the patio, staring out into the warm Greek night.

Iakovos stood next to the bed the following morning, looking down at his wife as she slept, snoring gently into his pillow, which she had confiscated at some point during the night. That was a regular occurrence of late—frequently he woke up to find himself pillowless, and Harry draped over every available pillow on the bed, her face buried in his.

He stroked her cheek, so soft, so sweet, and wondered why she had chosen yesterday to storm. Something had set her off, that much was clear, but just what it was eluded him. A brief conversation with Mikos had deter-

mined that at some point during the day, something upset her, but Mikos had no idea what it was, either.

It was probably the upcoming birth. No doubt she
was annoyed that he had been forced to miss going with
her to the doctor. She hadn't even called him to tell him
about the scan, nor had she put a note in with the DVD
Mikos delivered. But Harry wasn't the type to remain
silent when angry, and she knew he was trying to get
through a couple of ticklish deals.

Perhaps it was the language barrier. Although they had
been attending prenatal classes, he had to translate all the
instructions for her, and he knew it was frustrating to her.
Maybe she was just stressed by all of that. He would insist
that she hire an assistant of her own. He couldn't spare
Dmitri right now, when negotiations were so critical, but
there was nothing to stop her from getting her own assistant to help with things until she learned enough Greek to
get around.

"Harry."

"Nrf."

He smiled and stroked his fingers down the velvety
softness of her upper arm. "Is there something you want
to tell me, Harry?"

She opened her eyes, blinked to get him in focus, and
frowned. "What?"

"The living room." He sat on the edge of the bed, one
of his hands on her belly. He loved touching it, loved
feeling the occasional kicks and movements of the babies.

"What are you talking about?" she asked, groggy
from being woken out of a deep sleep. She blinked at

him a couple more times. "You must be going to work. You're in another one of those gorgeous suits."

He looked down at the navy suit. She'd given it to him for his birthday, saying that when he wore it with his hair swept back off his brow, his beautiful eyes, and perfect face, he looked like a model headed for a Paris runway. "I have to leave for work, yes. The living room, Harry?"

"What about it?"

"It appears to be gone."

"Don't be ridiculous," she said, falling back into the nest of pillows. "Rooms don't just disappear."

"They do if you call up movers and demand they take everything out of them."

A memory of her brainstorm the previous day obviously returned, for Harry struggled to sit up. He slid an arm behind her, helping her upright. "Oh. That. I . . . er . . ."

"I know you're anxious for Patricia to redecorate, but don't you think we should have new furniture before you move the old out?" he asked with a little smile.

The look she gave him was almost stricken. "I don't know what I was thinking. I'll have everything put back."

"There's no need. I'm having that done this morning." He stroked her cheek again. "Are you feeling well?"

"Yes. Just tired." She lay back, her eyes cloudy. He wondered what it was that was bothering her, but a reminder chirp from his phone warned him he'd have to leave now if he wanted to make the first of what would be many meetings that day.

"I'll be home for dinner," he said, leaning forward to kiss her sweet lips. "Wait for me?"

"Till the end of time," she answered, her lips curving under his.

He left with only the slightest sense of unease.

Harry called herself every name she could think of, and quite a few that came to her in moments of inspiration. How on earth could she even entertain the slightest suspicion that he was doing anything wrong when he was just as perfect as any husband could be? He was loving, he was thoughtful . . . he was her Iakovos, and nothing short of a signed, notarized statement by Iakovos and twelve independent witnesses saying he was having an affair would convince her otherwise.

"You could have just asked him what he was doing," she told her reflection as she brushed her teeth with her favorite cinnamon-flavored toothpaste. "Heaven knows you blurt out everything else to him."

Her reflection made a face.

"Yeah," she agreed with a sigh. "He would have been insulted to think I suspected him. Better to just keep your trap shut."

It was easier said than done, however. Especially when she returned home from shopping for the last few items needed for the nursery and she found Theo standing in the newly restored living room, his back to her as he spoke on the phone. She hadn't intended to eavesdrop, but when you walk into a room and you hear someone mention your name, it's hard not to stand and listen.

"—what if Harry finds out? No, of course I won't tell her, but she's smart, Jake, and she's bound to notice if you're not around much at night. My advice is to get Patricia out of your little love nest and just let Harry make a decision about what she wants to do."

Love nest? Patricia? Harry stared in openmouthed horror at Theo's back, then quietly, without making a solitary sound, slipped out the door. Iakovos wasn't planning on being around much at night? Where was he going to be? At his little love nest with Patricia?

She felt for a moment like her head was going to explode, then decided she had to do something. She loved Iakovos. He loved her. She knew that. But if he thought he could have a fling with Patricia at the same time, well, he just had better readjust his thought processes.

She flung open the door, making sure it slammed against the wall before strolling into the apartment.

"Hi, Harry," Theo said, spinning around as he put his phone away, guilt all over his face.

"Sober today, are you?" she asked with acid coolness.

He flashed her one of those heart-stopping grins that might have affected another woman, but not her.

Love nest? With Patricia? *Really?* That's the best he could do? If he was going to cheat on her, at least he could do it with someone spectacular, like royalty.

"I'm running some potential investors around town, so I figured I'd better be on my A-game. Thought I would show them the Parthenon. You want to come with us?"

"Another time perhaps. I'm going to be busy today." The doorman came up laden with the strollers, cradles, and changing tables she'd picked up.

"Ah. Baby stuff," he said, nodding as he scooted around the stream of men hauling the furniture in.

She directed them to the appropriate room, muttering to herself as she watched Theo slip out the door,

"That and I'm going have a long talk with your brother about whether he wants to keep that remaining testicle."

He called in the afternoon to say that he wouldn't, after all, be able to make dinner, but he'd be home before she went to bed.

During the intervening hours, she worked up and discarded any number of scenarios, some of them quite inventive in the revenge she was going to take. She was particularly fond of the one where she had him tied to a rock in the middle of the ocean, with a pack of hungry sharks circling around him.

"Hello, sweetheart. You look divine," he said wearily as he came in, tossing down his laptop bag and briefcase.

Harry watched silently as he collapsed onto the couch. His face looked drawn, the skin beneath his eyes appeared bruised. That's what burning the candle on both ends did to you, she thought to herself as she moved toward him.

"Did you have dinner?"

He nodded, closing his eyes as he leaned back. "Could you get me a couple of pain tablets? I've got a hell of a headache."

"Good."

He opened his eyes, lifting his head to squint at her. "Is something the matter?"

"Oh, yes."

He sighed and closed his eyes. "Not Theo again?"

"No, it's not Theo. How do you want to do this, Iakovos, the civilized way or the quick way?"

"Do what?" he asked, his hands rubbing his temples.

"Discuss your girlfriend."

His hands froze. "You saw us yesterday."

"Yes, I did."

He swore in Greek, looking at her with weary resignation. "Mikos told me today where you were planning on having lunch yesterday. I figured since you hadn't tried to come at me with a blunt instrument, you must not have seen us."

"Civilized or quick, Iakovos?" she asked again.

"How about neither?" he said, with a little smile.

"You really don't want that one remaining testicle, do you?" she said, coming toward him with murder in her eyes.

He laughed, grabbing her arms when she was within reach, easing her down so she was straddling his legs. "Does your back hurt?"

"Yes, you bastard. What's going on, Iakovos?"

He raised his eyebrows. "What, you don't think I'm cheating on you?"

"Of course I don't think you're cheating on me." She was silent for a moment. "You're not, are you?"

"No, I'm not. How about we make a deal—you rub my head, and I'll rub your back."

"Your testicle is at stake here, may I remind you, Mr. Papadomomu. There had better be one hell of an explanation to go along with that backrub."

"For the sake of any future children we might want, I will do my best, Mrs. Papaioannou." His hands were warm on her back as he tipped her forward until she was leaning against his chest. She put her thumbs against his temples and started rubbing in little circles.

"Your meetings with Patricia—are they related to work?"

"Yes, they are."

"Is she decorating a love nest for you?"

His eyebrows rose for a moment, then settled back down. "Theo."

"Yes. I overheard him this afternoon."

"Ah." He nodded tiredly. "Yes, she's decorating an apartment for me."

"And the work on that has been taking you there at night?"

"Yes. We've been so busy during the day with the two mergers and the acquisition, the only time I had to see Patricia was the occasional lunch and at night."

"You're very close to being a eunuch," Harry warned him, striving to keep both her voice and her hands gentle on his head.

He smiled, damn his delicious hide.

"Are you planning on living in this apartment that your ex-girlfriend is decorating for you at night?"

He nodded, his eyes closed.

She was silent for a few minutes, thinking about him, thinking about them. "It's for me, isn't it?"

His eyes opened, and she saw the exhaustion in them, but she also saw the love that shone so brightly that it warmed her to the tips of her toes. "Yes. You never seemed to like this place, and since it's Elena's and Theo's home as well as ours, I thought you would want a place just for us and the babies."

"I am happy to tell you that your testicle's future is now secure. Oh, Iakovos. I would love a little place just for the four of us. Not that I don't love Elena and Theo, but this has never really seemed like home."

"I know. That's why I wanted Patricia to decorate it.

Despite your feelings about her, she really is a talented decorator. It was just ironic that you had the same thought at the same time."

"So she's not going to redecorate this place?"

"She will, but I wanted ours done first."

"That's why she has been dragging her feet," Harry mused, feeling a hundred times like a fool.

A tired little smile pulled at one side of his mouth, his hands warm on her legs. "She thought I should tell you about the apartment, but I figured if she got your opinion on things using this one as an excuse, I could surprise you with it."

Does she know?

No.

You are going to tell her soon, I hope.

"Oh. You did surprise me." Understatement of the year, Harry.

"Mm-hmm." His eyes were closed again, his head back against the cushions of the suede couch as she rubbed his temples. His hands went slack on her legs.

He had done it all for her. He was working insane hours to try to build in some time to take off for the babies' arrival and to give her a home that she could love. He did all that, and still tried to give her everything else she needed from him—his time, his love, his devotion.

She leaned forward and said, "I love you, Iakovos Panagiotis Okeanos Papaioannou," before kissing him.

He gave a little jerk, waking himself up. "Sorry? Did you say something?"

"No." She got off his lap and held out her hand. "Come on, sleepyhead. Bedtime for you."

Chapter 24

The day he was finally going to let Harry see the apartment that he had worked so hard to get ready for her dawned with the promise of being a wholly glorious one, filled with her excitement, but life, as he was later to note, has a way of promising one thing and delivering another.

It was, in fact, the worst day of his life, surpassing the day his stepmother died of cancer, the day his father died from drinking himself to death, and the day he woke up in the hospital to be told he had lost a testicle and would never father children.

"Please, Yacky," Harry had begged him as he was leaving, batting her lashes at him and trying to look seductive despite the big belly and the fact that her hair, always a barometer of her inner tempest, was pulled back into a demure ponytail. "You went to all this work for me. I want to see it. I want to plan where to put all the baby things in it."

"You'll see it soon enough," he said, nibbling on her lower lip. "Patricia says the last of it should be installed today, and then it will be perfect for you."

"Just remember your promise," she told him with an arrogance that he found endearing. "She can't touch you. She can't put her head near yours. She can't kiss you."

"You're adorable, do you know that?" he said, kissing her, then collecting his laptop, briefcase, and a grinning Dmitri.

"Now would be a good time to tell me you love me!" she bellowed after him.

He gave her a cheery wave.

She yelled an obscenity in Greek.

He stopped at the door, gave Dmitri a long look, and made a mental note to line up a tutor for her.

"Can you take a break this afternoon?" Patricia asked him later that morning. She stood in his office, toying with the picture on his desk before she realized it was one of Harry that he'd taken out on one of his boats, her hair blowing around her as she laughed up at him. With a grimace, Patricia dropped the picture and leaned a hip against his desk.

"Is it done?"

"Done and ready for the walk-through. Sign off on it today, and it's all yours. Or rather, all Harry's."

Iakovos was silent for a few seconds before saying, "We wouldn't have suited, Patricia."

She shrugged a negligent shoulder. "No, we wouldn't have. But that doesn't mean I have to greet your blushing—if gigantic—bride with open arms."

"You like her, don't you?" he asked, leaning back in his chair, wondering how it was that he knew. Patricia had always been very careful to keep him at an emotional distance. It was one of the reasons their time together had come to an end, and why he fell so instantly in love with the unrestrained Harry.

"Of course I don't." She looked out of his window, her face serene. "She's horrid."

"She likes you, too."

Her gaze shot to his face. "You evidently haven't been on the receiving end of her slaps if you think that."

"She's a wild one, my Harry," he agreed. "She doesn't hold back."

Patricia sighed, slumping slightly. "She's perfect for you. And absolutely head over heels in love with you. You deserve each other. I just hope she appreciates all the work I put into making her a perfect home to love you in."

"She'll appreciate it." He sat up, consulting his calendar. "I'll cancel a meeting and be there at four."

He didn't tell Harry it was ready. He just sent her a text to tell her to expect him for dinner. After rushing through an important consultation and pretending that the connection to a Singapore client was sufficiently poor that it made a conversation impossible, he hurried out to the apartment.

He found nothing wanting, and immediately put in a call for Mikos to pick up Harry and bring her to their new home.

"I hope she likes it," Patricia said, making a face as she stood in the living room. "As much as it's costing you."

He looked around the comfortable room done in shades of eggshell, soft green, and marine blue. The apartment was half the size of his penthouse, with a master bedroom, nursery, and two guest rooms, one of which he had converted into an office for Harry. Two additional staff rooms were located on the other side of the apartment, one for a nanny, the other for a housekeeper.

"She'll love it," he said, filled with confidence. "She'll love everything about it."

Mikos called shortly after that. "I'm stuck in traffic," he said, yelling over the sound of sirens and horns blaring. "Explosion at a petrol station. We'll be here for hours."

Iakovos swore and told him to keep trying to get through. He was about to dial Dmitri when he remembered that he'd sent his cousin to Corinth for the day.

He called home. "Sweetheart, can you get a cab and come out to me?" He gave her the address.

"To the new apartment?" she shrieked, deafening him for a few seconds. "I'll be right there! Sooner!"

"I doubt that. There's been an explosion, and Mikos says traffic is backed up everywhere. Tell the cab to go via the north and you may miss it."

"I'll be there faster than you can say 'billionaire Greek playboy,'" she promised, and hung up.

He paced the length of the house, sitting in the little garden that was the main element that had attracted him to the apartment. That and the view of the Acropolis.

The sun started setting, and still Harry wasn't there. He texted her to find out where she was, receiving an immediate reply that they were caught in the traffic that he had warned her about, but that she should be there in the next hour.

The next hour came and went, and night began to fall. He swore to himself and called Harry to find out where she was. He'd go out to find her himself.

There was no reply. Nor was there a reply when he tried to text her. A call home was likewise not answered.

Where the hell was she? He was just trying the figure the likeliest route the cab would have taken when his phone rang with a number he didn't recognize.

"Mr. Papaioannou?" a cool voice asked.

"Yes? Who is this?"

"I'm the admitting doctor at the Agsavvas Hospital. We have a woman here identified as Eglantine Papaioannou. She's been in an accident—"

He listened to the voice telling him that Harry had been in a car with Theo at the wheel, a car that slammed into a light pole, leaving him with a broken collarbone and Harry unconscious, and possibly bleeding internally.

He couldn't speak, couldn't think. His heart stopped— nothing seemed real as he gave permission to save her life no matter at what cost. His storm couldn't die down, fading into nothing. He wouldn't let her leave him. Not now, not ever.

Two extraordinarily horrible hours later, he shoved a handful of money at the cab that had crawled its way to the hospital, and lurched into the emergency room.

He heard her yelling even before he took three steps.

"I don't care what you say, I am not having those babies before my husband gets here, do you understand me? No, I will not push! In fact, I'm sucking them back up into me, so you can just put the salad tongs away, because I refuse, I absolutely refuse to have these babies until Iakovos is here!"

He sank to his knees for a moment, his head bowed in

silent prayer as he heard the anger in her voice, her wonderfully belligerent voice. His storm, his tempest was alive and fighting, and that's all he asked for.

It took him a minute, but he managed to get to his feet again. "Eglantine," he said, rounding the corner of the room.

Her face, bruised and cut, lit up with joy as she saw him. "Yacky! Where the hell have you been?"

"Thought I'd take a stroll around the block. So you decided to have the babies early, did you?"

She grabbed him by his shirt, pulling her toward him, licking the spot above his upper lip, then kissing him with a ferocity that he more than matched. He wrapped his arms around her, ignoring the various tubes strapped to her, looking down at those beautifully stormy gray eyes. "Are you all right?"

"I am now that you're here. It seems the babies don't want to wait another month. Do you mind?"

"Not if you don't, no." He smiled at her, his heart light after what seemed like a lifetime of blackness.

Her expression sobered. "Theo . . . Iakovos, he—"

"We'll talk about my brother later," he said, not willing to examine the fury that threatened to crash over him when he thought of how close he'd come to losing her. Theo, who had sworn he would not take another drink . . . No. He couldn't deal with that now. "Later," he repeated when she was going to protest, kissing her hands instead.

"All right, but—" She stopped speaking and an indescribable look came over her face before she grabbed his hand and squeezed.

"That was a good one," the nurse told her. "Just keep

that up and we'll soon have these babies born. You're dilating nicely."

"Well, I'm so glad to hear that," she yelled, releasing his hand to glare at the nurse. "Because I don't know how I'd ever live it down if I dilated poorly!"

The woman looked to Iakovos to see if she was missing some nuance of the language.

"Where are you going?" Harry demanded as he moved down to where the nurse was peering between her legs.

"To see how you're dilating."

A couple of sheets had been draped over Harry's body to preserve her modesty, but if he bent down, he could see the fascinating sight of his wife's body preparing to give birth to his children.

"You are not! You are not to go down there and look at me, Iakovos! I'm splayed out here like some gigantic birthing whale, and I refuse to allow you to see things that will haunt you for the rest of your days. Iakovos! Don't you dare look at my private parts!"

"They're not very private right now, sweetheart," he said, leaning down with the nurse to get a good look.

"Argh!" Harry screamed in frustration, trying to kick him.

"Harry?" he said, looking up over the massive mound of her sheet-covered belly.

"What?" she snapped.

"I love you."

She sucked in approximately half of the available oxygen in the room.

"You dare!" she gasped, then took another deep breath and yelled at the top of her lungs. "You dare look at my vaginal parts bulging all over the place, and oozing god knows what, and bleeding and the babies about to come—you look at all that and you have the nerve, the gall, the outright *effrontery* to pick this moment to tell me you love me?"

He grinned. God help him, he loved it when she stormed at him. "Love me?"

"No," she bellowed, and with a dramatic sweep of her arm, pointed to the door. "I never want to see you again! I am divorcing you just as soon as I get out of this bed. Sooner! I'll make you rue the day you insisted on not having a prenuptial agreement! I never want to see you or your gorgeous face, or that spot on your neck or your upper lip dip ever again, do you hear me?"

"That won't make me stop loving you," he told her, taking another quick peek at her intimate parts.

"Now, you just listen to me, Yacky Papafroufrou! You are not to look down there again. Do you hear me? You look at that part of me just one more time, and so help me, god, I'll deck you like I decked your brother!"

By the time she got down to the business of having the babies, she did, in fact, inform anyone within earshot that not only were his parents *not* married, but they were actually Martians, that he was going to be so traumatized by the sight of the birth that he would never want to make love to her again, and last—and he had a hard time trying to figure out her line of reasoning—that if he ever so much as thought of being on another world's-most-eligible-bachelor list, she would personally geld him with an espresso cup and a dull table knife.

Through it all he held her up when she wanted to sit up, pushing back hard against him as she strained to birth the twins, helping her walk when she wanted to walk, wiping her face when she sat on the birthing chair, and telling her in both Greek and English just how much he loved her as the babies were, at last, born.

Twenty-two hours after he had rushed through the doors of the hospital fearing the worst, he looked down at the two blotchy little red bundles in the incubator, his heart swelling with love.

"I want to hold them again," Harry said, moving restlessly in her bed.

He left the babies and returned to her side, leaning down to kiss lips that were chapped and scraped from the flying glass in the crash. He thanked god for the makers of air bags, for the person who first thought up a seat belt, and for whatever angel's job it was to watch over his beloved goddess. "They just went to sleep, sweetheart. The doctor said we have to give them some time in the incubators so their immune systems are strong."

"I know, but I want to hold them again. I don't think I fed them for long enough. Maybe they're hungry. Are they crying?"

"No, they're sleeping. Which you should be as well."

"I couldn't possibly sleep. I'm too keyed up. We have babies, Iakovos!"

"Two beautiful daughters," he agreed, seeing the exhaustion in her eyes. He scooted onto her bed until she could rest against him. "Two little storms in the making."

Epilogue

Harry listened with half her attention to the voice droning in her ear. Elena, she thought, watching as the twenty-one-year-old leaped about in the pool, splashing and laughing with the same abandon as the two little girls in their water wings. Elena looked particularly happy. Could she have a boyfriend at long last?

A noise caught her attention. She glanced over to the massive cradle that sat next to her in the shade of the patio, the cool breeze from the sea making its draperies flutter.

Her eyes went again to the two little girls, sadness filling her at the thought of what should be a happy time—the first birthday of her son. Their friends and family were coming in later in the day to help them celebrate . . . all but Theo.

"Still at it?"

She made a face as Dmitri moved a chair next to her. She pulled off the earphones, turning off the MP3 player. "Trying. Do I have any earthly use for knowing how to say in Greek 'his feet are too big'? Because honestly, Dmitri, that's all I seem to be able to remember."

"I'm sure it's not that bad. How about something simple? Why don't you ask me who I've been talking to?"

"Um . . ." Her face screwed up as she tried to sort out the appropriate words. "Uh . . . what case is that in? Cases confuse me. So do declensions."

He laughed. "Never mind, then."

"Where's your cousin?"

"On the mainland meeting with the mayor about some repairs he's funding." Dmitri fell silent, and Harry had a feeling that he wanted to say more.

"Who were you just talking with?" she asked. "Iakovos?"

"No." He slid her a quick glance.

She sat up straight, her hand on his arm. "Have you heard from him?"

"Yes."

"Is he—"

"He says he hasn't touched a drop since that night Jake smashed all the alcohol."

Harry sat back, her heart heavy. "I've tried and tried to tell Iakovos that Theo hadn't been drinking that day the girls were born, but you know how he gets—he just won't listen."

"I know you've tried. I told him as well."

"You did?" She studied his face. "What did he say?"

"Told me that if I wanted to keep my job, I wouldn't mention it again." Dmitri shrugged. "I let it drop. I figured that in time Theo would prove himself innocent or Jake would figure out the truth for himself, but . . ."

"But he hasn't." She knew that immediately following the accident, Iakovos had coldly severed all ties with Theo, that he had finally reached his limit of tolerance, and didn't seem to care where his brother went, or what happened to him. It was the one subject on which they did not agree, a guaranteed argument starter, but as it had its roots in his father's history of alcoholism, Harry had learned to simply let it be over the three years of their marriage.

"After that night when the twins were born, I was sure I'd have to stop Jake from murdering Theo, but Jake never did go after him."

"No," Harry agreed sadly. "I think Iakovos knew that what we said was true—Theo hadn't caused the accident, hadn't been drinking—but it was just the last straw. So instead he told him to leave. But enough is enough." Her eyes rested on her daughters as they played with Elena. "If I don't do something, my children will grow up never knowing their uncle. What's Theo been doing?"

"What he knows—working in real estate. Sounds like he went to New York first, then somewhere in Asia, and ended up in New Zealand. Now he's back."

"Here?" Her hopes rose. "He's in Greece?"

Dmitri nodded.

"I've never been one to believe in signs, but if that isn't one, then I don't know what is." She was about to say more when her attention was caught elsewhere.

"Eglantine!" The voice roaring her name came from behind her, in the house. She turned, smiling as the tall, dark-haired Greek god—and former world's most eligible bachelor—stomped out onto the patio, lowering his voice only when he saw the sleeping child next to her.

"Yacky?" she said, raising her eyebrows.

He slapped down a piece of paper in front of her. "What is this?" he asked with furious intensity, his eyes sparkling with an unholy light.

She looked at the paper. It was a signed receipt, the kind you get when you pay for a meal with a credit card.

"That's from the lunch that Elena and I had in town yesterday."

"I know what it is. It was handed to me because the taverna owner thought someone might be impersonating you. What, if you don't mind explaining it, is *this*?" He pointed to the bottom line.

"My name, you mean?" It was almost impossible to keep her lips from twitching, but she made a huge effort to meet her husband's ire with innocence.

"That," he said with disgust, "is not your name."

"Harry Papamiaowmiaow isn't right? Was I close?"

"Not by any stretch of the imagination. It's not that difficult, Harry. It's P-A-P-A—"

The twins descended upon them, shrieking and laughing, throwing their wet arms around his legs, clinging to him and chanting with him in their high, sweet tones. "I-O-A-N—"

Elena joined them, her eyes sparkling as she added her voice to the others. "—N-O-U."

"I just don't know," Harry said, looking again at the receipt. "Honestly, Yacky, I think we should give serious consideration to changing our last name to something easier, like Smith, or Brown. Oh, I know—how does Jones grab you? Jones is a lovely name."

"Melina," he said, picking up one little girl and giving her a kiss before doing the same to the other. "Thea. I hate to break this to you, my darlings, but your mother is deranged."

"Deranged, deranged!" they shouted in glee.

"Don't like Jones?" Harry asked, watching the tell-tale sign of that quirky corner of his mouth.

He set the wet, squirming girls back on their feet, bent to give Harry a quick, hard kiss, kissed his sister's cheek, punched his cousin on the shoulder, and finally leaned over the cradle to deposit a kiss on his son's head.

Elena laughed at them both, giving her brother a wink before she herded the girls inside to change out of their swimsuits. Dmitri, with a significant glance at Harry, followed.

Iakovos towered over her, this tall, so-handsome-it-hurt man of hers. He said, with stern resignation, "You simply need to put your mind to it, Harry. It's really not that many letters."

"I love you," she told him in Greek.

He looked startled for a second. "What . . . what did you say?"

She repeated it, standing up so she could fling herself on him, wrapping her legs around his waist.

"That's what I thought you said." Passion kindled in his eyes as she licked first the spot at the base of his neck—the spot that still made her legs go weak if she looked at it too long—and then the lovely place between his lip and nose. "Sweetheart, what do you think you just said to me?"

She stopped kissing his face and frowned. "I love you. I said 'I love you.'"

"No, you didn't. You said, and I quote, 'The potato hangs below.'"

"I did not!"

"You did."

"What earthly reason would I have to say something like that? I couldn't possibly say that even if I wanted to. Thus, you're making it up. You may now apologize to me, and if I accept your apology, I will allow you to make hot, steamy love to me, and I will even let you be on top."

He hoisted her higher, laughing as he did. "We're getting you a tutor, so you can learn the language properly. I apologize for doubting your ability to speak Greek. And I will happily make hot, steamy love to you tonight, just as soon as Nicky's party is over. Happy now?"

She bit the end of his nose, the love shining in her face. "I will be completely and wholly happy if you do one thing for me."

"What's that?" he asked, sitting down with her on his lap, his fingers moving to the buttons on her shirt.

"Theo."

His fingers stilled.

She took his face in her hands, her mouth on his as she said, "He's back in Greece, Iakovos. Dmitri says he's been sober since that night the two of you fought. And he hasn't even seen his nieces and nephew."

His eyes, always so warm and filled with love, closed for a moment.

"It's time to start forgiving him, my most wonderful husband. He's your brother, and I want him back in our lives."

His hands were tight on her waist, but still he said nothing.

"He deserves another chance, my love. He deserves to have a family again. Especially since"—she pulled one of his hands around so that it rested on her stomach—"that family is going to be growing."

His eyelids snapped open at that. "You're not—"

"Oh, yes, I am. We are." She grinned at him. "I really am lucky you only have one testicle, because we'd end up with twelve kids otherwise."

"You are aware that it is the mother who decides the number of babies—"

"A mere triviality," she said, waving away such mundane things. "Please, Iakovos. For me?"

He sighed heavily, shifting her on his lap so that she rested back against him, his hands on her belly. "You're going to make my life hell until I give you what you want, aren't you?"

"Of course I am. It's what I do best."

"If I do this for you, will you learn how to spell our name?"

"Perhaps. Maybe."

"Harry . . ." He growled into her ear.

She laughed and turned around to kiss him again, this man she couldn't get enough of, content that he would do as she asked, and so much more.

Turn the page for an excerpt
from Katie MacAlister's next
Novel of the Light Dragons,

Sparks Fly

Coming from Signet in May 2012

"The lady is here to see you."

Baltic turned at the voice, obviously startled to
hear it, since he had been alone in the upstairs corridor.
"What foolishness is this?"

The heavily varnished paneling that ran the length of
the upper floor of the three-hundred-year-old pub melted
into a dirt yard dotted with odd wooden figures.

Baltic glared first at the figures, then at the man who
approached him. "Ysolde! Why have you drawn me into
one of your visions of the past? And why must you include that murderous bastard in it?"

"Don't blame me; blame my inner dragon." I sighed
to myself and folded my arms over the couple of shirts I
had been about to hang in the wardrobe, which, like the
corridor outside our bedroom, had faded into the scene
before us. "Although I have to say, if it's going to make
me watch episodes from your past, you might as well be
here, too. Who is that? . . . Oh, Constantine. And look—
it's Baltic version one-point-oh, all sexy and shirtless
and hacking away at something with a sword."

"I have better things to do than relive unimportant events," my Baltic, the Baltic of the present day, growled, transferring his glare from Constantine, the former silver wyvern—and once his friend, later his most hated enemy—to me. "Make the vision stop."

"I would if I could, but they never do until they're good and ready.... Hey, where are you going?"

Baltic, with a rude word, turned on his heel and marched away. "I have spent the past twelve days chasing Thala across all of Europe and half of Asia. I have work to do, mate. You may indulge yourself with this vanity, but I will not."

"Vanity! I like that! It's not vanity. And you can't just leave my vision like that!" I yelled after him, watching with a growing sense of injustice as he disappeared around the side of a building. "They're valuable sources of information! Kaawa says we're supposed to learn from them, to glean facts about what is important to us now. Baltic? Well, dammit! He left! That rotter."

I slapped my hands on my legs and spun around as the vision of Constantine approached the other man, who stood in a cluster of quintains and man-sized targets.

"Well, I'm not going to be so obstinate that I don't learn whatever it is that my inner dragon is trying to tell me. Let's see—what do we have here ... ? Obviously we're in some sort of training yard, and since Baltic isn't frothing at the mouth at the sight of Constantine, evidently this vision is from a time when they were still friends. Hello, my love. I don't suppose you can hear me, let alone see me?"

The vision Baltic didn't react, not that I expected him to. The people in the visions that my inner dragon self—

long dormant and only recently starting to wake up—
provided were just that: visions of events in the past that
I could watch and listen to, but not interact with.

Constantine, clad in wool leggings and a tunic bearing a gold-embroidered dragon on a field of black,
strode past the empty sword-fighting targets to the oc-
cupied one, his attitude cocky, while his face was ar-
ranged in an expression implying sympathy. "Did you
hear me?" he asked as he stopped at the side of the man
who was diligently hacking away with an extremely big
sword at a straw and wood target.

"I heard. It is of no matter to me."

I spent a few moments in admiration at the interplay
of his muscles as Baltic continued to swing and thrust
his sword into the target, his bare back shining with
sweat.

"It always did make my knees weak to see you wield
a sword," I told the vision Baltic, moving around to see
the front of him. His face was different yet familiar to
me, his hair dark ebony then, his chin more blunted. "I
like your hair the dark chocolate color it is now. And
your chin, as well, although you were certainly incredibly sexy before Thala resurrected you. And your chest . . .
Oh my." I fanned myself with a bit of one of the shirts I
was holding.

"Alexei says you have no choice. He says it is the
command of your father." Constantine cocked one eyebrow at Baltic, moving swiftly to the side when Baltic
swung wide.

"You look the same," I informed Constantine. "Evidently being brought back as a shade didn't affect your
appearance, whereas resurrection does. Interesting. I'll

have to talk to Kaawa about that the next time I see her. Still, you were handsome then, Constantine. But you didn't hold a candle to Baltic."

"My father does not control my life," Baltic snapped, his breath ragged now as he continued to swing at the vaguely human-shaped target. "Nor does Alexei."

I settled back against one of the targets, prepared to watch and learn what I could from the vision.

"He is our wyvern. You owe him your fealty," Constantine said, stiffening. "You must do as he says. You *must* meet the lady."

"Do not lecture me, Constantine," Baltic snarled, turning on him. Sweat beaded on his brow and matted the dark hair on his chest. Constantine took a step back when Baltic gestured toward him with the sword. "You are Alexei's heir, *not* the wyvern himself, and I do not take well to being ordered about."

"Pax!" Constantine said, throwing his hands up in the air in a gesture of defeat. "I did not come to argue with you, old friend. I wanted simply to warn you that the lady had arrived, and Alexei is expecting you to do your duty and claim her as mate."

I had been idly wondering to myself when exactly this moment had taken place—judging by the comments, it predated not only my birth, but even the time when Baltic had been wyvern of the black dragon sept. But as the two men argued, I had a sudden insight.

"This is about the First Dragon's demand that I redeem you, isn't it?" I asked the past Baltic. "This has something to do with whatever it is I'm supposed to accomplish to erase the stain on your soul. But that was due to the death of the innocent, and this . . . *a mate*?"

It took a minute before Constantine's words sank into my brain, but when they did, the hairs on the back of my neck rose. I stalked forward to the two men, glaring at the former image of the love of my life, uncaring that this was only a vision. "You were supposed to take someone else as a mate? Who?"

"I've told Alexei of my decision," Baltic said, snatching up his discarded tunic and wiping his face with it before sheathing his sword. "I have not changed my mind."

He turned and started up the hill of what was obviously the outer bailey of an early stone castle, stopping when Constantine called after him, "And what of the First Dragon? Will you defy him as well as Alexei? You are his only living son, Baltic."

"I know what I am," Baltic snarled, and continued walking.

"The lady wants you. The First Dragon is reported to desire you to take her as mate. Alexei has commanded it in order to avoid a war. Do you really think you have a choice in the matter?"

The word that Baltic uttered was archaic but quite, quite rude and, ironically, one his present-day self had spoken just a few minutes before. I watched his tall, handsome figure as he disappeared into crowds of dragons going about their daily business, my eyes narrowing as Constantine suddenly smiled.

"Why do I have the feeling that you know something?" I asked him.

He didn't answer, of course. He just continued to smile for a few seconds, and then he, too, strolled off toward the upper bailey, leaving me alone in the practice yard.

"Who was she?" I bellowed after them, achieving nothing but the venting of my spleen. "Who the hell was she?"

"Who was what?" a voice asked from behind me. I spun around, staggering slightly when the world spun with me for a few moments, finally resolving itself into a familiar, if uninspiring, bedroom atop the old pub. "Are you all right? You look funny, like you smell cabbage cooking."

"I'm fine, lovey." I smiled at the brown-haired boy watching me with eyes that always seemed to be far too old for their nine years. "And there's nothing wrong with cabbage, despite your stepfather's insistence that it was put on this earth only to try his patience. That stir-fried cabbage with peanut sauce that Pavel made last night was to die for, which you'd know if you had tried it."

Brom wrinkled up his nose. Always a placid child, if a tad bit eccentric, in the month that had passed since our house had been destroyed, he seemed to have adopted Baltic as a hero figure. I'd caught him more than once watching Baltic closely, as if fascinated with the way a wyvern acted, but I think it went deeper than mere curiosity about the dragons with whom we now found ourselves living. He'd started parroting Baltic's likes and dislikes, even going as far as to spurn food I knew he didn't really mind.

"Are you going into London today?"

"Nice change of subject, and, yes, I am." I shook off the last few dregs of anger over the idea that the First Dragon had tried to force Baltic into taking a mate, and finished putting away the shirts I'd bought in a local shop. "Where is Nico taking you today?"

"He wants to go see a history museum." Brom looked thoughtful. "It has ships and stuff, but no bodies, although Nico says there might be some surgeon's tools. When are we going to get our own house so I can set up my lab again? You said you'd start looking right away, and it's been forever."

"Four weeks is hardly forever." I smiled and gave him one of the three daily hugs he allowed. "But I'll ask Baltic again about a house. Would you mind if we lived outside England? He's likely to want to be near Dauva in order to oversee the rebuilding, and I hate to make him travel between here and Riga all the time."

"Are there mummies in . . ." His face screwed up in thought.

"Latvia?" I finished. "I have no idea, although it is close enough to visit St. Petersburg, which I know has some fine museums. Whether or not they have mummies is beyond me. You can ask Nico, though. Perhaps he'll know."

"OK. Will he come with us? Because he's a green dragon, and not in Baltic's sept, I mean?"

"I'm sure Drake will give him permission, since he's agreed to let Nico tutor you for a year. Oh, you probably want your allowance, don't you? Let me get my purse."

Brom's expression turned painful for a few seconds before his shoulders sagged, and he said with obvious reluctance, "Baltic gave it to me this morning when he got home from Nepal. But if you wanted to give me more, that would be OK."

I laughed and gave his shoulder a little pat. "I'm sorry to have burst your bubble, but you really don't need more than *one* weekly allowance."

"How am I going to buy supplies when we get a house?" he asked as I herded him before me back into the narrow hallway. The floor and walls were wooden and uneven, and made me feel like I was walking at an angle. I didn't complain, though; I found the small pub run by some human friends of Pavel, Baltic's second-in-command, charming and quaint in its Elizabethan Englishness. Baltic insisted we would be safe there should Thala, his former lieutenant, decide to try to kill us again. I had no doubt that he would keep us safe no matter where we were located, but, like Brom, I was growing tired of such a transient lifestyle, and yearned for my own home, where we could settle down once and for all.

"When we have room for you to set up another mummification lab, I'll buy you some supplies. Although, really, Brom, couldn't you find some hobby other than mummifying animals?"

"You said it was illegal to mummify a human," he pointed out as I tapped on the door to his tutor's room. "Besides, I don't know where to find a dead person."

Nico, an auburn-haired, studious green dragon who'd had charge of Brom's education for the past few months, greeted me and grabbed a small backpack. "Did Brom tell you that we're going to the naval museum today?"

"Yes, despite the fact that it won't have bodies." I shared a smile with Nico before reminding Brom to behave himself. "I won't be back until just before dinner, but Pavel said he was going to cook up something special, so be home by six."

"Absolutely," Nico agreed, and with a glance at his watch hustled Brom down the stairs. I heard the rumble of male voices drift upward after them and waited, wondering how best to broach the subject of my vision.

Baltic appeared at the head of the stairs, his hand quickly whipping away from his pocket as he spotted me.

"You didn't!" I said, frowning as he approached, with Pavel on his heels. "Baltic, really, it's too bad of you!"

Guilt chased across his face, followed immediately by a look of pure seduction as he swept me up in his arms and bathed me in dragon fire. "*Cherie*, what is it you're frowning over? Could it be that you have missed me in the past ten minutes as much as I've missed you?"

"Whenever you call me *cherie*, I know you're feeling guilty about something," I said, melting against him even as I giggled a little. "Of course I missed you, and not just for the past ten minutes. It's been a hellish twelve days while you were trying to find Thala, not only because I was worried sick about you, but because you weren't here to drive me wild with desire—but that's not the point. Brom did *not* need more money. And don't deny you gave him some, because I saw you putting your wallet away."

"We've spoken of this subject already," he murmured against my lips, pulling me brazenly against his hips. "Can you think of nothing more you'd rather discuss after my absence?"

"Why, yes, I can." I almost purred as I let him kiss me, amused that he thought he could distract me in such a way, before I realized that he had a very good record of doing just that.

I gave myself up to the sensation of his fire sinking into me, of the hardness of his body against mine, of his scent, that masculine, spicy scent that seemed to kindle my own dragon fire. And when his mouth moved against mine, I knew I didn't stand a chance. I kissed him with all the passion I possessed, making him growl into my mouth as I tugged on his hair, wordlessly demanding more of his dragon fire.

Pavel passed by us, murmuring something about waiting for Baltic in the sitting room, but even that didn't stop me from welcoming Baltic's fire with a little moan of my own. His tongue burned as it swept inside my mouth, his chest and legs hard when he pushed me up against the wall. I clung to his shoulders, rubbing myself against him, pulling hard first on my fire, and when that didn't come, I pulled on his to bathe us both in heat.

"Ysolde, if you do not stop attempting to seduce me in the hallway, I will take you right here," Baltic said in a low voice filled with passion. "And while I would be happy to fulfill this latest of your secret fantasies, we risk shocking anyone who comes upstairs."

I slid one hand down to pinch his adorable behind. "For the last time, you incredibly sexy dragon, I do not have sexual fantasies that are anything but perfectly ordinary, and certainly do not involve voyeurism. Besides, parts of me are still humming after the way you greeted me this morning when you arrived home. That was quite the homecoming."

"I merely gave you the attention you were due." Baltic raised an eyebrow seconds before he dived for my chest, his mouth and hands hot on my breasts. I squirmed against him, shifting his hands so I could have better access to his chest, wondering if I had time to indulge us both, but at that moment my phone vibrated in my pocket and bellowed out a recording of one word: "Ysolde!"

Baltic raised his head from where he was licking the valley between my breasts, frowning something fierce. "Mate! I thought I told you to change your alarm sound."

I giggled against his mouth and nipped his bottom lip. "But it's so perfect! Nothing catches my attention more than you saying my name. And speaking of attention, you should have stuck around that vision. It was *most interesting*."

He ignored the emphasis I put on the words, wrapping his arms around my waist and lifting me off the ground as he squeezed tightly. "You try my patience, woman. I have no time for reminders of what happened in the past. I have lost twelve days chasing Thala, and there is much work that I must accomplish in a short amount of time."

I took a deep breath. "I wish I could ignore them, but I can't. You're not the only one who lost twelve days, my darling. When the First Dragon demanded I salvage your honor—"

"I've told you before that my honor is fine as it is."

"When your father, the godlike ancestor of every dragon who ever was and who ever will be tells me to salvage your honor, I'm not about to ignore anything that might help me do just that. Especially since you aren't making it the least bit easy for me."

"If you choose to waste your time—"

"Waste my time? *Waste my time!*" I gasped, shoving at his shoulder. "I cannot believe that you would call my visions a waste of time!"

"You are being emotional, Ysolde," he said, stopping when I slapped both hands on his chest with a glare that by rights should have stripped the hair off his head.

"I am not being emotional!" I yelled. The echo of my voice along the wood-paneled hallway was quite audible. Baltic's glossy dark chocolate eyebrows rose. "Fine! I'm emotional! I can't help it. I'm hormonal right now."

"Are you having your female time? I hope it will be over soon. I do not like having to wait for it to cease," he said, passion firing in his eyes.

"People can hear us downstairs, you know, and you haven't *quite* embarrassed me to death. Would you perhaps like to inquire as to the state of my bowels?" I took a deep breath when he looked like he was going to do just that. "What were we talking about that didn't involve my bodily functions?"

"Your being emotional. It is a good thing that I am a wyvern, and thus am able to control my emotions where you cannot."

"Oh, I like that—"

"It is just like that time at Dragonwood when you tried to geld me with your eating dagger. You were most emotional then, as well. You remember that, do you not?"

I frowned for a few seconds as I tried to dig through what remained of my memory. "No . . . At Dragonwood? I tried to geld you? Are you sure?"

"Do you distrust my memory?" he asked. There was something about the innocent look on his face that made me suspicious, but there was nothing I could say to challenge his statement.

"Your memory of the past has never been in question, no," I said slowly. "If you say I tried to cut off your noogies, then I assume I did so, but I'm also sure I had a very good reason for doing it. What did you do that made me so annoyed?"

"You are going straight to the meeting and back again," he said, totally ignoring my question, returning me to the ground to escort me down the narrow stairs to the main floor of the pub. "The driver will wait outside for you. I would accompany you myself, but the builders are ready to leave the country, and I must check with them before they do so."

"You are getting more and more like Drake Vireo every day," I told him, alternating between annoyance and pure, unadulterated love. I decided that it was better to indulge the latter rather than former, and accordingly gave the tip of his nose a little lick before waving at Pavel as he stood talking to three men whom Baltic had engaged to begin the process of restoring Dauva.

"I am infinitely superior to the green wyvern," Baltic said loftily, nodding to one of the blue dragons he'd hired as drivers for us. "And you must remember that I will do anything to keep you and Brom safe."

"I know that, and I appreciate what it cost you to borrow some of Drake's men to watch over Brom and me while you and Pavel were tracking Thala, but as I told you before you left, we'll be fine. There's no reason for Thala to want to harm Brom, and really, that goes for me, as well. As for you . . . well, she went to the considerable trouble of resurrecting you, so despite that whole situation of her blowing up the house on top of us, I don't think she wants to kill you. I think she was just frustrated and angry, and felt cornered, and let loose on us because of that, not because of any murderous intent."

"She did an exceptionally fine job of making me believe otherwise."

I touched his shoulder. Although Thala's destruction

of the house hadn't killed us—dragons being notoriously difficult to kill—it had done so much damage to Baltic's back that even today, he still bore scars. "Well, I should say she has no reason to want to kill you, so therefore she can't gain anything by offing me. After all, you're not like the other dragons who cork off if your mate dies."

Baltic, who had been frowning at my slang, instantly switched into seduction mode, something he was wont to do whenever I mentioned the newly discovered fact that he was a reeve, one of the very rare dragons who could have more than one mate. "I would not survive your death again, *cherie*," he murmured against my lips, bathing me in a light sheen of his dragon fire. "Not a third time. It is for that reason I insist that you not see the archimage again."

"We may not have a choice in the matter," I said slowly, brushing off an infinitesimal bit of lint from his shoulder. "I didn't get a chance to tell you earlier, but I reached Jack this morning. Do you remember him?"

"No."

"He was apprenticed to Dr. Kostich at the same time I was—only Jack is a very gifted mage, and I'm . . . Well, you know how my magic goes all wonky because I'm a dragon. Jack is now a full-fledged mage, and very talented, from what I hear, but even he says there's just no one of the caliber we need other than an archimage to tackle Thala."

Baltic watched me closely. I kissed his chin, knowing he wasn't going to like what I had to say.

"There are other archimages," he said.

"Two others, and one is out of reach while he's on some sort of magi retreat. The other is a woman I have had no experience with, and I suspect wouldn't be overly easy to persuade to help catch a highly dangerous, partially psychotic half-dragon necromancer."

"Thala is not that dangerous," he said dismissively.

I pulled down the back of his shirt collar. "Have you looked at your back lately? That dirge she sang brought down an entire three-story house on top of us, Baltic. You can't do that if you're not able to tap into some pretty impressive power."

He made a disgusted noise.

"I'm just saying that I think Dr. Kostich is going to be our only choice."

"I do not like it." Baltic's frown was, as ever, a stormy thing to behold, but I had long learned to ignore it.

"Neither do I, but so long as mages wield arcane power, they are going to be the best bet for combating the dark power that necromancers use. I'm afraid, my delectable dragon, that it's Dr. Kostich or nothing."

His jaw worked, no doubt sorely tempted to tell me we'd do without my former employer and head of the Otherworld, but we had few choices open to us.

"You and Pavel chased Thala for twelve straight days and nights," I told him, my hands caressing his chest. "You know her better than anyone. You know what she's capable of; you know how many outlaw dragons follow her. Can we bring her to justice without the aid of people outside our sept?"

"No." I knew just how much it cost him to admit that. He took a deep breath, his eyes sparkling with the light of vengeance. "She has grown more powerful in the past month. I do not know where she is getting the members for her tribe of ouroboros dragons, but we encountered more than thirty of them in Belgium, and another two dozen in Turkey. That she can lose that many members and still have the number of dragons we saw when we finally chased her to Nepal . . ." He shook his head and didn't finish the sentence, clearly frustrated that he hadn't caught her to deal with her himself.

For a moment I was stunned by what he said. "You ran into more than fifty of Thala's ouroboros dragons before you lost them in the wilds of Nepal?"

"Fifty-eight."

"What happened to them?" I knew from the manner in which Baltic had greeted me upon his return that morning that he had no injuries, so it wasn't likely he'd fought the dragons.

His eyes grew hard and even shinier. "What do you think happened to them?"

"You didn't kill them?"

"Not alone. Pavel was with me."

I gawked at him. "Baltic!"

"They were trying to kill us," he pointed out, instantly quelling the lecture I was about to give. Although I had my doubts as to whether Thala's intentions in regard to Baltic were of a murderous nature, I knew from past experience that her gang of outlaw ouroboros dragons were much more cutthroat.

"I still don't like it."

"Your heart is too soft," he said, giving my behind another squeeze.

"That is not my heart, and you know full well I don't like killing. Which is why I wholly approve of the plan to bring Thala to the Otherworld Committee for justice.

They can banish her to the Akasha, or something appropriate like that."

Baltic made a noncommittal noise that had me glancing sharply at him, but before I could do more than wonder, he said, "You will ask the archimage if there is another who could deal with Thala now that we know where she is."

"I thought you said she disappeared in Nepal?"

His lips thinned a little. "She did. But I suspect she has taken control of an aerie high in the Himalayas."

"The one I saw in my vision a few months ago?" I asked, remembering the cold, bleak stone building.

"That is the aerie, yes. It used to be held by Kostya, before Thala confined him there."

I shivered at the thought of being held prisoner in such a stark location. "All of that notwithstanding, I will ask Dr. Kostich, but I can tell you now that there isn't anyone else to help us. And stop looking at me like that—I don't want to have to deal with him any more than you do, even though he's really not the horrible person you think he is."

"He is responsible for your death, mate."

"You know as well as I do that he wasn't responsible for my dying a second time. Well, not directly responsible. Besides, I apologized about that, so you can stop looking like you're going to yell at me again. It's not as if I die so often that I deserve a lecture. Honestly, Baltic, you really are becoming just as bossy as Drake, and you know that only irritates me."

"I do not like you going where I cannot protect you," he said in a low grumble that was softened by the look of love in his beautiful onyx eyes. I melted against him, unable to resist the emotions I knew bound us so tightly together. "The other mates should come here instead of your going into London."

"It's Aisling's turn to host the Mate's Union meeting, and even if it wasn't, I'm not going to live my life hiding in the shadows because Thala is on the loose." I kissed him quickly so as to avoid the temptation his mouth offered, and climbed into the back of the sleek dark blue car. "I'm going to do a little shopping before I meet with Aisling and May, and, yes, I'll be careful, so you can stop fretting. Thala is in Nepal, not here in England."

"There is nothing to say she hasn't escaped."

"You left a whole bunch of Drake's guys to watch the borders, didn't you? Stop worrying. They'll tell you if she leaves the aerie."

"Assuming they see her," he muttered darkly.

"I'm the first one to admit she's powerful, but I don't see her getting out of the country without someone noticing. I'll be back before dinner. If Brom and Nico come home early, remind them that Brom's vacation was officially over yesterday and it wouldn't hurt them to start on his lessons this afternoon. Oh, and Baltic?"

"Yes?" He leaned into the car.

I grabbed his head and pulled hard on the little core of dragon fire that slumbered inside me, letting it flow out to him as I kissed him again. "Perhaps later we can explore some more of *your* secret fantasies," I whispered, smiling to myself at the look of mingled surprise and passion that flitted through his eyes.